**"We just do** **need to settle for some random guy you meet online when..."**

Her voice trailed off as she looked to Reagan for backup.

"When what?" I asked, squinting my eyes at them both.

Reagan finally spoke. "When Brandon is right there, sis."

*Ahh. Brandon.* I should have known his name was going to come up in this conversation, though, because Reagan and Keisha were convinced that I was in love with him.

"Don't start with me about Brandon today. He's not the one for me. We have a great group dynamic. If he and I were to ever cross that line, and something went wrong, that would ruin everything. Then suddenly, it would be all my fault that the whole group can't hang out with each other anymore? Not to mention, I don't even know if he likes me like that. It's no secret that Brandon dates a lot—if 'date' is the word you want to use—and yet, he's never asked me out. When you put all that together, it's just a big heaping pile of risk with very low chance of reward."

"It's a heaping pile of something all right," Reagan whispered under her breath, just loud enough for me to hear it.

Dear Reader,

When I first started writing *A Risk Worth Taking*, I had in mind that the hero, Brandon, would be the kind of guy who says all the things that Giselle needs to hear (even when she's resistant to them). He is, after all, the person who understands her the best—one of the many reasons she initially hesitates to consider him as anything more. Who would want to risk losing that guy if it doesn't work out, right?

Well, turns out, he also ended up saying all the things I needed to hear!

Like "You should be, at all times, only pursuing whatever makes your heart skip a beat." Whew! Needed. But if you're anything like Giselle (and, ahem, me), that goes against all your practical sensibilities. This is how our heroine ends up in a love triangle with two great guys—one who checks off all the logical things she relies on for comfort, and one who's just...sigh...him.

Get ready to jump into the sixth installment in The Friendship Chronicles series! As it follows one of the friends you've loved since *Her New York Minute*, this story is an angsty take on a love triangle meets friends-to-lovers romance that's guaranteed to warm your heart. It also has those signature moments of the series when Giselle's dynamic girlfriend group makes you laugh and "mmm-hmm" as they nudge her toward the realization that all love requires risk. It's just about deciding when the risk is worth it.

Hope you enjoy!

*Darby*

# A RISK WORTH TAKING

## DARBY BAHAM

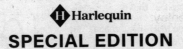

**SPECIAL EDITION**

Recycling programs for this product may not exist in your area.

ISBN-13: 978-1-335-18003-2

A Risk Worth Taking

Copyright © 2025 by Darby Baham

For questions and comments about the quality of this book, please contact us at CustomerService@Harlequin.com.

TM and ® are trademarks of Harlequin Enterprises ULC.

 Harlequin Enterprises ULC
22 Adelaide St. West, 41st Floor
Toronto, Ontario M5H 4E3, Canada
www.Harlequin.com

MIX
Paper | Supporting responsible forestry
FSC® C021394

**Printed in Lithuania**

**Darby Baham** is an author and storyteller on a mission to make women like herself feel seen and believe that love is possible for them—yes, them. The former *Washington Post* and *Times-Picayune* contributor uses her doubts, hopes and fears to connect with her readers and inform the themes in her Harlequin Special Edition series, The Friendship Chronicles. This series is a love letter to female friendships and offers an intimate look into the dynamic love lives of Black women.

### Books by Darby Baham

### Harlequin Special Edition

### *The Friendship Chronicles*

*The Shoe Diaries*
*Bloom Where You're Planted*
*London Calling*
*Her New York Minute*
*Falling for the Competition*
*A Risk Worth Taking*

Visit the Author Profile page at Harlequin.com.

To all the lovergirls, loverboys and loverpeople hesitating to go for the things they know will make their heart skip a beat, I see you. I hear you. I know it's scary, but do it anyway. You won't ever regret it.

# *Part 1*

"I think and think and think, I've thought myself out of happiness one million times, but never once into it."

—Jonathan Safran Foer

# *Chapter One*

"Soooo, I'm thinking about getting on the dating apps again."

After a bit of hesitation, I quickly blurted out my breaking news and then scrunched my face up slightly as I braced myself for my friends' reactions. Unsurprisingly, they didn't make me wait very long, with mere milliseconds passing before they replied in unison, like a well-rehearsed two-person choir, ready to jump in as soon as the preacher grabbed the mic.

"Wait, what?!" they asked, dropping their forks and staring at me from across the brunch table, their eyes widened in disbelief.

"You heard me."

"Yes, baby, but repeat it so I can make sure I heard you correctly."

With her thick New Orleans accent floating off her tongue—a blend of French, Native American, and African influences that playfully used words like *baby* in casual conversation—Keisha adjusted her leopard-print glasses and primed her face toward mine as she awaited my response. Her piercing brown eyes easily conveyed her skepticism (and implicit questioning of my decision) without her needing to say one more word. As my best friend since college, I'd been on the end of more than a few of these glances, all with good intentions, but intimidating nonetheless. In fact, in normal circumstances, that look on her face, combined with the fierce-ass curly pixie cut she usually wore slicked to the right, might have caused me to rethink my plans. Knocked me right out of my resolve and had me second-guessing myself. But not this time; I was as determined as I'd ever been.

"I think… I'm going to get on the apps again," I said, a little quieter but no less resolute.

"Okayyy! Well, that's a plot twist," Reagan said, chiming in from the seat right next to Keisha. "But you know what? I'm here for it. It's just that it's been, what, at least five years since you were on them, right?"

I chuckled to myself as I looked at my other best friend, the Creole beauty with ombré barrel curls who had a way of sneakily prodding people that she'd clearly mastered in her former life as a reporter. Like Keisha, who she'd known since high school, Reagan also spoke with a distinct New Orleans accent. But because she'd spent her life doing some sort of communications work since she was about fifteen, Rae's voice had blended into a mixture of a stereotypical journalist and a Creole Southern belle. This often meant that she could disarm people with her soft spoken tone and the way she decorated her speech with French colloquialisms like *cher* and *laissez-faire*, and the poor souls wouldn't realize she'd trapped them until it was too late.

I was onto her, though, and knew exactly the play she was trying to make, attempting to be the good cop to Keisha's bad, but both with the same intention. I paused to calculate the time in my head, figuring I might as well have a little fun if this was going to be their reaction, and stuffed my mouth with the best French toast I'd tasted above 165th Street before deigning to respond.

"Might be more like six years, actually," I mumbled, covering my mouth to finish chewing the last bits of my toast before continuing. "But… I truly do want to get serious about my dating life again. And that starts with letting God and the universe know I'm open for a real relationship, not just playing around with these same jokers I've had in rotation for the past few years. They've been good for *some* things, obviously, but a relationship? Not so much. And I can't even imagine wanting to build a future with any of them."

"Well, yeah, your rotation is filled with nothing but real-life boy toys, sis," Reagan replied, chuckling at her own wordplay, and giggling toward Keisha. "Between the two of you, I feel like I've been surrounded by more *toys* than I ever thought possible in the two years since I moved to New York City. You, *cher*, have spent the past few years snatching up every attractive man with at least nine inches' worth of fun attached to him, and Keish, the way you used to stockpile anything that vibrates…my God!"

"Used to?" Keisha and I blurted out at the same time, laughing at Reagan's reaction as she clutched the pearls she pretended were draped over her long-sleeve, black-and-white crop top Celine shirt. She'd paired that beautifully with some black trousers that tied above her waist—perfect for hiding her inevitable food baby after eating Republica's signature bottomless brunch, which came with two large entrees of Dominican food.

"Oh, well, excuse me!" she replied, joining me and Keisha in our laugh fest. "I just thought since you're in a relationship now, you had no need for *all* of them, my dear. And certainly, that you wouldn't be buying more."

"Ahh, but see, that's where you're wrong, Rae, because Julian very much enjoys every single toy that's in my pleasure box. It's like a fun surprise to see which one we'll use next."

Keisha winked at Reagan and burst into laughter again as our Southern belle grabbed her sangria from the table and quickly downed it in response.

"It's called compatibility, baby," Keisha added.

"You know what? That's fine. It's my fault for even bringing this up. Because I know you two, and I should have known better."

"Oh, please," Keisha said, waving her hand in the air. "Don't try to act like anybody at this table is a prude, least of all you, baby girl."

"No, I know! And I never said I was a prude. Tuh. I just...clearly need to step my game up a bit."

"And you do," I chimed in before stuffing another piece of French toast in my mouth, careful not to waste the sticky syrup or powdered sugar on my favorite Army green graphic tee.

Adorned with a huge dragon and bright red letters that read Court Me, the colors popped off my Fenty 390 skin tone and gave me the perfect excuse to rock my matching pleather pants that hugged my hips in all the best ways.

"Woooow, *et tu*, Gigi?"

Reagan looked at me from across the table with mock betrayal.

"I can't believe you flipped on me that quickly! And after I was trying to be on your side. Huh. I'mma start calling you Future from now on."

"Wait, no, Aubrey, don't!" I joked. "Truce. Truce!"

Laughing so hard tears were almost falling out my eyes, I reached over the table and tried to grab Reagan's hand, but before I could latch on, she snatched it away and shook her head with a smirk.

"Nah, nah. It's too late. 'I could never be your number-one fan…'"

Using Drake's words to Future after the public finally realized they were feuding, I knew Reagan had hit me with the ultimate "bet." I quickly wiped away my tears and prepared myself for the conversation to switch back to me, except, this time, I had a feeling Rae was done pretending to be the good cop. I loved her to death, but the woman was a Cancer sun; once she decided to be petty for the day, nothing was going to change that.

Without hesitation, Keisha grabbed her glass of sangria and swished it around as she turned her attention back to me.

"If you two are done, I think it's time we get back to more important matters," she declared before taking a large sip.

"Sure, let's do that," I replied with a deep sigh. "But can I just first say, I understand why you guys don't like the idea. But here's the thing, I need to do something different. And that's just what it is."

"All right, that's fair. And you're a grown woman, so it's not like you need our permission or anything. But riddle me this…you think getting back on Tinder is what's going to be the difference maker here?" Keisha asked, tilting her head with suspicion.

"Well, first off, it doesn't have to be Tinder. There are a ton of other options these days," I corrected her before taking a quick sip from my own glass.

Thankfully, our waiter, Niko, took "bottomless" to heart and was doing an excellent job of keeping us refilled. Something told me I was going to need him to bring over some more soon.

"But also, yeah…kinda," I continued. "At the very least, it'll be unlike whatever it is I've been doing most recently. That's gotta count for something."

"Hmm."

Keisha sat back into her chair and contemplated my response, sucking her teeth as she nodded her head and pursed her full lips. I knew this look all too well, too. It was similar to the one I saw on her face when we first met, and she'd walked into our freshman dorm room to find me working on a DIY bookshelf on a sweltering hot summer day in Los Angeles. I'd soon come to find out that while she was no stranger to working hard, my bestie from the bayou was not a fan of engaging in anything that would mess up her perfectly designed nails. She was just as skeptical of my choices then as she was now.

"Okay, I hear you," she added. "And listen, you're my girl. We've been riding with each other for fourteen years now. So, of course, I want you to meet someone who's not trying to give that same ol' sad storyline we've both heard a million times over. Talking about 'ma, you know you special and all, but I got a lot going on with me right now, so I'm just trying to keep it chill…'"

Keisha deepened her voice and hilariously attempted to change her accent and tone to sound more like the guys we were likely to meet in New York than the ones who might have grown up a few doors down from Lil Wayne.

"Exactly!" I said, giggling at her absolutely horrendous impression, but also sort of relieved she seemed to be coming around to my side.

Just in time, too, since I couldn't count on Rae at the moment.

"But…" Keisha continued. "The dating apps are literally a cesspool of trash mixed with large droplets of urine and a healthy dose of fragile male toxicity. You know this. That's *why* you haven't been on there in so long."

"She's not wrong," Reagan chimed in with a snort and a knowing nod. "It's a disgusting image, but it is true."

*Gah. Now she wanted to talk.* This was the double team I'd hoped to avoid but should have known was coming when I opted to tell them both at the same time. The way our friendship was set up, though, for better or worse, we always spilled tea as a group. And well, this was my tea for the moment. In any case, Keish was right; it wasn't like I needed my girls' permission, of course. But their encouragement certainly would have been nice. That seemed a long ways away, however.

"And what exactly would the two of you know about it?" I fired back, suddenly feeling the need to defend myself. "Rae, you're literally engaged to your college sweetheart. And Keish, I'm so happy for you, but you lucked up and found the man of your dreams when you left your full-time job to start business school last year. That's no shade to either of you, but it's not like you're out here in these dating streets with me anymore, so you don't know how it is. What would you rather me do? Audit a class somewhere so I can hopefully randomly meet someone like Keisha did? Look up one of my exes from college and see if by some miracle, he's a) not a dodged bullet and b) even still single?"

"Whoa, okay, that's a lot of bass in your voice, there, *cher*," Reagan replied. "Let's not act like my love story is some sort of grand fairy tale where I met Jake in college, and we've been together ever since. I spent many, many, *many* years solo dolo in these same dating streets as you two—well, mine were in DC, but that's not important—and on the same trash apps before he and I got back together. So, you know, I'm intimately aware of how frustrating it all can be and how you can find yourself wondering, like, why can I find guys to play around with all day, but no one who actually wants to work toward something meaningful?"

"Mmm-hmm," Keisha deadpanned as she sliced through the grilled steak that was perfectly plated next to her scrambled eggs.

She slowly finished chewing her bite before lifting her eyes toward mine, tilting her head again and calmly blotting the corners of her lips that somehow still had her velvet-red lipstick fully intact.

"You already know what I'm going to say, right?" she asked with a shrug, still staring into my eyes. "Because you, of all people, know that before Julian, I was right where you are. Actually, scratch that, I was worse off because the only man even remotely interested in me was the same one who'd taken my heart and stomped all over it. Did you conveniently forget that because I've been in a relationship for all of three to four months now?"

Okay, clearly this discussion had gone off the rails, I thought, sitting back into my chair with a sigh. Somehow, it had become about me insulting their relationship journeys and was no longer about me basically trying to admit how badly I simply wanted to be loved. The banter was still lighthearted to be sure, because ultimately, they *were* my girls. But while I knew they meant well, in all of the back and forth, neither had yet to utter anything even close to what felt like support. I wondered if they realized that or not.

Steadying my breathing, I cleared my throat and tapped my rose-pink-and-black, faux fur loafers onto the ground, trying to release any further tension within me before continuing. Then, with the calmest tone I could muster, I made one more attempt to reset the conversation.

"So, then if you guys get it—and you're right, I shouldn't have implied that you don't, that's my bad—then why are y'all acting like I said something so controversial? All I'm trying to do is get back in the game, and I can't do that simply waiting around for fate to magically send somebody my way while I'm out grocery shopping or at the gym. I want to take control here and do something that puts action behind my desire. I know y'all can understand that, right?"

They both nodded their heads in agreement.

"Okay, good. So, then, what I need most from both of you is for you to just be excited for me. Have my back! Tell me you can't wait to see who I match with…something!"

I held back the tears threatening to fall from my eyes and took another bite of my French toast to try to push down any remaining negative feelings bubbling under the surface. The last thing I was about to do was cry at this table while surrounded by a restaurant full of people dancing to reggaeton and bachata, especially since it wasn't even that serious. All I was saying was I was making a new dating profile.

"Okay," Keisha replied, reaching her arm over the table toward mine. "You know we love you, Gig, and we're not trying to be Debbie Downers, here. We just wouldn't be good friends if we didn't *lovingly* question this very random idea of yours."

"But that's the thing," I countered. "It's not random. I've been mulling over this for a while now. I just had a feeling that this was how this conversation was going to go, so I hadn't said anything to y'all yet…which is kind of crazy, since I was largely inspired by you two."

"Inspired by us? Really?" Reagan asked, just as Niko came by with another sangria pitcher.

She used one hand to cover her heart to express how touched she was by the sentiment while the other quickly scooped up the pitcher and poured full glasses out for us all.

"Yes," I replied with a sigh, happily accepting my refill.

"Well, that's what you should have started all this with in the first place," she added with a giggle.

"Hello?!" Keisha interjected. "You gotta know your target audience, baby. That's Marketing 101."

"Apparently so," I said, rolling my eyes in jest at them both and taking a sip from my glass.

"But for real," Reagan added. "We definitely don't want you to be scared to talk to us about anything. Like, of course we've got your back. That's not an even a question."

"Okay, good, because I know we joke around a lot, but genuinely, I look at y'all and see how loved you are by men who are not perfect but are perfect *for* you, and I want that. I'm not naive, of course. I know it takes work, but I want a partner who supports me and challenges me…who I can be myself around…who I can laugh and flirt with, but also just have real, honest, vulnerable conversations with. If I'm lucky, he'll also be someone who makes my heart flutter when I see his name come across my screen, but honestly? It doesn't even have to be filled with all the fairy-tale stuff—I simply want a stable love who's not going to disappoint me or leave like all the others. And I'm not getting that doing what I'm doing now."

"I hear you."

Reagan leaned her body into the back cushions of her chair, softening her tone as she stretched her arms out wide.

"And I want that for you, too."

"Well, of course," Keisha added. "We both do. We just don't want you feeling like you need to settle for some random guy you meet online when…"

Her voice trailed off as she looked to Reagan for backup.

"When what?" I asked, squinting my eyes at them both.

We'd been doing so well, I thought. But I had a feeling that was all about to change with the mention of one name. They each hesitated, but after a beat, Reagan finally spoke.

"When Brandon is right there, *cher*."

*Ahh. Brandon.* And there it was, just like clockwork. He was Jake's best friend and probably one of the most attractive and casually seductive men I'd ever met. Lord knows, there were days when just the sound of his voice made my knees weak. But Brandon was not exactly known for being the most monogamous person, either. As a matter of fact, as long as I'd known him, he'd had his own hefty rotation of men and women keeping him satisfied and occupied and totally not thinking about me. Reagan and Keisha didn't seem to care about that at all, however, and were convinced that we should be together—a sentiment they managed to bring up almost any time I talked about dating anyone other than him.

"Don't start with me about Brandon today, you guys. I don't know how many times I can say that he's not the one before you believe me."

"Well, that's because you never say why! And I may wear glasses, but I promise you that I can see things that are right in front of my face. Now, if you want me to pretend like I *don't* see the way the two of you are when you're around each other, then I'm going to need an explanation, sorry."

Keisha shrugged and then grabbed the pitcher from the table and poured herself a new glass before leaning all the way back into her seat as well, mimicking Reagan's stance. She moved slowly, careful not to waste any sangria on the white graphic tee she wore tied on top of her blush, midcalf satin dress, but I knew she was also trying to make a subtle point to me that she was "seated" for my response.

"Is it that I don't tell you why or that you never think my answer is sufficient?" I replied defiantly.

"Well, your answer really *isn't* sufficient," Reagan said, locking eyes with me even as she delicately scooped fresh strawberries and blueberries onto the last pieces of her pancakes and then went back to her previous position in her chair. "You want us to believe that if this were Keisha and not you, you'd just be okay with her avoiding quite possibly the love of her life simply because we're friends with him already? I'm not buying it."

"I love you, Rae, but a) that's super dramatic. The love of my life, c'mon."

"I said what I said."

"And b)," I continued with a sigh. "That's a gross simplification of things and you know it. There are a million reasons why Brandon and I could never be a thing. For starters, he's not just one of our friends, he's your fiancé's *best* friend."

I pointed to Reagan as she nodded in agreement, her mouth now full of food.

"Mmm-hmm. Go on."

"And as you know, that brings with it a lot of complications," I added. "For instance, we have a great group dynamic. We all go out together, and it's fun and lighthearted. If he and I were to ever cross that line, and something went wrong, that would ruin everything. Then suddenly, it would be all my fault that the whole group can't hang out with each other anymore? Nah, I don't want that kind of weight hanging over me. Second, he's also become one of *my* closest friends, and it feels too risky to even think about going beyond that. I know you might say that that's me planning for us not to work out before I even give it a shot, but let's be real—I'm thirty-two, and I've dated anywhere between twenty to thirty guys since high school. Where has that gotten me? Still very single. So, you know what that tells me? The chances of me and Brandon dating and things imploding are far greater than the opposite. I can handle that with some guy from a dating app…not him."

Reagan finished eating her pancake in silence while Keisha sipped on her drink, both clearly indicating that they wanted me to say more before they jumped in again. At least this was different from them ganging up on me earlier, but it somehow felt like it would have the same end result. Still, I happily obliged, hoping to, once and for all, end the Brandon talks, which had been going on for the better part of the past year. The truth was, I *wanted* them to be excited about me really focusing on getting out there again, but I *needed* them to stop bringing up Brandon as if he was a legit option for me.

"Not to mention, there's the fact that I don't even know if he likes me like that. You all say that he does, but *he* never has. And that's important. Because listen, it's no secret that Brandon dates a lot—if 'date' is the word you want to use—and yet, he's never asked me out despite plenty of opportunities to do so in the two years that we've known each other. He's never tried to kiss me. Yes, he flirts with me, but that's just Brandon. He flirts with everyone. Sometimes I don't even think he knows he's doing it. Outside of that, he's really never done or said *anything* to imply he has any interest in me at all. So, I know you two are convinced that I have this huge crush on him, but besides simply not being blind, that doesn't really add up to him being a picture perfect partner for me, either."

I paused to catch my breath after my soliloquy-level explanation and tried to determine if my friends had heard anything I'd just said or if it had been a big ol' waste of my energy. I couldn't quite tell as they each sat staring at me with little to no facial expressions, but I knew I'd learn soon enough.

"Soooo, to me," I added, pointing toward my chest for emphasis, "when you put all that together, it's just a big heaping pile of high risk with very low chance of reward."

"It's a heaping pile of something all right," Reagan whispered under her breath, just loud enough for me to hear it.

Keisha took another sip from her drink before sitting up straight and pouring her eyes into mine.

"Giselle Lewis," she said.

"Yes?"

I ran my right hand through my shoulder-length, jet-black twists as I waited for her to continue.

"Are you done?"

"I guess so. For now."

"Good. Because, baby girl, you know what all that sounded like? A lot of fear coming out of your mouth. Didn't it, Rae?"

Keisha spun her body toward Reagan, who couldn't wait to chime in again.

"Oh yeah. I'd go even further and say it was a heaping amount of malarky and fear."

"Okay, wait…what about what I said has anything to do with fear? You asked me why he's not an option, right?"

I glanced at them both as I let my rhetorical question breathe for a moment, partially hoping that it would remind them how we got into this conversation in the first place. It wasn't my idea to bring up Brandon, after all. I was simply explaining why I wanted them to stop trying to throw us together.

After a few deep breaths, I continued, knowing the exact mic drop words to use in my favor.

"Okay, so, then what's wrong with me answering you by saying that I want to date someone who makes it abundantly clear that he wants to be with me, who also doesn't carry the risk of messing up my friend group, and you know, someone who's just nice, sensible and maybe, possibly, adores me?"

"Nothing's inherently wrong with that," Reagan replied, her cheeks going flush either from the conversation or the multiple drinks she'd had…or both. "Except that you *absolutely* like Brandon. Now, maybe you don't want to admit that because of all the reasons you spelled out, but you can't deny it, not to us at least. We've seen how your face literally lights up when he calls you. We've been in the room when the chemistry between y'all is so electric, we all feel like we're invading your privacy or something. And don't the two of you talk almost every day?"

I nodded my head in silence.

"Okay, exactly. So, you want to talk about dating someone who supports you and adores you? Brandon is right there, all the time. He was the first person who suggested we go out and celebrate when you paid off your student loans. He's quick to compliment you and tell you how beautiful you look. Need I say again that you talk almost every day? But, sure, let's base his interest solely on whether he's kissed you or asked you out."

"You sound ridiculous, Rae," I replied with a laugh. "Him showing up for me proves that he's a *good friend*—nothing else. We've all seen him on the prowl. You know how I know when he's interested in someone? It's because he asks them out. That's the part that matters. Are you honestly saying it's not? You get how wild that sounds, right?"

"It's different, though, *cher*, because it's so obvious that y'all should be together."

"But it's not. It's not obvious at all, and frankly, I'm kind of shocked at you two. More than anyone else, you've seen me have to pick myself up over and over again after yet another relationship failed because the guy was inconsistent or started being distant or it turned out all he really wanted to do was Netflix and chill all the time. After seeing that and knowing how hard it's been for me, to hear me tell you that I just want someone who's intentional with me and it's easy and clear, and then to say it doesn't matter that Brandon has exhibited none of those things? That's wild. Seriously."

"Whoa, whoa, that's not what we're saying at all—" Reagan started replying before Keisha interjected, dropping her voice to calm the tension.

"It makes sense that that's what you hear, though, because you're scared," she said. "That's what I mean by the fear taking over. Don't get me wrong; I understand why. I was deathly afraid to be real with myself and acknowledge that I wanted to be with Julian last year, remember? I had excuse upon excuse for why I didn't like him, and it would never work out, anyway. But *you* were the one who called me out and told me to let my guard down and stop running from what was so clear to everyone else. All we're saying right now is we want you to stop stubbornly refusing to accept the truth, too—you're into Brandon, Gig! I mean, how hard is that to admit? Who's really the Taurus here? Me or you, girl?"

"And," Reagan added, jumping back in to complete her thought, "if you're talking about letting the universe know you're ready, I think it's far more important that you no longer fight your feelings for the person you truly want to be with than that you get on some random dating app. Now, will Brandon still have to step up? Of course! For all we know, Jake could be having this same conversation with him right now. But if I'm being honest, my focus is less on what Brandon will do and more on whether you're willing to at least be open to the possibility. That's about you more than it is about the outcome."

This was why it was incredibly difficult to take any two of us on when we'd banded together on an idea, I realized. We could be relentless! I didn't mind it when I was on the other side, as Keisha had alluded to, but being the one in the hot seat was torture.

"Okay," I said, relaxing my shoulders and jaw and trying to focus on the fact that I knew they meant well, even if we didn't agree. "So, what I'm hearing is that you think if I simply admit that I like Brandon, all of a sudden the rainbows are going to appear, butterflies are going to lovingly grace my presence and the world will be at peace again?"

"Ha ha, joke all you want," Reagan replied. "But there's something to believing that the things, and maybe the people, you want are possible for you. And if you don't want to do it for some pie-in-the-sky reason, can you just do it for me? Because I've been dying for you to just admit that the man is capital *F* fine, all right? And there are a lot worse looking people you could be enamored with than the deep caramel brown personal trainer whose locs have probably inspired countless dreams of folks holding on to them for dear life as he's stroking them deeply."

"Reagan!"

I screamed out in horror as she unknowingly described one of my very own fantasies that had gotten me through a lonely night or two.

"What? You don't like me talking about your man like that, huh?"

She winked at me and flung her barrel curls behind her shoulder, clearly believing she'd been the one to actually deliver the mic drop, not me. I rolled my eyes while giggling in response again, partially in defeat but also because I was out of words to protest. I just knew what they refused to see, apparently. No one in the world thought the man wasn't attractive, but Brandon was far too much of a risk for my liking. Even Keisha's comments lacked an understanding of what I was trying to say—yes, he was a good friend, a great friend even, and that's why I didn't want to risk losing him over something that felt so incredibly uncertain.

"Oh my God, no," I protested. "It's not that at all. I just… I don't know, y'all. Yes, he's fine! Okay, I'll give you that, but…that's…eh. I don't know…"

"Mmm-hmm, you're stuttering, Gig," Keisha said with a chuckle. "It's okay. It's cute even!"

Without realizing it, Keisha had thankfully interrupted me before whatever word vomit was surely about to spew out of me. That would have been the last thing I needed in that moment. As it was, I was still desperately trying to figure my way out of this part of the conversation and back to…well, really anything else.

My face must have given all of that away, because out of nowhere, Reagan finally put her petty aside and came to my rescue.

"Okay, okay, we'll stop badgering you for now," she said sweetly. "I will merely say this one last thing—over everything else, your explanations really just sound a little boring, and you, my dear Gig, are anything but that. I mean, do you know who's sitting across this table from me? A woman who is a housing advocate and a bomb-ass illustrator. A fashionista who commands attention when she walks in the room, even with a simple pair of loafers or tennis shoes on. One of the kindest, most giving people I know—"

"And my best friend, don't forget that part," Keisha interrupted, pointing her hand to the sky like she was giving a testimony at church.

"Yes, that too, of course!" Reagan continued.

"And…someone who's always trying to get everyone else laid," Keisha added, interjecting again as she took another sip of her drink.

"OMG, hello!? Exactly! And that woman… Giselle Catherine Lewis from Philadelphia, Pennsylvania, who moved all the way to LA by herself for college, then to New York with big dreams of changing the world…she deserves so much more than just— What were the words she used, Keish?"

"Someone who's 'nice, sensible and *maybe, possibly, adores*' her."

"Right. I mean what the hell was that? *Maybe, possibly*, if I could get a crumb of adoration, please, sir…just no passion or risk of me actually falling in love with you."

Reagan raised her hands into a prayer formation and mockingly pleaded at me while she waited for my response, but honestly, I had nothing. I was all out of fight, and especially thrown off by how my words repeated back to me sounded when they weren't coming from my mouth. Part of me wondered if I was too quickly settling for the idea of good enough before even trying to see if what I really desired was available for me.

I threw up my hands in defeat and settled into my chair.

"We're just saying you deserve more than that is all…" Reagan continued.

"Risk of disappointment be damned," Keisha added with a stern nod in my direction.

"Okay," I said, with yet another sigh. "I hear you both. I'm *still* going to probably get on at least one of the dating apps, but maybe with different intentions than before."

"I would expect nothing less," Keisha chuckled in response. "And maybe just consider what we're saying about Brandon?"

Now *that* I couldn't promise them, but she knew that already when she asked me.

Just in the nick of time, Niko walked up to our table again, ready to take our orders for our second entrée. I would have jumped up to kiss him on his cheeks if I'd thought it appropriate, but either way, I was immensely thankful for his interruption.

"All right, ladies," he said with a wink as his Dominican accent floated over the music blaring from the DJ. "What are we having for round two?"

We each quickly looked back at our menus to remember what we'd decided on earlier.

"I'm going to have the salmon *caribeño*," I replied, handing my menu over to his outstretched hands.

"And I'll have the *pollo al carbon*," Reagan added.

Keisha mulled over her menu a second longer, clearly trying to determine if she was going to stick with her first choice or change her mind.

"Do you like the *que chimi*?" she finally asked.

"Oh yes, it's *very* good. One of our more popular items."

"Okay, great. I'll get that then."

With that finally settled, she breathed a sigh of relief and handed her menu over to him as well.

"And more sangria, yesss?" he asked with a grin that implied he already knew the answer.

"Yes, please!" Reagan gleefully replied for us all. "It's not bottomless if the drinks stop coming, Niko."

"And we can't have that, now, can we?"

He quickly turned around and grabbed another pitcher nearby, refilling all our glasses with a grin.

"No, we can't," we all responded in unison, once again sounding like a choir, but this time with me in it.

Once Niko was gone again, I took in a short breath and looked at my girls.

"That last list of what I want really didn't sound all that good, did it?" I asked earnestly.

"Nah, sis, it didn't…like, at all."

Leave it to Keisha to bluntly, yet calmly, confirm my suspicions. This was why I'd kept her annoying ass around for all these years. Well, that, and I knew how much she loved me and wanted the best for me. I just also knew I was going to have to figure this one out my way.

## *Chapter Two*

Three hours later, I was back home in Hamilton Heights, sufficiently tipsy and feeling the need to reflect on everything that had come up over brunch. The girls had given me a lot to think about, but before I could deep dive any further, I was in desperate need of some water. Once I crossed the threshold at my door, I immediately exchanged my loafers for my nude-brown, fuzzy house slippers that always felt like heaven when I slipped my feet inside. Then, almost as if in a daze, I seamlessly glided toward my kitchen, politely asking Alexa to turn on my favorite R&B playlist along the way.

The refreshing coolness of the water instantly lulled me into a feeling of euphoria, where I found myself closing my eyes and simply reveling in the stillness of the moment. It was nice to be back home. I'd, of course, enjoyed our brunch, lively as it was, but honestly, there was something so peaceful about a Sunday afternoon in my apartment with nothing but a bunch of singers extolling about love reverberating off my walls. I stood for a beat and took in a deep breath as I let the feeling of calm wash over me.

*This is exactly what I needed*...especially after I'd spent what felt like at least an hour defending my decisions to my well-meaning, but very opinionated, best friends. Probably the only thing that would have made the moment better, I realized, would be if my next move involved walking to my bedroom and curling into the arms of the boyfriend that had been patiently waiting for me to come home.

That wasn't yet the case, however, so I slowly opened my eyes, poured myself another glass of water and began walking to my living room. I had every intention of plopping onto my sage green sectional, lying back and letting the likes of everyone from Jodeci to Summer Walker sing me through my feelings when a curious idea hit me like a ton of bricks: I needed to sketch...and now.

I didn't exactly have a plan to draw anything specific, but the urge to pick up a pencil and let my hands do the "talking" was so intense, there was no way I could deny it. It probably also wasn't a coincidence that the desire came so strongly over me just as Mary J. Blige began singing her classic '90s hit, "Be Happy." Like other babies of that era, who weren't initially old enough to understand that song when it came out, I'd fallen in love with it much later on and found it to be a great reminder of what I actually wanted in love and in my life. And so, with the Queen of Hip-Hop Soul egging me on, I knew exactly what I needed to do. Without another thought, I quickly pivoted from my original plan, put my glass down and started scouring my place to find my most recent sketchbook and my favorite set of colored pencils.

Room by room, I looked. I checked the drawers in my coffee table first, recalling the nights I'd sat on my living room floor and drawn everything from what I saw on TV to what I'd walked past on my way to work that day. But unfortunately, all that I found in there were old DVDs and Wii games that I probably needed to recycle. Next, I went to my hallway closet. Ever since I'd moved into my own apartment and had the ability to make sure almost every-thing had an organized place where it belonged, that closet had served as my de facto catch-all spot. A place for misfit items or even sketch tools that I hadn't used in...

I paused my search briefly to consider how long it had been since I dared to draw something.

At least a year, I realized. Maybe more?

*Wow, that's a long-ass time.* Out of the many things Reagan had gotten wrong in her speech at Republica, her brag-ging on me as an illustrator in addition to being a housing advocate was probably one that had struck the hardest be-cause I knew what she didn't. I hadn't picked up a pencil to draw anything in quite some time.

As much as that realization felt like a gut punch, it also helped me remember where my sketchbook and pencils just might be. In a flash, I ran to my bedroom and crouched down to see under my bed. After moving several items out of the way, I finally found the clear box I'd placed them in the year before. Tucked behind my Christmas tree bag and the litany of color-coordinated decorations I'd purchased throughout my time in the city.

As I grabbed the box from its hiding spot, all the mem-ories of why I'd buried it behind some of my favorite sym-bols of joy came flooding back to me almost as if someone had reverse engineered the *Men in Black* neuralyzer and used me as the guinea pig. A little over a year before, as the sunsets were beginning to color the April sky slightly later in the day, I'd gone on my seventh date with one of the most gorgeous men I'd ever met. His skin was a deep cocoa brown with golden undertones, and his eyes had a way of boring into my soul that made me feel completely exposed but also sent thrilling sensations down my spine whenever he looked at me. More importantly, in the few months that we'd known each other, he had opened up so honestly and vulnerably that he'd managed to convince a very jaded me that I could trust him. That maybe all the tears I'd secretly cried over the men before him who'd let me down or the times when I hadn't even allowed them to get that close to me had all led to me being the person I was when we met, and so it had all been worth it.

Inspired by this date, I had come home and drawn pages upon pages of beautiful rose-and-white cherry blossoms, hoping that a love made just for me was finally starting to bloom in my life. Not two weeks later, that same relationship had turned into a telenovela storyline, complete with one woman DM-ing me on Instagram to let me know that she was six months pregnant for him and another leaving a "Hey Barbara, this is Shirley." type message on my phone. I had no idea how either woman knew about me or how to contact me, nor did I care to find out. Because what I did know was a simple truth: he'd tricked me into trusting him, and he'd been lying all along.

I never said another word to that guy. I simply blocked him, and them, from ever being able to communicate with me again and packed my sketchbook and pencils away, shoving them far behind everything else under my bed. By the time I was done, I'd rather successfully locked all my feelings away into that very same clear box and had moved past being a woman completely dejected by yet another man. Instead, I'd shifted into one who was able to get up, wipe her tears away and do what she needed to do to continue showing up in her job and with the people still in her life.

Fresh off that disaster of a memory, I sat up straight, leaning my back onto my bedframe, and opened the box as if it were a treasure that had recently been rediscovered.

Then, without hesitation, I flipped to the first empty page, palmed the closest colored pencil to the top and began to draw, letting my hand guide my strokes. As I did, I thought about how Reagan and Keisha had described me at brunch, and how as much as I hated to admit it, they were right about some aspects—I *had* come to the city a decade before, bright-eyed with my hopes set on changing the world with my drawings and finding a great big love. But now? At thirty-two, my desires were for things far more attainable.

Truthfully, the longer I'd lived in New York, the more sensible I'd become, slowly learning to choose small wins over lofty fantasies. I'd long ago given up on my dream of being a professional illustrator. And now, as an advocate, I knew being practical sometimes meant I had to be okay with getting twenty people access to housing instead of focusing on a pipe dream of what I wanted to do for the whole city. Maybe that wasn't as inspiring, but what I'd come to understand over time was that a lot of my big ideas weren't based in reality. They had no foundational grounding—couldn't exist except in the dreams of a young woman who wanted a better world. And that could sound great on the surface, but it had never been enough to actually make change happen. Not in my world, at least. Instead, what was real, what created tangible results, was the day-to-day work I put in, fighting for housing access for every single person my small company had the resources to help.

In that same way, my experiences had taught me to stop getting my hopes up too high when it came to love. So, now, all I really craved was a good, kind relationship that would complement the life I'd built and loved in New York and that wouldn't rip my heart into tiny, little pieces if it didn't work out. That wasn't going to win me any lover girl awards, but it was a twenty-two-year-old's folly to live with your head in the clouds all the time. And I was far from that now.

I looked down as my hand continued to scratch and shade in the image coming together on the page, and I thought about all the dates I'd gone on in the past decade, as well. The men who I'd hoped were "the one," and the guys who it had been clear from minute two that I'd never see again. The ones who'd graced the comforts of my bed and learned the inner workings between my thighs for months, sometimes years, at a time, but who never had intentions of building something long-term with me. Occasionally, I recalled, there *were* the guys who adored the ground I walked on, but unfortunately for them, they'd usually met me right after I'd survived another heartbreak by numbing so well that I couldn't possibly give them what they wanted. These were all the relics of a woman once filled with pipe dream aspirations that had left me perpetually single and resistant to risking my heart again.

And then, of course, there was Brandon. Sweet, confident and capital *F* fine, as Reagan had called him. I could remember the first time we met like it was yesterday. Only a few months after Reagan had moved to New York, and after what would become one of our signature bottomless brunch outings, she'd convinced me and Keisha to come with her to cheer on Jake at a pickup basketball game in Harlem. She was so tipsy and cute, sauntering up to the basketball court and yelling out his name, that neither of us had the heart to tell her she'd clearly distracted him from hitting the winning shot. Of course, his boys were all too willing to point this out in great detail, good-naturedly clowning him after the game. But anyone looking at the two of them for even one minute could tell that Jake didn't care.

Brandon, who had been on his team, and who I later

learned had been one of his fraternity brothers, came running over to us not long after the game, still dripping with sweat. It was like watching a camera move in slow motion as he casually, but very seductively, used his towel to wipe off his face, then neck and finally his hands. Once he was relatively dry, he turned toward us and introduced himself. I remembered wondering at the time if he'd lingered a little longer when he took my hand, but then quickly assured myself that it was all in my imagination. After all, I looked amazing, standing tall at five foot seven, face card never declining, and clad in a pink-and-red floral shorts set that made my legs look they were made to be on fashion runways. But this man, with his chocolate dreads swinging past his broad shoulders and his shirt clinging to his chest from the perspiration he hadn't bothered to wipe up, was beyond what I thought *attractive* could even mean. He was stunning, and he knew it.

"Man, Rae, next time, you gotta either be here for the whole game or wait until it's over, because my dude here can't think straight when it comes to you," he said, flashing a large Colgate smile as he tapped Jake on his chest and then retied his locs into a top bun.

"My bad, B," she replied with a sly smirk. "I guess I just got a little excited seeing my guy with the ball in his hands about to make big moves. I'll remember that in the future."

"It's all good, sis. My bro is in love, you know. That's how he's supposed to respond."

Jake laughed and waved off Brandon's comment before gripping Reagan by her hips to bring her closer toward him.

"Don't let this dude fool y'all," he said with a chuckle. "Brandon knows a lot of things, but he wouldn't know love if it hit him upside the head."

"Damnnn. Now, why would you disparage my character like this in front of these beautiful ladies," Brandon responded, glancing at me before taking my right hand in his again. "You never know, maybe I'm just a hopeless romantic waiting for someone like Miss Giselle here to walk into my life and cure me of my playboy afflictions."

He spun me around playfully, stopping me right in front of his face so that I found myself staring into his deep, penetrating, dark brown eyes for a moment too long. When he let my hand go, it took everything in me not to let out an audible sigh.

"Hopeless romantic?!" Jake blurted out. "Sure, sure, I'll believe that when I see it."

"Jaaake," Reagan chided him. "C'mon now. Brandon's a lovable guy, I could totally see him falling head over heels for the right person. Maybe even a brown-skinned cutie from Philly."

She winked my way, and I instantly felt myself slide back over to Keisha. The guy was strikingly handsome, but everything about him read "danger zone," especially the way he'd expertly lured me into that mutual stare for just a second too long. This was a man who knew how to seduce subtly but was also clearly used to getting everything he wanted. I had all the information I needed to know that I should keep my distance.

"Nah, he's right, Rae," Brandon countered. "I'm a menace, but hey, also a damn good time. Some people find that a worthy trade-off."

He shrugged and flashed another smile that sent chills down my spine and caused goose bumps to form on my exposed skin. Confirmation received, I thought, making a mental note even then that this guy seemed like he could be fun to hang around, but I better not ever allow myself to have anything even close to feelings for him.

The next song on my playlist began, interrupting my memories with a sweet guitar riff that eventually mixed with a familiar blend of low drums and soft piano notes all before Yebba's voice rounded out the melody. For my purposes, she and Lucky Daye had made one of the best-sounding heartbreak songs when they came together to sing "How Much Can a Heart Take." It was as if their tones were meant to seamlessly float over the chords in perfect harmony while they gut-wrenchingly detailed how much love could hurt when it was ending. I knew all too well about that.

Suddenly taken out of my trance, I looked down at my sketchbook and marveled at the image I'd created, almost unconsciously, as if my hands had taken over the reins from my brain, knowing that only they could truly illustrate what was in my heart without logic and sense getting in the way. There, before me, was a meticulously drawn depiction of two people lying out in the greenest corner of my favorite park in the city—Fort Tryon, located in the northernmost part of Washington Heights—flanked by the flowing streams of the Hudson River to the left and rows upon rows of bright orange, yellow and pink flowers to the right.

The guy's five-foot-eleven, athletic frame was positioned perfectly between the woman's long, brown legs, which practically glistened under the bright sun, making it so that she could comfortably run her hands through his waist-length locs as they lay across her neon yellow shorts and folded onto their blanket. Next to them on that blanket was a bottle of champagne, a wicker basket of snacks and two half-full flutes that I'd drawn to look like they could almost tip over with a strong gust of wind but were magically secured in their place. The sky above them was a beautiful shade of azure blue and filled with only a few clouds that had dutifully parted to allow the brightest sun to pierce through.

Like any artist worth her weight, I'd even added small details to the picture that indicated they were in a park filled with other people, despite the fact that it was clearly meant to show they'd created their own world in the midst. To their right, on one of the park's walking paths, a young woman strolled past two giggling friends with her Pomeranian dog while at least three different-sized groups of people lay on their own blankets around the central couple, filling out the background of the image.

The focal point was obvious, however. All while barely realizing it, I'd drawn near identical versions of me and Brandon—capturing everything from the way my jet-black twists fell slightly past my shoulders, accentuating the pronounced dips in my clavicle, to the way his goatee curved around his full lips as he looked up at me. Mostly I was stunned by how I'd drawn our bodies, which appeared as if they were practically created to be entwined with one another as we spread our limbs across the blanket. On our faces were looks of equal parts peace and tenderness.

"What in the world did I just draw?" I asked myself out loud, staring at the illustration wistfully.

At first, I was excited by the image and how detailed it was, impressed that over a year later, I could create something so beautiful without overthinking it. How effortlessly I'd allowed my hands take over and drive every stroke of the pencil, every color decision, every re-creation of what I could so vividly see in my head from all the days I'd spent in that park, walking its paths and longing for someone to join me. But that feeling didn't last long. Eventually, it shifted to concern as I was suddenly confronted with reality while Yebba and Lucky Daye sang softly about hearts changing with the moon. Before me was this beautiful and lovely illustration, but what it represented was far too risky to even allow myself to fully want it.

*What was the point of hoping for what I knew couldn't be? Right?*

That was just the remnant of my twenty-two-year-old folly rearing its head all over again.

. Recognizing my mistake, I snatched the page out of my sketchbook, crumpled it into a tight ball and tossed it aimlessly over my shoulder into my open closet. I didn't need to waste time dwelling on that image for too long. Instead, what I needed to do was refocus my energy on goals that had actual potential and possibilities I could legitimately see happening in my future.

With a deep breath, I gathered myself, grabbed another pencil, closed my eyes and asked myself a very important question: "What's a more realistic manifestation, Gigi? Better yet, what would feel safe and nice and comforting to you?"

It took a little while for my mind to get there, but after a few minutes, I had another vision to work with…one that didn't involve Brandon. I gratefully opened my eyes and, with an energy that felt intentional, began to sketch out the first details of the Little Red Lighthouse, which sat to the side of the George Washington Bridge, right off the bank of the Hudson River. From there, I added myself into the image laughing alongside a beautiful, but random man. My face was filled with joy while his body curled over with glee. And while you could barely see his expression, you could instantly tell these two people were happy and enjoying a simple, carefree moment together.

"That's much better," I noted, removing my hands from the illustration, finally satisfied with the results.

This was more of what I could handle. And it would do just fine.

# *Chapter Three*

"Giselle! Wait! Wait!"

My ears perked up as I heard my coworker screaming my name, first from afar but then growing louder as he drew closer to me, repeating it with an urgency that was so alarming, it prevented me from taking another step. This was despite the fact that it was already two hours later than I'd wanted to be leaving work. But after hearing his voice go up a full five octaves out of nowhere, there was no way I could simply jump on the elevator and pretend I hadn't heard it.

With deep curiosity, I turned my body 180 degrees and immediately saw Antonio racing up to me, completely flustered, but with a distinct expression of gratitude rising on his face. I watched him as he stopped in his tracks and attempted to catch his breath while I waited to learn what all this commotion was going to mean for my ability to make it back uptown before my grocery store closed for the night.

"Whew, I'm so glad I caught you," he said, his breathing still quite heavy. "You didn't hear me calling your name all that time?"

"My bad. I guess I was in a daze, just trying to get out of here. But what's wrong? Are you okay?"

"Girl, it's not about me. You dropped your keys!"

Antonio raised his hand and held out a small bundle of keys, connected only by a simple brown heart keychain that my mom had given me when I first moved to New York. It had been her way of reminding me that she was always with me. Sadly, it had become that much more important when she passed away soon after my twenty-eighth birthday. I don't know what I would have done had I gotten all the way home only to find out that I didn't have it on me.

"Oh my God, thank you," I said, politely taking them from him and clutching them to my chest. "I totally wouldn't have realized until it was the exact wrong time to do so."

"Yeah, I know. That's the only reason you had me out here running like I'm freaking Usain Bolt trying to catch you. What's got you so in a rush, anyway? Hot date? And you have to tell him big news?"

Antonio's eyes shone brightly as he looked toward me, clearly anticipating that I was about to regale him with some amazing story about how I was late to meet up with a new Prince Charming, and I just *had* to get out of there before he erroneously believed I was standing him up. I almost hated to break his precious little heart, but the truth was a lot more boring than that.

"Absolutely not," I replied with a chuckle. "I just don't have anything cooked at home, and I've ordered off Uber Eats three nights in a row now. So, I'm trying to make it to my grocery store in time to avoid the same fate tonight or having to pick up some fast food on the way."

"Oh."

Antonio's once beaming face fell so quickly, I didn't have the stomach to continue looking at it. Plus, for such a short word, his response was loud and clear. I quickly checked my watch to both avoid continuing that conversation and to see just how much time I had left.

"And...now I only have about forty-five minutes before that happens. So, I hate to run, but..."

"Oh, yes! Go do what you need to do," he said, waving a hand in the air to whoosh me away. "But try not to drop anything else, okay? I won't be around to save you next time."

"I'll do my best. Promise."

Grateful to have maneuvered myself out of a longwinded explanation of how I was too young to be acting so old—an Antonio signature at this point—I quickly winked goodbye and hopped on the open elevator that had been waiting for my arrival.

"See you tomorrow!" I called out as the doors closed in front of me, and I prepared myself to make a run for the train as soon as I got downstairs.

If Antonio had considered himself Usain Bolt just minutes before, I was Sha'Carri Richardson, racing through my building's lobby and onto the streets of Hell's Kitchen, desperate to make it to the Port Authority terminal in time to catch the next A train. Despite it being after 8:00 p.m. on a Thursday night, I still found myself dodging a sea of tourists as I maneuvered my way through the glass doors of the building, expertly swiped my MetroCard so that it only took me one try to get through the turnstiles and then zoomed down the stairs to get to the A platform for trains heading uptown.

I couldn't have timed it better, as the train pulled up almost at the exact moment that my suede sneakers touched the last step, giving me just enough time to slide through the opening doors and find a seat for my twenty-plus-minute ride.

Thank God I'd chosen an outfit almost tailor-made for

running through the streets of New York that day, I thought as I settled into my seat and finally took in a long and grateful deep breath. That morning I'd decided to pair my tan sneakers from Zara that had a fun little fringe situation happening on top with my loose-fitting, turquoise, satin midi skirt and a lightweight graphic sweatshirt featuring a mock turtleneck that helped keep me warm enough for our always frigid office but didn't suffocate me once I walked outside. Little did I know then that my sneakers and the "flowyness" of my skirt would come in handy when I needed to run like my life depended on it, but then again, the day had been full of surprises that had somehow felt fate-like.

I dug around in my bag and found my earbuds so that I could listen to some jams for the rest of my train ride as I thought back on just how wild the day had turned out to be.

It had started off like any other day at work, with me reviewing a bunch of case files on the latest group of people we'd connected to a rapid rehousing center while I sat in one of the office stations, looking out onto our completely open floor plan. Our company had made a big deal about remodeling the office space a few years before, taking out all the individual offices and replacing them with glass-windowed conference rooms and making it so that no one person had ownership or claim over a particular area on the floor. It was supposed to make for more transparency and greater collaboration among your team members, but truthfully, a lot of times, it simply meant that people were sitting right next to each other with noise-canceling headphones on and Slacking about their frustrations.

Since we only had to be in the office a few days a week, I normally didn't mind it, but I had learned by now how to go into my own little world to make sure I wouldn't be distracted by all the activity around me. That was how it took me a minute to notice when my boss walked up to me around 11:00 a.m. with the biggest grin I'd probably ever seen on his face.

"Giselle," he whispered, attempting to get my attention but not cause too much of a scene.

I didn't really make that possible, though, as I nearly jumped out of my skin when I finally realized he was standing directly next to me. How long he'd been there, I genuinely had no clue. But I knew as soon as I looked at him that he had capital *B* big news.

"Oh! Hi, Silas," I said, hoping to quickly regain my composure. "Sorry, I didn't see you there at first. Did you need something?"

"It's all good," he replied, pulling a chair up to me and plopping down in it so that we would be eye to eye. "I know you're doing good work, Giselle. I see it. We all see it."

In the ten years since I'd graduated from college and moved to New York, Silas was my first ever Black male supervisor, and I appreciated how he just seemed to intrinsically understand the ways that different power dynamics could influence your work. He never situated himself standing up to talk to me while I sat, for example. And he almost always asked for my opinion before giving his own. In a career that could be really difficult on the days when, despite my best efforts, I couldn't help more people, it was little things like that that kept me showing up for work and wanting to give it my all.

I turned my chair toward his and waited with bated breath for whatever was coming next.

"And I'm happy to be the one to give you some news that might just make you start running through the hall," he said, his grin growing ever wider.

"Oh my God, Silas, spit it out, please. I'm a nervous wreck over here."

"Okay, okay," he replied and leaned in closer. "We just heard back from HUD, and our proposal to pitch them an idea to address homelessness in New York was accepted."

"What?!"

I sat up straighter in my chair and stared Silas down, telepathically signaling to him that he better not be playing with me.

"I know. It's almost surreal, except it's not. We're one of five companies that have been selected for this opportunity, so we've got to make sure that we hit this out of the park."

"Well, yeah," I replied, stunned but also incredibly excited. "This is what we've been working so hard for, to have this shot at partnering with them so we can finally make a bigger difference in this city."

"Exactly. And because it's such a big deal, I want you to run point on it."

My eyes widened as I tried to comprehend what he'd just said to me.

"I'm sorry, what?" I asked, feeling literal goose bumps pop up onto my skin.

"You heard me. You're the one who led the effort for the proposal, Giselle, so it's only right that you would lead the next stage of the process. And besides all that, I know that if anyone here is going to come up with something that will blow their minds but will also be doable, it's you. Now, I have every faith that you can do this, but I didn't want to put you on the spot in front of everyone until you said yes."

I stared back at Silas, speechless as every part of my body tried to catch up to what I was hearing. My brain was still stuck on the fact that we'd been selected. I barely had the capacity left to handle the news that I was being offered the reins on something so important to not only our company but the thousands of people in the city who just wanted a place to call home. My heart was trying to grasp how much Silas and, I assumed, the rest of the senior leadership team, believed in my ability to get this done. My legs wanted to do exactly what he'd joked about minutes before—jump up and hit a praise dance while I ran through the hall in glee. And my mouth, well, that was frozen in place as I tried and failed to come up with any words to say in response.

"This is the part where you say yes," he laughed, thankfully realizing that I'd lost all ability to find that one word on my own.

"Ye-yes," I finally replied, relief and panic flowing through me all at once.

"Good."

Before I could say anything else, Silas jumped up from his chair, cleared his throat and immediately drew everyone's attention toward him.

"All right, everyone, today's no longer just another Thursday. It's the day that I get to tell you everything's about to change around here."

I watched as each person's eyes lit up around me, their whole beings completely enthralled by this six-foot, slender, deep-chocolate-toned man as he delivered the news to them that he'd just given me. The wonder on their faces was both inspiring and a little terrifying, especially as I knew I was going to be the one to have to corral all this energy into something concrete, and as much as I was excited to take on the challenge, I also knew it wasn't going to be easy.

"It's now the first week of May, and we've only got until July to pull this together. I want us to be so prepared that when we walk through those doors in Washington,

DC, the only outcome possible is that we walk out of there with a new partnership and, most importantly, the funding to change the lives of so many people in this great city of ours," he continued. "So, let's not waste any time."

With those final words, Silas turned toward me, smiled once more and officially declared me the project lead to everyone present in the office that day. For my part, I stood up next to him, determined to look like the very definition of confidence, thanked him for the opportunity and calmly but assuredly explained my thinking to the rest of my colleagues.

"This is going to be an all-hands-on-deck, team effort," I said. "But I believe we can get it done. No idea is too big or small right now. I want us to consider them all and the implications each will have, from what it will take to effectively communicate it to the public down to the partnerships we'll need to establish or shore up to realistically make the idea work and the data we'll have to collect to accurately show how many people can be impacted by what we propose. Deal?"

"Hell yeah," I heard Antonio whisper as others nodded with excitement.

I tried my best not to giggle at his outburst. My nerves were working overtime, attempting to invade my brain waves as reality hit me. Not only were we going to have to figure out what this proposal would entail, but also I was going to be the one in charge of keeping our folks energized as we finalized it and managing their expectations of what could actually work in a city with a lot of low-key NIMBYism at play.

*No pressure, right?*

"Great," I replied, straightening my posture and conjuring up a smile that my mom, who'd spent twenty years on stage as a ballerina, would be proud of. "Well, let's get to work then."

From that moment on until I sat down on the train, my butt hadn't touched a seat for more than two minutes at a time. Instead, I'd spent the next several hours listening and brainstorming with every department that would have a say in this proposal. It was why I'd left the office as late as I did, and why I was most thankful to have found an empty spot on the train so that my body and brain could finally rest as I headed home.

Thee Sacred Souls' "Can I Call You Rose" began playing in my ears as I brought myself back into the present, staring out into the train's windows as it whooshed past the next station. I had two more stops before I needed to get back into running position, and I was determined to enjoy the sweet melody as it temporarily calmed my nervous system before the necessary chaos resumed.

# *Chapter Four*

With exactly fifteen minutes to spare, I bounced into the Key Foods Supermarket on 146th and Broadway, my R&B playlist still ringing in my ears and pushing me forward to what felt like my finish line for the evening. Indeed, I was a woman on a mission, ready to scoop up only what I needed for a quick stir-fry dinner and walk back out of those same doors before they began putting the locks on them. On my mental list: a frozen bag of mixed vegetables, preferably containing everything from sliced carrots to peas, green beans and broccoli; a large cut of fresh salmon; some cauliflower rice; a jar of soy sauce and a dozen eggs.

It was a staple go-to meal that Keisha and I used to make when we lived together in our first apartment in Harlem and needed to cook something quick, easy and relatively healthy. Of course, with her Louisiana taste buds leading the way, as we both started making a little more money, she began throwing more seafood into the mix. Sometimes, she'd combine shrimp with the salmon or even occasionally, add some scallops too. But tonight, I was going to keep it simple and go back to the basics. That's really all I had time to shop for anyway.

As I made my way through the aisles, I piled the items into my basket as fast as I could, not wanting to get to the store's countdown-to-closing before I had everything I needed. But once I'd successfully tackled that part of the mission, I added a box of Cap'n Crunch and a half gallon of 2% milk at the last minute, figuring that it might be good to have some quick breakfast food on hand since I was going to be working from home the next two days. Then, with an extra pep in my step, because I'd somehow pulled off what felt damn near impossible an hour before, I sauntered to the only cashier still open and quickly began loading my groceries onto the checkout conveyer belt as the person before me punched in their debit card information.

I slid my earbuds out and turned off my playlist just as PARTYNEXTDOOR began singing his sultry-sounding but conflict-laden classic "Come and See Me" with Drake. Despite the lyrics, it had become one of my favorite tunes to sing, but I had a thing about not wanting to be *that* person who walks up to the cashier clearly intending to avoid any real, human interaction. So, as I waited for my turn, I carefully placed the buds in their cartridge and watched as my items began slowly moving on the conveyer belt.

It was at that exact moment that I heard the person behind me chuckle deeply from something that sounded like the depths of his stomach.

*Oh no*, I thought to myself, had I done something embarrassing as I was pausing my playlist? As distracted as I'd been, there was no telling what I could have done.

I turned to him sheepishly, ready to give a preemptive look that said *Hey, don't judge me; it's like that sometimes*, when I was suddenly stopped dead in my tracks by a handsome man whose smile made me forget anything else I had in mind. Dressed like a J.Crew model, he wore a pair of slim-fit, black dress pants and an open gray blazer with an untucked white T-shirt and crisp white Air Maxes that somehow, someway actually all really worked together.

It was his smile that was most captivating, though, as it stretched across his whole face, crinkling his nose in the most adorable way. I had to literally bite down on the side of my cheek to stop myself from word vomiting what would surely have been the world's most awkward compliment ever.

"That's one interesting combination of foods," he said, winking at me and then nodding toward my groceries on the conveyer built. "Do you have a kid and an extremely healthy husband waiting for you at home?"

"Neither," I replied, letting out a high-school-like giggle that, try as I might, I simply couldn't contain. Call me presumptive, but it seemed like he was trying to figure out if I was single or not, and for some reason, I found it kind of cute. "Everything you see here is all for me. I like to call it balance."

"Ohh, okay, balance huh? That's one word for it."

The two of us laughed as he started unpacking his basket onto the moving belt as well, and I soon realized that Mr. Handsome didn't have any room to judge my choice of groceries.

"I'm sorry, you were laughing at me, but do you want to explain the frozen pizza and wings you've got going on? Kinda hypocritical, no?"

"I'd like to think I'm laughing *with* you," he corrected me. "But you know, touché. I didn't have a ton of time to grab something, so I just went with the first thing that came to mind."

"And so, you decided to get the same thing you could have ordered from any number of local pizza spots in the neighborhood?"

"Well, when you put it like that…" he replied, laughing again. "I guess I'm a man who's in desperate need of a good woman's wisdom. Maybe even one who likes children's cereal."

"Ha! Oh, so you're a smooth talker," I surmised. "Good to know."

"Or maybe I'm just willing to say whatever I need to to keep you smiling."

I looked back at this guy briefly, amused and intrigued, before dutifully turning my attention to the cashier, saying my pleasantries and waiting as she rang up each item. As she did so, I quietly used my peripheral vision to study the man who was unknowingly trying to blow up my theory that the universe wasn't going to just send someone my way as I casually shopped in the grocery store. Only three weeks had passed since I'd made that very case to Keisha and Reagan over brunch, and I just knew they were going to get a kick out of this story if it continued the way I hoped it might.

*Ugh. I hate it when they're right*, I thought. *Except maybe in this moment.*

After only a couple minutes—more than enough time to notice the way that his thick eyebrows framed his face or the slight curl pattern peeking through the top of his fade—I tapped my card on the machine and moved to the side to let Mr. Handsome take my place. Slowly and deliberately, I took my time packing my reusable bags so that if he wanted to, he certainly had the chance to make another move.

The only question was if he was going to take it.

"You know," he said, turning toward me as I placed the very last item in my bag, "you should do me a solid and let me see you again. I'm not going to be able to go home and rest knowing I let you walk away without at least asking for your name and number."

"Oh, is that so?" I asked, relieved that I hadn't been wrong about our connection, and that he'd finally spoken up. "Because I was starting to think you had intended on doing just that."

"Nah, I just had to let you sweat for a bit after I revealed the hold your smile had on me, and you batted those pretty eyes of yours and turned away."

"I did not," I replied, biting my lower lip to keep me from grinning like a Cheshire cat.

"Hmm. If you say so."

The look on Mr. Handsome's face made it clear that he was observing me and fully aware of the predicament I'd found myself in, desperate not to let on just how much I was enjoying our interaction. More importantly, I could also tell that he relished the effect he was having on me even as we both stepped to the side of the cashier line to make room for the next person.

"Well, I mean, I had to pay for my groceries," I protested, attempting to turn down the chemistry I felt radiating between us so that I wouldn't lose my composure in a grocery store. I could already feel the butterflies starting to tumble in my stomach, but I'd just met the man, so I couldn't exactly let him see me squirming already.

"I hear you."

"That didn't mean I didn't appreciate the compliment, though."

I watched as Mr. Handsome's green eyes flickered before me, traveling lustfully from mine down to my lips and then back up again. It was as if he wanted me to know what it might be like to be under his gaze as he made love to me for hours. Something that I realized my body craved as a shiver flew down my spine that was almost too sinful for the venue we were in.

"Oh, I know you liked it," he said, smiling back at me with one raised eyebrow. "That part was clear. I just pointed out that you turned away, so that meant I didn't get to properly introduce myself at the time. I'm Phillip, by the way."

The calm confidence he exuded as Phillip shifted from calling me out to something far more benign left me speechless for the second time that day. With his mischievous smirk still plastered on his face, Phillip raised his hand to meet mine, however, and I very quickly snapped out of my trance and responded in kind.

"I'm Giselle," I answered, immediately feeling a spark as our fingers wrapped themselves around one other. "Most people outside of work call me Gigi or Gig, though."

"Okay, Gigi," he said a with a head nod of approval. "Do I get the pleasure of getting your number as well?"

Almost too smoothly, as if it was his go-to move, Phillip then pulled his phone out of the inside of his blazer, unlocked it and handed it to me so that I could input my digits into his call log. If I hadn't been so caught off guard by the gesture, I might have said something slick in return. Instead, without even bothering to put up a fake fight, I dialed in my number, pressed the call button and handed it back to him. There was no use in denying it; he'd caught me hook, line and sinker.

"Thanks," he replied, tucking his phone away as he stepped in closer to me. "I have just one more request."

"Wow, you're relentless."

"Hey, what can I say? I'm used to negotiating all day."

"Okay, then. I'll bite. What else would you like?"

Before Phillip could respond, I grabbed one of my reusable bags and swung it over my shoulder so that it was perfectly clear that I was prepared to leave the store if he said something dumb. Then, I smiled back at him and braced myself for whatever was going to come out of his mouth next, hoping it wouldn't be anything that completely ruined what had been a really nice interaction thus far. In fact, the last ten minutes had been just the right amount of cute and flirty mixed with a bit of intrigue, but some guys didn't know how to stop while they were ahead, and I so didn't want him to be one of them.

"Don't worry, I'm not going to ask you for anything untoward," he replied, almost as if he had been able to read my mind and knew that he needed to defuse my spidey girl senses. "I was just wondering if you'd be interested in joining me for dinner tonight...virtually, that is."

"Oh."

I didn't bother acting as if Phillip's request hadn't caught me off guard. In less than a minute, I'd gone from assuming I might hear from him a couple weeks from now—a tried and true supersuave guy move that was totally meant to make a woman feel like the man wasn't pressed about her—to anxiously hoping he wouldn't say anything weird before I had a chance to walk away. I hadn't even considered the possibility of him simply wanting to FaceTime me in a few so we could continue our conversation.

*Whew, the way my brain worked overtime to try to protect me, it's so obvious I've been put through the ringer one time too many by the men I've let into my life.*

"Actually, you know what? I'd really like that," I replied, shaking all the negative thoughts that had been swirling around in my head. "I'm heading home now, so just call me when you're free. I'll be around."

"Bet. I'll see you again soon then."

"I guess you will."

I looked up into Phillip's dashing eyes and flashed him another smile before I grabbed the remainder of my bags and began walking. I could feel his eyes on me, and so I subtly but intentionally swung my hips as I sauntered away. He may have had the upper hand in a few of our interactions so far, but I knew that the satin fabric of my skirt gave him just enough of a glimpse of my curves that he'd be thinking about them until we spoke again.

If nothing else, I figured that might encourage him to be a man of his word and actually ring me tonight. But even if it didn't, I was at least satisfied knowing that I wasn't going to be the only one left speechless during our encounter.

I'd take that win.

By the time I heard my phone buzzing a little over thirty minutes later, I'd already changed into a light pink sweatshirt adorned with the words "Cozy Season" in script along with my most comfortable, but cute, heather-gray leggings. I'd also seasoned the salmon, cut it up into pieces and placed it covered into my oven while I began working on the rest of the stir-fry in the deep skillet I'd inherited from my mom when she passed. There weren't too many things that couldn't be cooked in that thing, so other than my beloved heart keychain, it had become one of my most favorite ways to make sure she was included as part of my usual routines.

Leaning over my kitchen counter, I scooped up my phone and did a quick face check before answering the incoming video call. From the looks of it, Phillip had changed as well and was now wearing a long-sleeved white shirt scrunched to about halfway up his forearm. It was a simple top, but the way it hugged his biceps, I almost had to stop myself from melting instantly.

"Hi," I said, initially attempting to hold back my smile but then changing my mind as I repositioned my phone so that I could still cook while talking to him.

He'd actually called, and when he said he would, so what was the point in pretending I wasn't happy to see him.

"Hey there," he replied, grinning into the camera as he very visibly scanned me with his eyes, clearly enjoying the effect he was having on me once again. "Now, that's what I've been missing for the past thirty minutes."

"I'm going to interpret that as 'It's really good to see you, Gigi,' and not something else."

"What's the other way you might take it?"

Phillip stared into the camera with a mischievous smirk on his face as he awaited my reply, his deep voice sending small shivers down my spine.

"I think it's best that I do not say what else I think you could have meant."

"Really? Because now, I would very much like you to."

"Oh, I just bet you would," I answered, rolling my eyes in jest. "I have to ask you something before we go any further, though."

For a hot second, a flash of disappointment and maybe concern seemed to spread across Phillip's face, and I realized that my awkward attempt to pivot our conversation could have come off very abrupt and even alarming. Thankfully, he quickly recovered and smiled brightly toward me.

"Okay," he said. "I'll bite. Hit me with your best shot, Gigi. I think you'll come to learn that I'm a pretty open book."

"All right, well, that's good to know because open and honest dialogue is like tops for me these days."

"Above all else?"

"It's right behind being attracted to the person."

Phillip nodded in understanding and leaned in closer to his phone.

"Hopefully you'll consider me two for two then."

"Time will tell," I replied, staring back at him with my cheeks rising up to the sky once again. "That said, my question right now is nowhere near that serious. I really just wanted to know why you stayed in the grocery store when I left. It's not like you had more things to buy, right? Plus, they were getting ready to close, so I know the cashier wanted us out of there!"

I couldn't explain why, but that question had been lingering in my mind ever since I turned the corner from the store and walked the few minutes between it and my apartment. While I'd certainly enjoyed teasing Phillip on my way out, it dawned on me afterward that it was kind of odd I'd even had the opportunity to do so. After all, we'd both obviously finished paying for our groceries at that point.

Phillip chuckled with that same velvety smooth tone I'd heard while we were in line. The same one that had stopped me in my tracks and literally forced me to turn around and see who was behind me.

"Great question," he said with a shrug. "I think, mostly, I was just trying not to come off as a creeper."

I watched in anticipation as Phillip leisurely walked from his kitchen to his living room, and then quietly fell onto his brown leather couch. The whole time, he held his phone high and in his left hand like a pro, never dropping it so far that I didn't see his face but also not bringing it so close to him that I could see inside his nostrils. For a moment, I briefly caught a glimpse of what looked like the waistband of a pair of gray sweatpants, but just as quickly, the focus was back squarely on his chest and above. I wondered what kind of arm exercises he must do to have that kind of bicep control, and then briefly considered what that might mean for his ability to pick me up and sustain his hold before brushing off the thought and bringing myself back to our present conversation. The fact that I could almost picture myself climbing on top of him on that sofa as he lay flat against one of his side cushions and stretched his other arm behind his head definitely didn't help my cause, but I was determined to persevere through it.

I had enough boy toys to last a lifetime if that was all I wanted, I reminded myself. With Phillip, I hoped there might be a chance for more than that, and I didn't want to risk that possibility by jumping into talks of sex or intimacy too soon.

Once he was finally settled in—and thankfully not a moment too soon for my heart's sake—Phillip continued.

"Uhh, my assumption is that we both probably live somewhere around here, and so, I didn't want you thinking I was trying to follow you home or anything like that. You'd already given me the *oh dear God, please don't let him be a stranger danger dude* look when I asked you for my last request, so I guess I just wanted to put your mind at ease a bit. I didn't stay inside too much longer, though. Maybe a couple minutes."

"Wow, okay," I replied, a little shocked and impressed with his answer. "That was actually really thoughtful of you."

"Yeah, but don't give me too much credit," he added. "I had the added benefit of being able to watch you walk away, too."

"I *knew* you were looking at me!"

"And I knew that you knew. That's what made it fun," Phillip countered with a wink. "I see that we both also changed when we got home, so clearly, our great minds are continuing to think alike."

"Yeah, I guess so. I don't generally like to sit around my place with clothes I wore outside if I don't have to, so it doesn't take long for me to change into something comfy when I get home."

"Hmm. And I don't like to sit around wearing anything, but I decided to be a gentleman tonight."

"Please!" I said, bursting into laughter before catching just how big I was cheesing into the camera.

It was almost shameless how much I couldn't stop smiling around this guy who I barely even knew. And it certainly wasn't my typical M.O., which had lately been not to let anyone get too close for fear they'd play me like ol' boy from the cherry blossoms. Something about Phillip felt different, though. And I had to admit, it was nice to connect and laugh and slightly flirt with someone new. Someone who hadn't already told me that he wasn't looking for something serious. Someone who just seemed to want to get to know me.

"I'm so glad you made that choice because if I had turned on my phone and saw you without any clothes on—"

"Oh, I know, it would have been a wrap," he interjected.

"Like, call that thing a tortilla because…"

I let my sentence trail off as we each laughed at the idea and my very corny way of confirming his suspicions. I even thought I might have heard Phillip snort at one point as we both tried and failed to regain our composure. This, of course, only made him all the more adorable.

"Don't worry," he added. "Again, I'd like to reiterate that my goal here is to actually get to see you again. I won't accomplish that by doing creep shit."

"I'm glad you are very aware of that."

"I'm damn near forty, Giselle. If I didn't get that by now, we might need to be having an entirely different conversation."

"Like one about having you committed?"

"You know, that might be a *little* dramatic, but...then again, maybe! I wouldn't exactly blame you if you thought that was the best course of action considering all the weirdos that I'm sure you've dealt with over the years."

"Ugh. You have no idea."

I smiled briefly into my phone, acknowledging Phillip's accurate assessment and pleased with how he not so subtly tried to make it clear he was an ally. What I hadn't been prepared for was the realization that his gaze would have just as much of an impact on me through a camera as in person. So, before I risked getting lost in it again, I quickly drew my attention back to my pan and went about the business of stirring my mixture of veggies and soy sauce to ensure all the pieces were evenly coated. It was a decent enough distraction, especially for someone who'd very recently realized she hadn't eaten anything since before the HUD announcement.

With only a few minutes left before the salmon finished cooking, I also whipped up my eggs and tossed them into the pan, scrambling them off to the side of the veggies as Phillip continued talking.

"Nah, but for real," he added. "I don't want to sound too cliché, but I've heard enough horror stories from my sisters that I never want to be that guy for someone else."

"I appreciate that. And unfortunately, it's not all that cliché. There are a lot of guys with sisters who still manage to do things that are either incredibly immature or harmful, or even just indicate that they don't think past their own experiences."

"Sounds like you've had your fair share of all three."

"Honestly, I don't know many women my age who haven't," I replied softly, raising my eyes back up to meet his. "But... I don't want to talk about that tonight. I'm more interested in hearing how your quote,unquote 'cooking' is going on over there as you lay with your feet up on your couch."

I made a point to punctuate the word *cooking* with air quotes as I not-so-subtly acknowledged the stark difference between the fact that I was still chugging along in the kitchen while Phillip was the picture perfect definition of comfortable.

"See, you joke, but you're not over here. So, you don't know how hard it was for me to open up both of those boxes, pour the wings into a baking pan and gently sit the pizza on the oven rack so that it wouldn't overcook or undercook in the twenty minutes it's meant to be in there."

"Oh, you're right. It sounds like such a hard-knock life," I replied, once again unable to stop myself from giggling at him.

"I'm telling you, girl. Life over here's no crystal stair."

"Okay, that's it. The fact that we just referenced Jay-Z and Langston Hughes, and we haven't even been on the phone for ten minutes yet..."

"I know," he said staring back at me as we telepathically shared an exchange that said *Damn, this is nice*, without ever having to actually utter the words.

In the brief moment of quiet between us, I absentmindedly began humming the chorus to Jay-Z's "Hard Knock Life," twisting my fingers around a couple strands of my hair as I relished our unspoken connection. It wasn't until my oven timer suddenly went off, alerting me that the salmon was ready and jolting me out of my inner thoughts, that I realized the tune wasn't just playing in my head, however.

For a split second, I wondered if Phillip had heard me, but once I looked up and saw him straightening his back and staring at me suspiciously through the phone, I immediately knew that wish had been a pipe dream.

"I'm sorry, did you just casually start singing 'Hard Knock Life' perfectly in tune with the melody?" he asked with a look of both wonder and fascination.

"Well... I was humming it, but yes."

"Woman."

"What?!" I replied with feigned innocence.

"You know what I meant."

"No, I know. You're right."

I paused momentarily, halfway considering if I should just play things off or admit yet another fun fact about me. The con to being honest was the uncertainty of whether he'd think *I* was now the weirdo. But the pro meant the potential for having someone see me and like for me for who I was. That felt worth it to me.

"So, ummm...yes," I admitted with a bit of hesitation. "It's kind of a thing I inadvertently do when I'm comfortable around people."

"You just burst into song?"

"Yeah, kinda."

"And you hit every note, like all the time?"

"Well, I studied music as a kid, so also yeah. You probably think that's super weird, right?"

"Are you kidding me? The only thing I'm thinking right now is that you are easily becoming one of the most interesting people I've ever met. Well, that and I'm pretty sure you just admitted that you feel comfortable with me. That makes a brother feel good, like maybe I'm doing something right so far. But to be clear, the first thought is what's most important."

I smiled back at Phillip as I tossed the salmon pieces into my pan and began mixing everything together. He didn't know it, but talking to him was starting to feel like the best kind of sprinkles on an already amazingly cake-like day. So, I guessed we were both experiencing some pretty amazing realizations about each other.

"Interesting in a good way, right?" I asked, wanting to make sure we were definitely still on the same page.

"Yeah, Gigi. In a very good way."

Phillip stared at me through the phone, his eyes once again capturing and holding my attention so that it felt like he was seeing into my very soul.

"My only problem now is somehow I'm going to have to stop myself from asking you to sing me to sleep tonight."

"You should definitely try to stop yourself from doing that," I replied.

"I mean, obviously. I can't promise it won't be on my mind, though."

"Well, that's all right. I've had things on my mind tonight that I haven't been able to discuss, either, so I guess now we're even. Especially when I saw you might be wearing gray sweatpants over there."

I raised an eyebrow at him in jest, which suddenly caused Phillip to very visibly begin to blush, a tiny but distinct rosy hue flushing under his light brown skin.

"See? Now, look at you trying to treat me like a piece of meat," he joked in response.

"Don't act like you didn't know what you were doing!"

"What? Can't a man just like how a certain pair of pants feel on his body without it meaning that he's trying to show off his goods?"

"Sure, he can! But not if they're gray and hug certain parts of his thighs. That's the male equivalent of a formfitting sundress on a curvy girl, and you know it."

Phillip could barely contain himself as he threw his head back in a laugh that once again ended with a snort. This time it was loud and clear, however, so there was no question it was real.

"Okay, so am I supposed to pretend I didn't hear that?" I asked, tears forming in my eyes as my giggles turned into roaring laughter as well.

"Woooow. A brother can't snort now, either!"

"Oh no, you don't. You don't get to flip it on me like that," I protested through more giggles, all while attempting to dry my cheeks at the same time. "I just want to make sure it's not off-limits to talk about, that's all."

"Gigi, I already told you I'm an open book. That means that there's nothing off-limits with me," Phillip replied. "You can randomly bust out into song, and I'll still think you're absolutely gorgeous. Maybe a little nuts, but by far one of the most beautiful people I've ever laid eyes on. All I ask is that you offer me the same courtesy with my snorts."

"Deal," I answered, still grinning but finally calming down from my chuckles enough to plate my food.

As much as I was enjoying our banter, I was also very ready to be able to join Phillip virtually in my own living room so that I could finally eat the food that had been calling my name for the past thirty minutes. As I walked into the next room, I thought about how easy it felt talking to him. How seamlessly we just seemed to enjoy one another's presence and get the other's sense of humor. In fact, if the two of us hadn't been balled over in laughter, I'm sure that someone overhearing our conversation would have seriously wondered if there was something wrong with us. But as it was, the glee we were experiencing through the magic of FaceTime seemed to overshadow almost anything else.

Over the next few hours, that joy never waned, even as we finished our meals and our eyes got heavier and yawns increased. It was almost reminiscent of the days in high school when you'd find yourself on the phone with the guy you liked for hours, way past your bedtime and alternating between *no, you hang up* declarations until someone either eventually gave in or the two of you ended up falling asleep with the phone pressed to your ear.

Phillip and I were good and grown, so I wasn't exactly worried about us getting to the point where I'd see him passed out and snoring on the other end of the video. But we did make it through a third round of goodbyes before we finally ended our call, committing at the last minute to an in-person date when he returned from his work travel.

"Don't forget, next Wednesday," he said, stifling another huge yawn as he rose up from his couch and began making his way to his bedroom.

"Trust me, that date is etched into my brain at this point."

"Good," he replied, "because I cannot wait until I get to see you again."

And with that, Phillip made the first move and ended our call, leaving me seated on my sofa, mind blown at all that had happened in just twenty-four hours.

"Score one for manifesting," I said to myself as I slowly began to drag my body upward so that I could head to my own bed. "In one day's time, two things I'd been wanting for the longest came right to my 'doorstep' as if they had been intentionally designed just for me."

That couldn't have been a coincidence, I thought as I walked into my bedroom, removed the decorative pillows from my bed and climbed under my covers.

One thing was for sure, though; I would have to give the girls the stats on Phillip ASAP. Otherwise, I was going to burst trying to hold in the anticipation all on my own. That announcement would come with another update that they hadn't been made aware of just yet, however. For what they didn't know, what no one knew, was that I'd finally started my profile on Hinge just two days before.

So, yeah, maybe they'd been right that I could still meet someone randomly in the grocery store. But in the grand scheme of things, I hadn't been all that wrong about my theory that making a move would signal to the universe that I was ready.

Time would tell which of us won out in the end. And if Phillip turned out to be a bust, there were at least ten guys on the app, waiting for me to reply.

# Chapter Five

The following Wednesday, I spent more than a few minutes checking out my reflection in the office full-length mirror before leaving to meet Phillip at Barn Joo in Union Square. Even though we'd already technically had a date over video, this was going to be the first one in person. So, I still felt every single bit of pressure to make a good impression. And while logically I knew how attracted he was to me, it had also been a week since our first encounter. Since then, he'd seen me rock different variations of lounge clothes around my apartment through a phone screen, with no makeup on and my hair barely done. This time around, he was going to be an arm's length away, and I wanted the pleasure of watching his jaw drop when he first laid eyes on me.

Doing another quick fit check, I scanned over my choice of clothes and marveled at the way I'd put each item together to complement something about my body that I absolutely loved. The Army green graphic tee that I wore with a bright orange-and-red image of Flo Jo crossing the finish line perfectly accentuated my golden brown skin tone, as did the gold hoop earrings and the matching slender chains I wore that fell right at my bosom. At the last minute, I'd also decided to add two gold rings on my left hand and one emerald one on my right, all serving to bring out the jewel undertones in my complexion. I topped off the T-shirt with a brown-and-tan plaid blazer that highlighted the angular structure of my jawline and was sure to subtly draw his attention to my neck—often considered one of the most feminine parts on a woman—as my jet-black twists, hanging just below my shoulders, framed it.

For my pants, I'd chosen a pair of acid-washed, slim-fit jeans that showed off the definition in my long legs, courtesy of my mom's genes and several years spent on my high school track team. I hadn't been good enough to compete in college, but if nothing else, that time laid the strong foundation for the enviable limbs I had today—something that I quite enjoyed showing off with every type of short I could find as long as it was the right setting.

For my final accents, I selected my cream-and-pink Astro sneakers from Axel Arigato and a pale burnt-orange lipstick that made my lips look as if they were almost as full and plump as Keisha's. The sneakers were a fun homage to the '90s, with their chunky silhouette and overlapping suede and leather panels, helping to tie the whole look together as an elevated but casual play on Hilary Banks's style from *The Fresh Prince of Bel-Air*. They were also a very subtle nod to the Philly connection between me and Will Smith. And the lipstick, well, that just looked damn good on me, so, really, it was one of the first things I knew I'd be rocking once we settled on meeting up in person.

Just a few days earlier, I'd finally spilled the beans to my girls, who were both very excited about Phillip's stats— what we'd for years called our first physical impression descriptions of any guy Keisha and I met—and most especially how the meet-cute had gone down.

"Can we say 'fate'?" Keisha asked, as she casually scooped up a meticulous combination of grits, eggs and fried catfish.

"It certainly felt that way," I admitted, trying not to cheese too hard, but honestly probably not doing a great job of it.

For the next half hour, I gleefully gave them the full rundown about how we'd talked every day since, divulging everything from our full names to our ideas of the perfect first date. He'd even convinced me to go on video sometimes early in the morning before I'd had barely a sip of coffee. From my perspective, the fact that he was purposely making time for me, while on a business trip no less, added twenty-plus points in his cool book. So, not only was I down to honor that by jumping on a video call without having sufficient time to beautify myself, but I was also beyond amped to finally show him what I could look like with just a little more preparation and effort.

To their credit, Reagan and Keisha also liked these facts about Phillip and seemed to be having just as hard a time as I was not grinning from ear to ear as I continued to describe our interactions. I was happy, but suspicious, that we'd gone almost our entire brunch without either of them uttering Brandon's name. Unfortunately, that didn't last forever.

"I love every single bit of this," Reagan said, her eyes gleaming and freckled cheeks rosy from smiling so much, "except that…"

*Oh no*, I thought to myself as she hesitated. *Here it comes.*

"I guess I'm just curious about what this pending date might mean for our hopes and dreams about Brandon."

She scrunched up her face like a kid who knew they'd said something their sibling didn't want to hear, but Reagan wasn't one to cower, either. Her expression was more about trying to soften the blow for me than it was about her not wanting an actual answer to her question.

"Hopefully, it means you'll finally give those up," I countered and then gently reminded her about the very sexy man who'd taken initiative to express his interest in me from day one.

"When my phone buzzes, and I see it's him, I can't stop smiling," I added. "That's partially because of how much I enjoy talking to him, but it's also because I don't have to question if he's into me. In one week, he's shown me that in ways Brandon never has."

"Okay, Gig. Well, I definitely can't argue with that," Reagan replied, tilting her head to the side with a nod that made it clear she wasn't going to try. "I really and truly hope you have an amazing time on this date with Mr. Handsome."

"Oh, is that his official nickname now?" I asked, happy with the idea. If he was being given a nickname that meant they were expecting to talk about him some more.

It was a blessing of sorts, in the way that only me and my girls could understand.

"Well, you practically named him yourself as you were running through his stats," she added. "Who am I to deny a fantastic nickname when it's right there in our faces?"

"Rae's right, it's pretty good," Keisha chimed in.

"That's true. My only concern is...you know what happens as soon as you make the mistake of actually starting to like a guy."

I bit my bottom lip anxiously as my brain quickly conjured up a series of worst case scenarios.

"He immediately embarrasses you," Keisha replied, already knowing where my head was at.

"Exactly. It's like they have some kind of radar. 'Oh snap, she's talking to her friends about me. Let me go ahead and ghost her now.'"

Reagan and Keisha laughed as I continued on, likely recalling their own dating woes before coupling up with their beaus.

"Wait, so does that mean you *don't* want us to give him a nickname?" Reagan asked in between her giggles.

"No, I mean that's already done. I guess I'm just saying, I don't want to jinx things with this guy. And I'm already feeling a little squeamish that things are too good to be true."

"You won't," Keisha said, gently grabbing my hand. "I promise."

"And if Mr. Handsome does do something stupid, we'll be a phone call away, ready to talk so much crap about him, it'll almost certainly permeate through the universe and smack him upside the head."

I smiled at their attempts to both root for the man and be prepared for his demise. What more could a girl ask for among besties?

"For the record, though, I'd like to second Rae's *well-wishes* for this upcoming date," Keisha chimed in with a wink. "Just as long as you know we're going to need the deets as soon as it's over."

"Please," I replied.

Like there was any way I would ever get away with doing anything differently.


At 7:00 p.m. on the dot, I walked into the famed Korean BBQ restaurant and saw Phillip standing next to the *Wheel of Fortune*-style game they had posted at the front, giving patrons a chance to win free drinks and other prizes simply by checking in online. Clad in a powder blue suit that popped off his light brown skin beautifully, I immediately noticed that he'd once again created a look that paired the formality of a suit with a casual air, thanks to a simple white T-shirt and a pair of crisp white sneakers. This time, his shoes were Nike dunks instead of Air Maxes, but it was clear that the man knew something about a style uniform and that he was well aware of what worked for him.

*And boy, did it work.*

The way his trousers and matching single-breasted jacket fit as if they'd been made specifically for him, I wouldn't have been surprised if an image of Phillip showed up in a Google search of what a man should look like when he was wearing a suit as opposed to the suit wearing him. It also didn't hurt that both items of clothing seemed to hug every part of his body that I'd secretly considered holding on to in the still moments at night when I allowed my brain to wander, from his shoulders and biceps, all the way down to his thighs.

"You're punctual," Phillip said, taking my hand in his and flashing a smile that could have lit up a mile-long block if he wanted it to.

"And you're early," I replied, instantly reveling in the warmth of his fingers intertwining with mine as we walked toward the hostess stand.

"I may have been a little excited to see you tonight."

Phillip glanced at me sheepishly with a look that read as if he was desperately hoping I might feel the same before quickly turning his attention to the woman standing before us, waiting with a pen in her hand. While he officially informed the hostess that his full party had arrived, I took the opportunity to breathe in slowly and quietly, attempting to steady my nerves even as my body wanted to respond every time he ran the tips of his fingers in the palm of my hand.

At least I'd avoided embarrassingly losing myself in Phillip's gaze, though I'd come far too close to being mesmerized by the flash of vulnerability I saw in his eyes. It had been so quick, but the honesty behind his expression had almost made me want to reveal just how much I'd been looking forward to our date, too. That I hadn't been able to think of much else since we'd confirmed the details, and that there was a small but persistent part of me that was eager to see if this night might lead to more.

Maybe an admission like that would have been normal for a lot of women, but with my dating patterns, I still felt like I needed to keep some kind of guard up, albeit one that was steadily withering away. Thankfully, for my psyche and my panties, Phillip's gaze hadn't lingered, and so I was able to recompose myself as the hostess said we'd be seated in a few. Dutifully, we stepped to the side, our hands naturally falling from around each other, as she moved on to greet the next patrons behind us. As weird as it felt to battle with myself internally, I struggled to decide if I was more grateful or sad to no longer be bonded with him physically.

"Did your excitement translate to us winning anything on the wheel?" I asked as we moved into a position where we stood side by side.

While I turned my face toward Phillip and awaited his response, I was careful not to directly face him. This way, I could subtly gaze into his eyes when needed but still keep my wits about me. The last thing I wanted was for him to realize I was oh so close to being putty in his hands, especially since all he'd really done so far was look amazing, ask me for my number, follow through on it without hesitation and call me a few times while he was out of town. These were all good things, yes, but the fact that they'd felt rare in comparison to what I'd been dealing with simply meant that the bar had gotten so low, it didn't take much to clear it.

When I was honest about my desires, however, I wanted

someone to soar over that bad boy. I longed for someone who would wow me with his intention and his sincerity. Who would make my rotation of guys feel utterly pointless. Who could barely breathe without thinking of me. Deep down I knew, if I had any chance of that being Phillip, I couldn't jinx things and let on so early how much he'd managed to capture my entire attention.

The way his pearly white teeth shone brightly under the low lights of the restaurant as he returned my smile certainly didn't make that decision very easy, though.

"Actually, yeah," he replied. "Our first drinks are on them."

"Ohh, okayyy. Well, look at you!" I responded with a wink, swallowing down my desire to do something, anything, that would keep him smiling at me. "Way to start us off with a win tonight."

"Well, you may not know this yet, Gigi, but I'm a man who generally comes out on top because I do what I need to do to get what I want."

Phillip's voice was smooth and velvety as he slowly and deliberately delivered his response, his eyes catching mine and refusing to let them drop at the same time as he shrugged off even the remote possibility of him not winning one of the prizes on the wheel.

"Is that so?"

My voice barely rose above a whisper. I was very clear on the implication in Phillip's statement—that he wasn't just talking about his luck at the wheel or even with work, but he'd also meant me—and yet something in me wanted, no needed, him to verify it.

"Mmm-hmm," he replied with a quick lick of his lips and a twinkle in his eyes that seemed to have a direct connection to my knees, which were suddenly struggling not to buckle under me.

"Okay. Noted."

For a few more seconds, I returned Phillip's gaze, content to let the silence between us speak volumes. But eventually, and likely for self-preservation, I diverted my attention to the gold ring on my left middle finger, dropping my eyes toward it as I fingered it with my thumb. What was most interesting to me was a realization that neither of us had said anything explicitly flirty to each other as we waited off to the side. But there had been so much subtext in our interactions that I was increasingly nervous I'd give in to my basest instincts and pull him so close to me all he could possibly do was kiss me right then and there.

It was all so subtle, but as he raised his eyebrow when he spoke about getting what he wanted or dragged his eyes up and down my body when he thought I wasn't paying attention, I became almost powerless to stop my desire to grab his head and suck his lips into mine. I chose to nibble on my bottom lip instead, hoping to tamp down the heat building within me. But I was also more than sure that anyone around us could literally picture the flames rising between our bodies.

Finally, and not a moment too soon, our hostess walked up to us, indirectly saving me from myself as she casually informed us that our table was ready. Then, with a polite smile on her face, she led us up the stairs toward a quiet section of the restaurant that was clearly meant to provide us with a certain amount of privacy even though it beautifully overlooked the first-floor dining area. Something told me that Phillip's early arrival and the fact that we were being seated in quite possibly the best part of the restaurant were interconnected.

As much as I was interested in confirming my theory, I was far too distracted by the fact that I could feel his eyes on me the entire walk to our table, up the steps and all. It was clear to me, and probably anyone paying attention to us, that he was enjoying his view as he steadied himself a few paces behind me. It was adorable, flattering and exactly the reaction I'd been hoping for as I got dressed earlier.

*Score one for my slim-fit jeans.*

"I feel like you're trying to memorize every inch of my body," I noted once we were settled in our chairs.

"Ha! Was I that obvious?" he asked sheepishly, his green eyes practically begging me not to say yes. "I just couldn't stop thinking about seeing you again the whole time I was gone, and now that you're here, right in front of me, it's hard to believe you're even more beautiful than I remembered. I didn't know that was possible."

"Well, you did meet me when I wasn't exactly at my best, and you've insisted on seeing me before the sun even wakes up, so really I could only go up from there."

I giggled at my own joke, fully expecting Phillip to join in. Instead, as I peered at him across the table, all I saw was his head shaking slowly but sternly at me.

"Nah, I can't agree with that," he said, his tone calm but direct. "First of all, you're drop-dead gorgeous at any time of day. You do know this, right? Or do I need to spend all night telling you as much?"

"I'm aware that my face card rarely declines," I replied, giggling again as I tried to deflect my eyes from his intense stare. "But even the highest paid supermodel can have a bad day."

"Hmm. That brings me to my second point. I don't need a supermodel. I want a woman who's just as hot when she's not trying as she is when she's dolled up. So, I'm actually really glad I got to see you be naturally you early on because now I know you're not just a product of L'Oréal and some designer clothes."

"I don't know if I should take that as a compliment or an insult."

"I hope you take it as a compliment because that's what it's intended to be. I'm just saying that you're beautiful with or without trying. I like that."

"Okay," I obliged. "But for the record, I'm wearing designer clothes and Fenty tonight, not L'Oréal."

"Either way, you're not a product of them," Phillip countered. "That said, I can't lie—I definitely appreciate how you look this evening."

"Oh, you *appreciate* it, huh? That's a funny way to say, 'Damn, Gigi, you look good as hell.'"

I raised my eyebrow to emphasize my point and then watched as Phillip's lips turned upward into a mischievous smirk.

"So, you *do* need me to spend all night telling you how beautiful you are. Okay. Got it. Well, how's this—Giselle Catherine Lewis, you are the most beautiful woman, not just in this restaurant tonight, but quite possibly that I've ever met. And maybe it has something to do with the fact that I can look at you as much as I want to without coming off like a weirdo this evening, but I could swear it's almost like you're glowing in front of me. I don't want to stop looking at you. I didn't want to stop holding your hand. And all I can think about is how much I'm attracted to you and how badly I want to know everything there is to know about you."

"Wow," I whispered, completely unable to control the word from seeping out of my mouth.

That was surely the nail in the coffin of any further resistance I had left in me. Not only had Phillip stunned me with his words, but he'd also very obviously remembered me telling him my middle name during those first hours we spent talking on the phone. If he was going to pay attention to little details like that, I could very easily see myself falling for him. In fact, if we'd been anywhere other than a very public restaurant, I'd have been tempted to climb on top of him and tell him to have his way with me. As it was, I could barely stop myself leaning over the table and pulling his incredibly kissable lips into mine.

"Umm, so about the glowing..." I said, clearing my throat as I tried to shake away all the thoughts running through my head. "That's probably just a testament to my gold jewelry. I wore it tonight because I happen to love how it complements my skin."

"Hmm."

Phillip tilted his head to the side as he stared back at me, visibly contemplating if I was right. He was probably also wondering if he should call me out for trying to talk my way out of my initial reaction to his words. Thankfully for me, there seemed to be a part of him that rather enjoyed my attempts at deflection. What was understood didn't have to be explained, after all.

"You may be right," he finally replied. "But now you just gave me another reason to stare at you all night. To see if your theory is true, of course."

"Ahh, I see. So, the fact that you can't keep your eyes off me is all my fault now, huh?"

"Pretty much."

Phillip's lips curled up again, slowly at first and then culminating in his very irresistible smile.

"Well, that's fine."

I smiled back generously.

"I suppose a dinner date is a fairly acceptable occasion to get away with egregiously looking at someone for hours."

"I'm so glad you agree," he said with a wink, eyes brightening before me as he drew himself closer to the table. "Because as far as I'm concerned, the FaceTime dates don't count, so I've got a lot of making up to do in this regard. It's not like I could spend as much time as I wanted taking you all in while we were at the grocery store, and on video, it's mostly been just your head and shoulders."

"No knees and toes," I added with a giggle.

"None. Not even a thigh," he answered, laughing along with me.

"The horror! You poor man. However did you make it through?"

"Memories. And thoughts of seeing you, here, tonight."

Phillip's grin shifted into an intense stare as he once again looked at me with a seductive lust in his eyes, the kind that seemingly had power over my thoughts and panties. I cleared my throat to pivot our attention elsewhere again.

"You're right about the grocery store part," I noted. "I would not have given my number to Phillip the creeper."

"See? And I knew this, so I was careful then," he replied. "But now... I mean, look at you. I just realized you have the cutest dimple in your right cheek."

"Oh wow. Should I prepare myself to hear more of these kinds of observations throughout the night?"

Despite my best attempts, I'd yet to stop grinning.

"They may not all be as G-rated," Phillip admitted.

"I'm a big girl."

"Oh yeah?"

He nodded slowly, keeping his eyes on mine the whole time.

"All right then. Noted."

Before either of us could say another word, our waiter showed up to our table, very obviously interrupting whatever fire had started brewing between me and Phillip. He quickly went over our options, offering recommendations as he went along. But it was clear he did not want to be there. In fact, by the time he was done writing our orders down, I was convinced he would have taken them with his back turned toward us if it meant he could avoid making eye contact. With one hardly audible rundown of our selections, he then awkwardly pivoted on his left foot and walked away so fast I was sure that he was going to have some sort of whiplash when he got home.

Phillip and I burst into laughter almost immediately once we were alone again.

"I think we made him a little nervous," he noted.

"I guess so, but wow. Poor guy."

"Poor guy? Don't you mean 'poor Phillip'? Should I expect to have to deal with people falling all over themselves when I'm out with you from now on?"

"Only if you keep looking at me like you want to slowly savor every inch of me."

"Oh, so now you're blaming me?"

"I'm saying that I think that kid was responding to the vibes between us both, but yes, mostly you," I replied, laughing again. "I don't know if you're aware of this, but the way that you look at me is pretty intoxicating. I can see how he might have felt as if he were walking into our bedroom."

"Hmm. So, the answer is yes again then. Okay. Got it."

Phillip paused, tilting his head toward me, and suddenly, it was as if I could see the effect of his troublemaking thoughts growing across his face.

"But just so we're clear," he added. "Our waiter wouldn't

find me simply *looking* at you if he ever did walk into our bedroom."

I giggled again at Phillip's brazenness, and then cleared my throat to help settle myself in front of him. What exactly had I gotten myself into agreeing to a date with this charmer? It was admittedly very flattering hearing how much he desired me, but there was an element to his charm that also triggered my dating PTSD and reminded me of my tendency to date men who talked a good game but couldn't—or, more to the point, had no desire to—back it up. While I certainly wanted to give him the benefit of the doubt, there was a reason I had the rotation of guys in the first place—not because I wanted to settle for pieces of each, but because as much as I'd dated, I'd yet to meet a man who maintained what he started when he was actively pursuing me. So, I'd done what any rational, slightly jaded millennial would and made the last few years work by simply not requiring or expecting them to do so.

My tactics helped reduce the disappointment when the guys ultimately lived down to my expectations, but they also made me wary of anyone who came on too strong out the gate. Only time would tell, I supposed, if Phillip was going to be like the rest or if he would surprise me and actually keep up this level of enthusiasm beyond the first couple of months. It did make me a little nervous, however.

"Ha! Okay, maybe let's bring the heat down a little," I replied, attempting to finally spin our conversation beyond our attractions to each other. "I know we both like to flirt, but I really want to hear more about your trip, especially now that you're back."

My pivot was a bit of a gamble, but as much as I enjoyed the chemistry bubbling up between us, I needed to know that Phillip and I had more in common than just that. Since he'd already told me he had been on a recruiting trip for the sports agency he worked at, I had a feeling that a recap might be the perfect opportunity to learn more about the man in front of me, his relationship to his job and what he wanted out of life. Plus, if I'd soaked up anything from being friends with Reagan—the writer and former reporter—it was the ability to come up with several questions on a given topic.

"How many prospects were you planning to see again?" I asked. "Was it five?"

"Close. It ended up being six once my agency realized we might have a chance to represent the kid who's projected to come out as the number-two pick during the NBA draft."

"Oh my God."

"I know."

"Phillip! That's such a big deal. Look at you!"

I watched as Phillip's cheeks turned a subtle but distinct rose hue under his light brown skin, which only managed to make me smile that much more. He was blushing, but this time, it wasn't because I was flirting with him. It was simply because I'd acknowledged his efforts at work. Seeing this side of the debonair charmer always looking to sweep me off *my* feet was especially refreshing and a reminder that he too was someone who likely craved compliments that had nothing to do with his looks.

"Yeah, man, it was a very good trip," he replied bashfully.

"I see! Your agency must really trust you if they threw that on you at the last minute. My goodness."

I paused to make sure my enthusiasm didn't have the unintended effect of adding more weight to Phillip's own personal expectations of himself.

"No pressure, though, of course," I added.

"Nah, it's every single bit of pressure," he admitted with a slight chuckle. "But, honestly, it's all good. This is the part I revel in. So much about being a sports agent can be exhausting that when I get the chance to, I really try to enjoy what got me excited about becoming one in the first place. It probably sounds corny but having a chance to talk to young people and their parents at one of the most pivotal moments in their lives, when they can almost touch the future that they've been dreaming about for years, that is what energizes me. I had that exact experience when I met with the last guy. So yeah, there's a lot of pressure on me to make sure he signs with us. But I'm also excited for what I know I can do for him, and it just pushes me to go that much harder."

"I love that. Correct me if I'm wrong, but it sounds like the trip was a great reminder of your purpose beyond simply making everyone a lot of money, right?"

"Exactly," Phillip replied, his gaze having turned from one of lust to something that at last felt to me like an appreciation for being understood.

"The money is really important, too, of course," he added. "It is my job to make sure they get paid, and then by extension, we get paid. But when I'm sitting down in family living rooms or dorm rooms and explaining to the student athlete and their parents the real-life opportunities before them, and how my agency can help them with everything from endorsements and advertisement deals to contract negotiations, that's when the exhaustion turns to fun. That's when I really feel like all the long nights and time away from home are worth it. It's also where I shine because I don't just walk in these folks' houses with fantasies. I always have my receipts ready."

"Okayyy, let me find out you're an actual superstar!"

I caught myself cheesing once again as I listened intently to Phillip describe exactly what he loved about his job. I was envious, really. I knew my work was important, but often, and especially lately, I had a hard time remembering what I enjoyed about it when all I could feel was the exhaustion that came with it.

*Must be nice to know that so clearly,* I thought. Maybe it was something I could learn from him.

"Well, I kinda have to be in order to be sitting here on this date with you right now," he replied with a wink.

"Oh, no, you don't," I interjected. "Don't try to turn this moment around so that it becomes about me. I actually really enjoy hearing what makes you happy, and this clearly does. It's inspiring."

"I appreciate that," Phillip admitted, throwing his hands up in mock defeat. "I don't exactly get told it very often."

"Well, say less, because I'm nothing if not an excellent cheerleader."

I paused upon seeing Phillip smirk at my choice of words and realized I'd set myself up again. To his credit, however, he somehow managed to stop himself from blurting out his very obvious thoughts, which absolutely warranted a gold star in his book in my head.

With a knowing nod, I cleared my throat and attempted to get back to my actual point.

"What I mean to say is that I think maybe we don't divulge this kind of stuff to the people closest to us because in some ways it feels kind of cheesy to do so, right? Like, we know that we're all out here trying to do our best, so you never want to be the one to look like you're gloating. That, or it feels too vulnerable to talk about it, as if bringing it up will somehow jinx the good parts away. Maybe I'm projecting a little, but I know I have definitely been guilty of only telling my friends about the frustrating times at my job. So, I'm glad you opened up to me about your love for yours because it gives me a chance to cheer you on...and not in a sexual way."

"I know what you meant," Phillip said with a smirk. "And you're probably right. I think it's also easier for me to talk to you, as a woman, about my feelings. It's not like me and my boys are talking about the last time I smiled at my job while we're shooting hoops."

"Okay, but if y'all did, that would be amazing to see. Could you imagine?"

"I really can't, but if it ever happens, I'd definitely want you there."

Phillip flashed yet another irresistible smile at me, and I instantly felt a small shiver run down my spine.

"Well, I think you've got yourself a deal. In the meantime, though, I'll gladly be your listening ear. How many of the six do you think you secured?"

"Mmm, cards on the table, if I had to guess right now... I think at least four."

I waited for a moment, staring at him with my eyes squinted as I tried to determine if he was being modest or not. There was still so much to learn about Phillip Evans, and yet, I was already starting to understand little bits and pieces. For one, I could tell that he was someone who believed in being prepared for every situation. It was why he'd arrived early for our date and how he'd been able to seamlessly add his agency's highest prospect to his plate, at the last minute, while he was already on the road. For most other people, that would have been incredibly nerve-racking. But not Phillip. He seemed to revel in proving that he could be given such a big task and kill it without breaking a sweat. That led me to my second conclusion: there was no way he didn't think that he had secured all six players.

"I don't know if *I* believe that *you* believe that," I finally said.

"Oh? Why not?" He smirked again.

"I don't know. I just think that what you actually believe is you nailed all of them, but you don't want to come off as arrogant."

"Wow, I didn't know I'd be getting read while we waited for our food tonight," he said with a laugh.

"It's just an observation," I noted, taking a page out of his book and purposely using his language from earlier as well.

"Mmm. Well, you may be right," Phillip admitted with a slight grin.

"I know I am!"

"You can't give away my secrets, though."

"I got you. Don't worry."

Our poor waiter walked up to us again just as we were in the middle of yet another sexy staring contest, this time with several trays of food that he proceeded to strategically position on our table. Just as awkward as before, he silently went about his business, placing the strips of uncooked pork, sirloin, chicken and shrimp closest to the barbecue grill. One by one, he then added the basket of lettuce, bowls of rice, various sauces and egg soufflé in the few empty spaces remaining on the table. Just when I thought he was done, another waiter came by with our drinks, and our original waiter, just as quietly, took those and passed them to us. I noticed how he seemed to easily remember who'd ordered what—me a gin cocktail that tasted like the fancy version of a gin and juice, my actual go-to, and Phillip an old-fashioned—despite the fact that he was clearly trying to avoid eye contact with us. It made his interactions with us all the more interesting.

"Do you all need anything else?" he asked, briefly raising his eyes to meet ours.

"I think we're good, man," Phillip responded with a chuckle that made it very hard for me not to join in.

Just like before, he clearly took that as his cue and scurried away as fast as he could. We never even got his name.

"I'm dying," I said, finally breaking my composure and letting out the laugh I'd been holding in for several minutes.

"I don't know if we should be offended or what…"

"I think it's just clear he's trying to give us space," I interjected before the conversation took a turn I didn't want to go down. "We're hot, you know. I can only imagine how uncomfortable it has to be for someone who's just trying to do their job to realize he is a disruption to the sexy vibes practically heating up the barbecue grill on their own."

"Yeah, you're probably right," Phillip said, conceding to my theory pretty easily.

I was sure all the verbal butter I put on it helped it go down smoother.

"Besides," he added, "there are more important things to discuss anyway. Like, how *you're* doing. I'm hoping the fact that you're here right now means you'll have less late nights in the office this week?"

"I appreciate you, but we don't have to do the weird pivot to talking about me just because I was asking about you. Your trip is far more exciting than anything going on in my world."

"I'm going to have to disagree with you yet again, Gigi," Phillip said, leaning toward the table. "I want to know everything there is to know about you. So, how about you let me decide if I think it's boring or not?"

He looked at me from across the table with eyes that poured deep into my soul, and for the first time, I didn't giggle in reaction to his words. I simply believed him and obliged. For the next several minutes, I explained how my team had been trying to figure out which route to take for our HUD proposal as Phillip listened intently. Even as he began searing strips of meat on the grill, he rarely took his off eyes off me as I further described how we needed to settle on our direction soon so that we could proceed forward.

From my perspective, we now had two choices before us: one that was sensible and doable, but probably far less impactful, or the other one, which was shooting for the moon as if we were being given a magic wand even if it might be a pipe dream. For the past week, we'd been all-hands-on-deck going over the pros and cons of both pathways, and yet, still hadn't decided which way to go.

"Ultimately, I think it's going to come down to me," I admitted. "I was the one my boss asked to lead the initiative, so I can't let us linger on too much longer."

"What are you leaning toward?" Phillip asked.

"Right now, my answer depends on the exact moment when you ask me. My head says to go with the sensible direction, that it's the only logical choice, and they'll appreciate someone coming to the table with concrete ideas that are actionable right now. But my heart? I don't know. I can't seem to shake this feeling that going that route is just me operating in fear."

"I can understand that dilemma," Phillip replied. "All I can say is that in my line of work, I would never feel comfortable presenting an idea or proposal to a client that I wasn't 100% sure I could pull off. Maybe it's different in housing advocacy, though? You're not looking to meet one person's needs, but hundreds and thousands, right?"

"Yeah, it's a greater number of people, for sure, but I've been working in it long enough to have experienced the disappointment when big ideas go south. Not only does it make it less likely you'll get funding from that organization to try again, but what's worse is, you're no closer to helping anyone get access to housing. It's a failure all around. I think that's why my brain keeps telling me to go the sensible route because the last thing we want to do is win the proposal from HUD and then fail. I don't think we'd get another chance. And that doesn't benefit us or the people we're trying to help."

"I think you have your answer then," Phillip said quietly as he started removing our first strips of meat from the grill and placing them on my plate and then his.

"Yeah, I guess I do."

I sat in silence as I contemplated my decision. Phillip was absolutely right about everything he'd said, and I so appreciated his honest assessment of the situation. But deep down, I think something in me really wanted him to just tell me I could do whatever I put my all into. Instead, he'd walked me toward the most rational conclusion, which was great and probably what I needed. It just didn't really feel like it.

"I don't think you should look at the sensible direction as a bad thing, though," he added. "You're just managing their and your team's expectations."

"No, you're absolutely right. And honestly, that's as much a part of my responsibility as the leader as anything else."

"This is true," he said with a wink. "And I think if you remember that, you'll do well. But in the meantime, you need to try that shrimp before it gets cold."

"Ahh yes, you are so right yet again."

I smiled back at him, maybe not as bright as before, but genuinely.

"I try very hard to be," Phillip remarked, in almost exactly the same tone as he'd used when he said he generally comes out on top.

For some reason, it seemed a lot sexier then. But that probably had more to do with me than him. Without another word, I grabbed a piece of lettuce and one of the butterflied shrimp, meticulously adding some kimchi and bean sprouts to it, and then gently wrapping it all together. Once that was done, I took the biggest bite I could fit in my mouth, stuffing my whole face with it, as I chewed into the deliciousness.

"Wow, I guess somebody was hungry, huh?" Phillip asked with wide eyes.

"Seems so," I mumbled with my mouth still partially full.

The silliness of the moment caused us to burst out laughing, which was a much-needed break after the seriousness of our conversation.

"Damn, I guess I need to catch up then," he replied, his eyes still beaming toward me.

"You can certainly try!" I said. "But I don't think you will."

# *Chapter Six*

Hours later, Phillip and I exited the train at 145th Street with full stomachs and genuine smiles plastered on our faces. We'd practically shut the restaurant down, stuffing our faces and talking about everything from our Philly and DC hometowns to which podcasts we listened to while traveling on the train—his faves were *Higher Learning with Van Lathan and Rachel Lindsay* and *A Way with Words*; mine, *Slow Burn* and *Black Girl Songbook*. But the conversation hadn't stopped there; we were absolute chatter bugs the whole way back uptown, and I, for one, couldn't have been happier about it.

"Which way is your place?" Phillip asked as we walked out into the brisk, spring night air.

"I'm off Frederick Douglass. You?"

"Broadway."

"Ahh, of course, total opposite directions," I said, still smiling, despite the realization this meant we'd have to part ways soon.

"Yeah, makes us meeting at the grocery store feel that much more like fate," he noted.

"Honestly, it really does."

Standing face to face, with a light wind blowing through my hair, I looked up at Phillip and marveled at the man before me. He was kind, attentive, incredibly handsome, very practical and, by all accounts so far, seemingly especially interested in me. It was almost as if I'd dreamt him up and someone, somewhere had decided to create a real person out of my fantasy. The only question I had now was what was his next move going to be? Would he try to kiss me? Grab me toward him and teasingly run his fingertips down my spine until I pleaded for him? Ask to walk me home and then conveniently need to use the bathroom? Or...would he completely flip the script on me, simply dap me up and walk away, never to be seen again? At this point, anything was on the table.

"I hope you've had a good night," he said, with eyes that once again bore into my very soul.

"I have."

My voice came out barely louder than a whisper as I tried to keep my composure, even as shivers flashed down my spine the longer that he held my eye contact.

"Thank you very much for dinner and the great company," I added.

"I promise you the pleasure was all mine."

Phillip subtly licked his lips as he took my right hand in his, intertwining our fingers once again. This time, however, there was no hesitancy in his movement as he gripped my hand tightly and pulsed his palm into mine.

"I would really love to see you again," he said. "Maybe Saturday?"

"Saturday sounds good. Do you have something specific in mind?"

"I do, yeah. But let me look into it a bit more, and I'll get back to you on that."

"Oh, ending the night with a little suspense, I see?"

"You know, I gotta try to keep you on your toes."

*How audacious of him to use the word* try *when he's been very much succeeding at that since the moment we met.*

In between hand pulses, Phillip gently pulled me closer to him until I could practically feel his breath on my forehead. Then, as if he knew exactly what to do to melt my resolve down even further, Phillip leaned down and softly placed his lips right where he'd seen my dimple earlier—in the little corner between my lips and my cheek. For my part, I did the only thing I could do. I stood in silence and closed my eyes as I breathed him in for one, two, three, four, five seconds.

"Will you let me know when you make it home safely?" he asked, breaking my trance before he stepped back and released my hand.

I opened my eyes in time to see Phillip moving a few inches away from me, and it was, all at once, exceptionally clear to me that he'd chosen this to be our final interaction of the night. I was disappointed, but there was no way I was going to let him see that.

"Of course," I replied. "And you the same?"

"You got it."

This time, I backed away from Phillip. Then I said goodbye and started on the five-minute walk to my apartment. One thing was for sure: if by keeping me "on my toes" what he really meant was punch me in the gut, he'd succeeded. I was stunned, not only by the gentlemanly way he'd chosen to end our date, but also by how soft his lips felt on my skin. And the fact that he'd just…stepped back.

I'd walked about a block, just coming up on Jackie Robinson Park, when I felt my phone vibrating in my pocket. Had Phillip changed his mind about calling it a night? I pulled out my phone, hoping to see his name on the screen.

Maybe he'd realized that, despite his best efforts, he needed to feel his lips on mine just as much as I did and wanted me to turn back around.

I swung my body back toward the train station as I eagerly looked down at my phone, ready to say yes to whatever he asked, when reality hit me square in the face.

It wasn't Phillip that was texting me at all; it was Reagan and Keisha.

I quickly unlocked my phone and opened our text chain, appropriately labeled Boos Who Booze, and prepared myself for the playful interrogation I knew I was about to be subjected to, just at the exact wrong time. In fairness to them, I'd already missed a few of their messages, so I knew they were on the edges of their beds, anxious to hear the details. I just wasn't sure how ready I was to jump into the hot seat after how things had just ended.

With nothing else left to do, I breathed in deeply and scrolled through the texts to see what I'd missed so far. Unsurprisingly, the duo had been talking to themselves as they awaited my reply.

*10:15 p.m.*

Reagan: Soooo??

Keisha: Yeah, I think we've waited long enough. How'd it go?

*10:31 p.m.*

Keisha: Wait, you haven't replied to us yet. Does that mean you're still on the date with Mr. Handsome?

Reagan: Aww shucky ducky, that's got to be good news. Send us a signal when you can, cher.

*10:50 p.m.*

Reagan: Now, all right, we're over here on pins and needles. Give us something, Gig!

Keisha: You think she went home with him tonight? Maybe that's why she's not answering yet.

Reagan: Ooooh, I hadn't even thought of that possibility. We'll really need the deets if that happened.

Keisha: Uhh yeah lol

*11:10 p.m.*

Keisha: Giselle. Catherine. Lewis. Have you lost your mind?

Reagan: I mean, hello?! Even if Mr. Handsome is on top of you right now, you need to let your besties know where you are. Stat.

Keisha: This is why the younger generations all share each other's locations, because the way that I'm stressed right now...

Reagan: You know what? You're right. Because I know she's not still at no damn Barn Joo at this time of night.

I chuckled to myself as I turned onto Frederick Douglass Boulevard, mere steps away from my building. If there was one thing me and my friends didn't take lightly, it was one of us not responding to the group chat in a timely fashion. I'd been on the other side more than a few times as well, so I damn sure knew not to wait until I got settled in my apartment to reply all.

I'm literally walking up to my building, I typed back furiously. Sorry for the delay. We took the train home together, so I didn't have a chance to text y'all until now.

Reagan was the first to respond, less than twenty seconds later, just as I walked into the lobby of my building.

Oh, well would you look who's alive! she replied.

Me: Don't do me like that lol

Keisha: No, no, it's cool. You just almost had an APB out on you, that's all.

Me: Well, I'm home now, so no need for all that.

Reagan: Thank God. Now, does your late arrival home mean that you made a pit stop somewhere else first? Maybe to Mr. Handsome's place?

Me: Not at all, actually lol. Y'all aren't going to believe this, but he didn't even kiss me goodnight [eyes emoji]

Keisha: Wait, what?

Reagan: What do you mean? Was it a bad date?

Me: Nope. We had a great time, or at least I think we did. We even made plans to see each other again on Saturday. I just think that he might really be, like, a nice guy? IDK.

Keisha: Wow. That's a change.

Me: I know lol

Reagan: I mean, nice guys don't like to kiss, though? Is that what we're saying?

I laughed out loud as I walked into my apartment, sliding my sneakers off my feet at the door and replacing them with my slippers. Leave it to Rae to say the thing we'd all probably been thinking but didn't want to admit. In fact, I could practically hear her soft voice through our texts, as if she were right in front of me, dumbfounded at the suggestion.

I slipped off my blazer and made my way into my living room, plopping down back-first onto my couch and taking in a deep breath before jumping back in to respond.

Well, I typed. I guess it wouldn't be totally fair to say he didn't kiss me. He just didn't kiss me on my lips.

Keisha: Oh no, was it a forehead kiss? [eyes emoji]

Me: It was in the crease between my lips and right cheek.

Reagan: Shit. That's worse!

Me: I knoooow. And he was sooo close to my bottom lip, y'all. I almost started quivering. Like, dude, if you'd just slide over less than an inch...then we could do this thing for real. We don't have to stand out here and pretend like we don't both desperately want each other!

Keisha: Yeah, he totally did that mess on purpose.

Me: He did say right before that that he had to keep me on my toes.

Reagan: Oh, so Mr. Handsome is diabolical? Bet.

Me: And now I can't stop thinking about it, and how badly I wanted him to put me out of my misery.

Reagan: Damn, sis.

Keisha: He's good.

Me: Too good.

Reagan: So, what now?

Me: Nothing. I told him I'd let him know when I got home, so I guess I'll do that and then wait to hear what our plans are for Saturday.

Keisha: Gig, you gotta stand up, my girl.

Along with her text, Keisha replied with a gif of a Black woman sitting in her car yelling "Stand up!" It was the perfect reaction, and one we'd been using ever since the video version went viral of the same woman admonishing her counterparts not to let a bunch of men leave us weak in the knees.

Ugh I know, I know. I can't let him treat me like I'm the yellow Laffy Taffy! I replied, using another part of the video in my response.

Keisha: Exactly. You need to take back some control of this thing! You like him, right?

Me: I do, yeah.

Keisha: Well, then you gotta be yourself, Gig. And you know damn well you're not some wallflower who sits around waiting for a man to dictate everything in the relationship.

Me: Sigh. You're absolutely right. Thank you for that reminder, and don't worry, I will. For now, though, I'm just going to lay here on this comfy ass couch because your girl is tired, I was out late on a school night, and I actually have to go into the office tomorrow.

Reagan: All right, I guess that's fair. We'll let you go but keep us updated about Saturday.

Keisha: And…we still need the rest of the details about this date. How about happy hour on Friday?

Me: That works for me.

Reagan: Me too!

Keisha: Okay, great. Get your rest. We'll talk to you later.

Me: Bye!

Reagan: Bye!

I blacked out my phone and shut my eyes momentarily,

taking in another deep, calming breath, until suddenly I remembered that I hadn't texted Phillip yet.

"Shoot," I said aloud, and promptly raised the phone back up to my face.

Me: Hey, I made it home safely a few minutes ago. My girls were texting me as I was walking through the door, so I got caught up for a moment.

All good, he replied back within a couple minutes. Thanks for letting me know. And I'm home too.

Me: Oh good, I'm glad you weren't scooped up by some aliens looking specifically for men with green eyes wearing light blue suits.

Phillip: Nah, thankfully I seem to have dodged that particular bullet tonight. But you do bring up a good point; you can never be too careful. Maybe next time, I'll wear a different colored suit to be safe.

Me: hahaha, good thinking. And thank you again for tonight.

I paused for a moment and considered my conversation with the girls. They were absolutely right about me not showing him the full Gigi, who would at least have made a joke about our exit. This felt like the perfect time to make up for the past, though. So, before he could reply again, I hurried up and sent a second text.

Even if you did try to leave me hanging at the end… I added.

Phillip's reply came through about a minute later, in a series of three texts back to back.

Ha! You know, I was wondering if you were going to call me out about that.
Let me be perfectly clear, Gigi. I very much want to kiss you, in case you're at all worried about that.
I just didn't want our first kiss to be out on the street in front of the train station.

Me: Okayyy, I'll give you that. I suppose there are better venues for a first kiss.

Phillip: Plenty. But trust me, the amount of willpower I had to tap into to stop myself... I think I could have won a strong man contest tonight.

Me: hahaha, well that is good to know. Is that the reason you stepped back from me so quickly?

Phillip: Yes. I couldn't continue to be that close to you and still walk away.

Me: I know the feeling. Don't forget to let me know about Saturday when you can.

Phillip: I got you.

It took everything in me not to type back "not yet" and continue our cute banter, but I was exhausted, and I assumed so was he. Instead, we said our goodbyes once more, and with barely enough energy left to get up and get ready for bed, I dragged my tired body off my couch and headed toward my bathroom.

I knew at that point there was no way I was going to bother with my full nighttime routine, consisting of brushing and flossing my teeth, then flushing my gums with my electric water flosser, cleansing and exfoliating my face, applying my favorite serum before using my gua sha stone roller and then topping everything off with my favorite Perricone MD moisturizer. But a truncated version of that, I could at least try.

I was almost done with my first task when my phone began vibrating again.

*Is there no rest for the weary?* I asked myself as I leaned over, mouth full of toothpaste, and tapped my screen to see who was on the other end. To my surprise, it was a text from Jake, Reagan's fiancé. Now, we were cool, but not "text each other at almost midnight" cool, so that immediately seemed suspicious. I quickly unlocked my phone and hoped that nothing was drastically wrong.

Hey, everyone, apologies for the late night text, his message read. I had to wait until Rae went to bed so she couldn't ruin my surprise. Y'all know she's nosy.

Phew! I breathed a sigh of relief upon realizing a) nothing was wrong and b) he wasn't just texting me. Both good signs, but also indicators that this text probably could have waited, but whatever. I rinsed out my mouth and joined in on the conversation.

Keisha: Now, Jake, you know I love you, but this better be good.

Leave it to Keisha to say exactly what I was thinking, I thought.

Jake: It will be good and QUICK, I promise.

Keisha: All right then, tell us what you need.

Me: Umm, you scared me there for a second, my guy. But I'm here, too. What's going on?

Jake: My bad y'all. But I appreciate you both.

Keisha: Mmm-hmm go on…

Jake: Okay, so, I want to do something special for Rae's birthday this year, especially since the wedding is coming up in November, and I think she's a little overwhelmed to try to figure out something herself. I was thinking of a cabin trip upstate sometime in June.

Me: Oooh, okay, I like this. Tell us more.

Keisha: Wait, now when you say cabin…

Jake: Don't think cabin as in log house. I saw this one place online that had 5 king-sized bedrooms, all modern appliances, a hot tub, grill, the whole nine. And it's only a 10 minute walk to this really beautiful lake.

Keisha: All right! Now you're talking. That's the kind of cabin we can get behind.

Jake: Trust me, I know my fiancée…and her friends. I wouldn't dare try to have y'all in anything less than the best.

Keisha: See, this is why we love you, Jake lol. But where do we come in?

Jake: I'm glad you asked. I'm putting together the plans to rent the house and buy all the food and drinks, etc. I'll also work on inviting everyone and coordinating rides up there. What I need you guys' help on, mostly, is the activities. That is not where I excel, but between the two of you, I know we'll be set on all the fun stuff she would want to do beyond the house.

Me: Oh, yeah, we can definitely help plan the activities.

Keisha: For sure! We got you. Just send us the details of where the cabin is located, so we can start seeing what's nearby.

Jake: You two are the absolute best. I'll text you when I know who can make it and who can't.

Me: You better believe it.

Keisha: Yeah, c'mon, you know we'd do anything for our Rae. But next time, maybe try texting during the workday?

Jake: You're right. My bad. I just got so excited. I'm not trying to have any beef between me and Julian. I don't need him thinking I'm trying to get at his girl.

Keisha: He's right here and laughing at this whole exchange, so I think y'all are straight. I'm talking about me! It's past my bedtime lol

Jake: Oh. Okay, I gotchu. And, tell J I said what's up, and that I'd like him there too if he can make it.

There was a slight pause in the texting as I presumed Keisha was relaying the message to Julian, but it wasn't lost on me that I didn't have anyone for Jake to want to include in the festivities. That kinda stung, not gonna lie. Yet, something about my interactions with Phillip had me finally feeling hopeful about the future. This trip was probably going to be too soon for him to attend, but the next group event? If things kept going in the right direction, it didn't seem like a far-fetched idea, which was kind of wild considering I'd just come off my first in-person date with him.

Either way, I was determined to have somebody on my arm at least by the wedding, even if it wasn't Mr. Handsome. In the meantime, and while we waited for Keisha to respond, I took the opportunity to finish up the rest of my truncated routine, washing my face and rubbing in my moisturizer.

Keisha's reply came through just as I'd completed my final task.

Keisha: Julian says he wouldn't miss it for the world, and if you need some help on the grill, he's got you.

Jake: Bet. I can't wait. Okay, thanks you two. We'll talk again soon, and I'll email you both the cabin details in the morning.

Keisha: Gnite!

Me: Night!

With my nighttime routine done and my last text sent, I once again blacked out my screen, then happily turned off my bathroom light, and began making my way to the bed that had been calling my name since I stepped foot in my apartment. I didn't even bother to turn on my hallway or bedroom lights, walking through my place seamlessly in the dark, buoyed by the anticipation of how amazing my sheets were going to feel as I wrapped them tightly around my body.

I easily slipped out of the rest of my clothes, placed my jewelry on my nightstand and then, like a kid excited to see their gifts from Santa in the morning, climbed into bed with the biggest smile ever on my face. As my head hit my pillow, I briefly thought about the fact that I probably should have taken a shower, but as I sank into my memory foam mattress, that guilt flew right out of my head. What replaced it was a feeling of pure bliss as I settled in comfortably and thought back to Phillip's admission that he'd wanted to kiss me so badly, he had to step back to stop himself.

It felt good to know we'd shared the same thought, like just maybe, all the messy relationships I'd had before this were leading me here—to a man who was ready for me but also so intentional, he wasn't going to let temporary pleasure upend his plans.

Now, that was sexy as hell.

I shut my eyes and felt myself starting to doze off when my phone began vibrating yet again, this time from my nightstand.

"You've got to be kidding me," I said aloud. "Who is this now?"

With a long stretch of my arm, I grabbed my phone,

my eyes still partially closed, and once again, I tapped my screen to see who was on the other end.

Brandon.

You'll probably see this in the morning, but I hear we're headed upstate this summer, his text read. Wanna ride in my car?

I didn't respond. I simply put the phone back in its place and curled my body back into my sheets and comforter, shut my eyes and started back on my slumber journey. The only problem now was that Brandon's face had replaced Phillip's in my head, and that, I realized, was probably not a good thing.

# *Chapter Seven*

"I've lived in New York for more than ten years, and I can honestly say I've never done this before."

I stared out of the massive windows in front of us as our dinner cruise floated by the Statue of Liberty, lit up beautifully and practically glowing under the night sky. For the past hour, Phillip and I had been taking in the breathtaking skyline of the city from the vantage point of the Hudson River as we feasted on an incredible meal of grilled sea bass with heirloom tomatoes, crab-stuffed eggplant and roasted asparagus. With our dinner now complete, we moved to a secluded spot on the yacht, where we could marvel at the sights before us in our own little nook away from everyone else.

"Me either," he replied. "It's one of the reasons I thought this might be a nice thing for us to try together. I feel like when you live here, it's so easy to miss out on stuff like this because it's seen as just something for the tourists to do. But hey, I want to view the Financial District from a boat while smooth jazz plays in the background, too."

"You're right," I said, laughing in response, particularly about the music accompaniment. "I don't know if I necessarily need the smooth jazz part, but there's so much I've probably missed out on because it seemed uncool to do as someone making New York their home."

"Exactly. And hey, don't hate on the smooth jazz, there's nothing wrong with a lil Kenny G every once in a while."

"I mean, he's aiight. But you can't tell me this night wouldn't be so much better with the sounds of Musiq Soul-child playing in the background or even some Jill Scott instead. Whew! Imagine, cruising down the Hudson River with 'sobeautiful' or 'It's Love' literally caressing your eardrums."

I shimmied just from the thought of how romantic of a vibe that would have been. I mean, we were already at about an eight on a scale of one to ten, with the champagne flowing throughout the night and the stars lighting up the night sky. To me, that might have taken things to a level even the best rom com couldn't compete with.

"I think your Philly bias might be showing a little, Miss Lewis," Phillip replied with that dangerous smirk of his only serving to egg me on further.

"Absolutely not, Mr. Evans. I just know good music. And don't get me wrong, my man Kenny is a legend, but would I pick any song of his over D'Angelo's 'Untitled' under a full moon? Tuh. Not in this lifetime."

"You have a point about 'Untitled'—I'll give you that one. But you don't think it's funny that all your examples just so happen to hail from the same city?"

"Oh. Well, I can't help it if we make world-renowned musicians where I'm from."

I turned my head toward Phillip's and smiled brightly, hoping all of this talk about romantic songs would encourage him to move just a few inches over and wrap me up in his arms. What I wouldn't give to relax in his embrace as we looked out on the river, our breaths moving in sync while we quietly and peacefully enjoyed each other's presence. Sadly, though, he didn't take the hint and remained where he was.

At least my current view of him gave me the opportunity to watch the lights from the Statue of Liberty sparkle in his eyes. That was one helluva consolation prize. It was also the perfect complement to the more muted outfit he'd chosen for the night—a khaki, long-sleeve tee with a crew neck collar that looked like one of those shirts that seemed simple on the surface but probably cost a couple hundred bucks, and a pair of gray slacks that hugged his thighs just enough to be enticing but not so much that he couldn't sit without risking busting through them. It was a far cry from the sky blue suit he'd worn the other night, but it fit him just as well.

Maybe it wasn't that Phillip had a style uniform after all, I theorized, but just that everything looked so damn good on him, you'd be hard-pressed to think each piece of clothing wasn't designed and sold just for him.

"Hmm, if that's the criteria for the music you'd rather hear on our cruise tonight, then let me throw some DC legends into our imaginary playlist. I'd love to add some Backyard Band or Rare Essence to the mix," he replied with a smile.

"What? No!"

"Oh c'mon, don't tell me you have something against Gogo, Gigi. We might have to part ways immediately."

"Please, of course not," I scoffed. "I'm a millennial from Philly, so I love to pretend like I know how to beat my feet. But that's not the music that's going to bring you closer to me so I can snuggle up against your chest while you whisper sweet nothings in my ear. Now, if you want to add somebody from DC for that? I feel like it's gotta be someone like Tank, and maybe very specifically his song 'Slowly.'"

Phillip eyed me mischievously as I stood tall in my khaki, linen, high-waisted pants, totally not backing down from what I'd just said. While he'd gone for a more subdued look with his, I'd paired my khaki attire with a long-sleeve, champagne-colored top, embossed with gold-and-hunter-green leaves that I tied between my breasts, multilayers of slim gold chains that also fell between my chest and marigold feathered earrings that dropped right at my collarbone. I'd wanted my outfit to make it clear he was no longer dealing with the wallflower whose friends had admonished her to *stand up* just a few days before.

"Oh, I see what type of time you're on now," Phillip said moving toward me, his eyes never leaving mine.

*Finally*, I thought. *I've only been waiting for you to get it for two weeks now.*

I stared back at him defiantly, undeterred by his slow, but intense progression.

"But the thing is," he added, carefully licking his lips as his body came ever so close to mine. "One, I'm guessing you've never heard UCB perform 'Sexy Lady' before because, trust me, if you had, you wouldn't casually throw away the option of adding some Gogo music to your hypothetical playlist. And two...well, instead of, what was the word you used again, *snuggling*? If I'm that close to you, I think I'd much rather do this."

Without another word, Phillip lifted up my chin with his right hand, and before I could finish my sigh of relief, planted his lips directly on mine. The kiss started off gently at first, sweetly reminding me of the first time I had the pleasure of experiencing how soft his lips felt on my skin, but the longer it went on, the more urgency I sensed behind his touch. Eventually, he abandoned all pretense and pulled me into his chest, sucking on my bottom lip and darting his tongue in and out of my mouth. Closer and closer, our lips and bodies intertwined until I could barely breathe without his help.

This went on for several minutes, both of us unfazed by the very public setting, grabbing at each other and locking lips as if our very lives depended on it. Nothing else mattered in that moment. Not the scenery we were missing out on or the potential eyes that would most certainly be on us if anyone dared look toward our little corner on the boat.

All along, I realized, I'd been wondering how amazing it would feel to finally experience Phillip just like this. Unguarded, uninhibited, solely for me. And boy, was it worth the wait.

"Wow," I whispered as we finally came up from air. "So, that's what I've been missing?"

Phillip chuckled and kissed me on the lips once more, short and sweet, like he needed to punctuate the moment before we fully untangled our limbs from each other.

"Now you see why our first kiss couldn't have been the other night, right? I love New York, but inevitably, someone would have started honking a horn at another car or some neighbors would have begun yelling at each other. And I needed you uninterrupted and free to give wholly into your desires."

"Yeah," I sighed. "There's no way that could have compared to *this*."

"Even with the elevator music playing in the background?"

Phillip smiled again as he looked at me, allowing his eyes to drag the length of my body before coming right back up to my face. I was sure that he could see how flushed I still was from the kiss we'd lost ourselves in…and I didn't care at all to hide it.

"Honestly? I think the smooth jazz made it better somehow. I don't understand it, but apparently a saxophone solo is just what you need when you're in the throes of passion. I guess maybe you really are right about everything," I said with a giggle and a shrug.

As the boat turned, I suddenly had an even clearer view of Phillip under the moonlight, allowing me to gleefully watch his face light up again once he processed my latest reply.

"Say that one more time for me," he responded, his voice gritty and low, but with a smirk building on his face.

"I will not."

"C'mon, you know want to."

"I do not."

Protests aside, I hadn't been able to erase the big, fat grin off my face since our lips parted. So, as Phillip drew closer to me once again, I found myself smiling even brighter, overcome by how adored I felt in his presence. Clearly, I'd figured out his kryptonite, but he'd also assessed mine. And suddenly, we were two Supermans caught in each other's traps, with only time to reveal if we would use our knowledge for good or evil.

Phillip pressed his warm body on mine and then wrapped his arm around my shoulder, turning me so that my back was to his chest, and enveloping me in his embrace.

"Are you sure about that?" he asked, whispering into my ear as his breath tickled the back of my neck.

"Mmm-hmm."

A moan escaped from my lips as I felt myself melt under his touch again. Gripped tightly between his arms, I was desperate to keep my knees strong and my girls proud, but damn it, I was losing ground, and fast.

"Okay," he replied, releasing me from my mental anguish. "I won't push...for now."

"Good."

I cleared my throat and stood taller, still wrapped in his arms but with my wits about me again.

"Because then I can tell you about some big news that I have without worrying it will go to your head."

"Oh? Well, please, do tell."

"I took your advice, and we decided to go the practical route for the HUD proposal," I said, slightly tilting my head up and to the side so that I could view his expression without removing myself from his embrace. "There were a few team members who were disappointed at first, but they ultimately understood the reasoning behind it. So, now we're starting to work on what I think will be a pretty solid idea."

"Gigi, that's great. Congratulations. Do you have any specifics on it yet?"

"We're still figuring that out, but the crux of it is that we're going to look to target one neighborhood as a pilot program instead of trying to oversell what we could do for the whole city. And then, if we're able to get good outcomes with forty or fifty people over the next few years, those results can be used to scale up the program, hopefully with line-item budgeting from the city and the state."

"I'm sure that wasn't an easy decision," Phillip replied, squeezing me tighter in his arms, maybe for validation, reassurance or just because he liked it. I wasn't quite sure yet. "But you made it as the leader of your team, and not for nothing. It definitely sounds like the start of a solid idea to me."

"Thank you."

Smiling once again, I turned my face back toward the water and rested my head on Phillip's chest. It really was a remarkable view of the city. And if nothing else, it helped put a lot about life and all the people striving within it into greater perspective.

"You're right, it wasn't easy. There's still a part of me that wants to shoot for that giant, bright circle in the sky right now. But I think this route is what's best—for my team, our company and the people we want to impact— and all those things are far more important than my big dreams."

Phillip leaned his head on top of mine and breathed in deeply as he continued holding me in his arms.

"Who knows," he said. "You might just find that the two end up being one and the same."

"Yeah, I might. It's not like you've been wrong about anything else, yet."

"See," he said with a chuckle. "I knew you wanted to say it again."

"Orrrr...maybe I knew you really wanted to hear it."

"Tomato, tomahto. Either way, I'll take it."

# Part 2

"It's always the mind that needs quietening and the heart that needs listening to."

—Rasheed Ogunlaru

Part 2

# *Chapter Eight*

"Ayee, the crew's all here!"

Jake's face was lit up like a Christmas tree as he greeted the lot of us, gathered in front of his building and preparing for the two-hour drive up to the Catskills for Reagan's birthday trip.

"I'm really excited for this next week," he said. "And I can't thank you all enough for being here and celebrating my baby with me."

He paused to look around the circle of friends he'd pulled together from various parts of Reagan's life: me and Keisha, her New York City besties who'd been inseparable for the past two years; Julian, Keisha's boyfriend; Jennifer, one of Rae's closest girlfriends who she'd known since college, and who had just last year married the love of her life; Lucas, Jake's best friend from college who'd been around Reagan for so long, they'd become like brother and sister; and then of course, Brandon Clark, Jake's fraternity brother turned big brother turned second best friend.

The last two may have stemmed from Jake's friendship tree, but he and Rae had a way of integrating their lives together so seamlessly that it was sometimes hard to remember who'd brought who in first. I envied that about them.

There were, of course, some important missing faces—

ones we'd expected to have to skip it like Robin and Liv, who were living their best lives in London; ones who couldn't make it at the last minute, such as Jennifer's husband, Nick. And then there was Chrissy, Reagan and Keisha's best friend from high school, who'd tragically passed away a few years before, the result of a chronic disease that finally caught up to her. All in all, however, Jake had done a pretty great job rounding up the right squad for a fun-filled week upstate. I, for one, couldn't wait to let my hair down and breathe in some fresh air.

"Now that we're all together, I just want to run through a few things, and then we can get going," he added, his smile turning to more of a businesslike expression. "That good with everyone?"

A round of head nods passed through the group and gave him all the verification he needed.

With his clipboard in tow, Jake spent the next several minutes detailing everything from what food we'd ordered from the grocery store to the activity schedule that Keisha and I had planned out, the breakdown of the rooms in the cabin, and more. I had to admit, I was pretty impressed with his efforts leading up to the trip, and especially how he'd planned everything specifically around what Reagan would enjoy and how he could help give her a relaxing week away with some of her closest friends. He'd even managed not to let her in on the big secret until two weeks before, when she'd started trying to make her own birthday plans and he'd finally had to spill the beans.

When I talked about wanting a man of intention, this was exactly what I meant.

That didn't mean he was perfect. Rae and Jake had had their share of ups and downs when they were younger, first splitting up as they graduated from college, and then going through a few rounds of "will they or won't they get back together?" nonsense. But as they'd gotten older, they'd figured out how to better communicate with one another and prioritize the other person's needs. On top of that, anyone standing near them for even ten minutes could easily tell how much he loved her. And Reagan the same.

So, it wasn't that I desired their exact relationship, but I was certainly inspired by them and wanted to make sure I found something that fit *me*, with a man who was ready to choose us on a daily basis. Thankfully, even though we weren't yet exclusive, in the month-plus that Phillip and I had been dating, he was already showing me glimpses of this, making sure to carve out time for us even when he was busy and planning dates that gave us fun opportunities to get to know each other.

In fact, despite him being on the road a lot, so far, we'd tried everything from cooking classes to sculpting blindfolded, all new experiences in New York that we could say we did together. That knowledge made it a lot easier to be on a trip full of couples, one married person and the only guy who could somehow still interrupt my dreams of Phillip with a simple text. As charming and attractive as Brandon was, however, I knew I wanted more than just to fall for yet another alluring man who wasn't going to put me first. Any wandering thoughts of him were easily squelched by the reality of what Phillip was consistently bringing to my table.

"Okay, one last thing," Jake continued, looking down at his clipboard once more. "Since Nick couldn't make it anymore, I switched up the car assignments. Lucas, I figured you'd rather ride with me, Rae and Jenn now that there's room. That means, Keisha and Julian, you can consolidate with Brandon and Gigi if you want. I know you already rented a car specifically for the trip, so completely up to you."

I hadn't had a chance to peek at it, but the way Jake was clutching that clipboard like it was a security blanket, I wouldn't have been surprised if it included a full-on diagram of who was in what car and what they were bringing with them, how long he thought it would take them to arrive to the cabin and what shape they might be in once we did. Not to say that I thought he was over prepared, but he was definitely a little on edge. And the more I looked at him, the more his smile started to seem like a cover for something I couldn't quite put my finger on.

"Noooo, I think we'll let them have their own space, right babe?" Keisha replied, winking to Julian before darting her eyes toward me and then giggling her way over to Reagan's side.

Somehow, Jake's very innocuous question had turned into yet another opportunity for those two to tease me about Brandon. I swear, I loved my girls, but they were incessant. This wouldn't have been so annoying except for the very real fact that I knew he did not want me. That could not have been clearer if it were underlined, starred and broadcast in the sky, and yet, somehow, the two people who spent the most time with both me and him seemed completely oblivious to it.

I flashed Keisha a quick smile that read *I love you, but also hate you right now, k?* In return, she mouthed a feigned innocent "what?" that totally made me want to "accidentally" step on her foot. Really, I felt like I should crawl into a dark dungeon to escape how embarrassing it was to have been put on the spot in front of our whole group. It may not have even been so apparent if her initial response to Jake hadn't been in such a singsongy tone. But since it was, it had raised almost everyone's eyes to attention, including Jake, who seemed to want to avoid the discussion almost as much as I did.

"Plus, there's not enough room in Brandon's car for all four of us anyway," Keisha added, a little too late for my liking.

"All right then," Jake replied, clearing his throat and attempting to get everyone back focused on him. "Let's get these cars packed up, so we can be on our way. If we can get on the road in the next fifteen to twenty minutes, we should be good to beat any traffic that might cause the grocery delivery to be sitting out at the front door for too long."

"Aye, aye, captain," Brandon answered dutifully, tapping Jake on his shoulder in a move that seemed to instantly calm him. "Don't worry, we won't let the bears get to the stockpile of meat you've ordered."

With Jake's spiel finally complete, the rest of us moved into action, packing up the cars and trunks as if we were little ants on a mission, all with our own special assignments. Many of us were even dressed alike, despite never having discussed coordinating attires for the trip. That sort of unplanned matching had become par for the course the longer I spent time with this crew.

Like the rest of the Howard grads in the bunch, Jake was wearing an HU sweatshirt—something I'd come to realize they all did when traveling, even in the middle of June—with a pair of charcoal gray joggers. His sweatshirt was a dark blue pullover with a hoodie attached that featured a large white stripe over the chest, where the word "Howard" was emblazoned in red. On his left sleeve, the designers had vertically positioned "Est." on the side of his upper arm. The numbers "1867," the year the school was founded, lay parallel on the right.

Reagan, Jenn and Lucas—all Howard grads as well—
had their own variations. With her hair pulled up into a
loose, high bun, Rae had on a dark blue crew neck sweatshirt with a bright red *H* on the front that she'd paired with
simple light gray leggings, somewhat, but not completely,
matching her fiancé. Jenn, meanwhile, had tucked a loose-
fitting tan sweatshirt with blue lettering that read "Howard"
above the school's seal into her acid-washed mom jeans.
And Lucas had found probably the reddest sweatshirt I'd
seen in my life with the words "Howard University" etched
across it in white letters. He'd combined that with a pair
of blue shorts that weren't quite "hoochie daddy" level but
were very much teetering on it.

As the two University of Southern California grads in
the bunch, Keisha and I had learned the hard way that
we needed to come with our own 'nalia if we didn't want
people to assume our whole New York crew had gone to
Howard. So true to form, we'd also shown up to Jake's
wearing our own college's sweatshirts, with Keish rocking an oversize tan top with cardinal-and-gold letters spell-
ing out "USC Trojans" above a side profile illustration of
a Trojan warrior's head and garb. Like me, she believed in
showing off her thick thighs, so I wasn't surprised to see
her in a pair of cutoff jean shorts with her high-top, crisp
white Chuck Taylors and her signature leopard print glasses
setting her outfit off right.

I'd opted to keep things fairly simple and had pulled the
top of my jet-black twists into a high pony, which allowed
the bottom half to cascade down right onto the collar of my
favorite goldish-yellow crop top sweatshirt. It didn't feature
a bunch of designs like some of the others but modestly included the word "trojans" written in all lowercase letters in
our signature cardinal red across the top—the combination

of colors literally popping off my skin. I also had on my own pair of jean shorts, though not quite as short as Lucas's or Keisha's, and some rose-gold Birkenstock sandals that were the perfect shoes for road-tripping.

I laughed to myself as the eight of us packed each of the trunks with suitcases, coolers, blankets and more, thinking of how a bystander could have easily pictured us in someone's college alumni magazine, colorful and bright, and moving in sync with one another as if this were something we did every day. Even Julian, someone relatively new to the crew, had come through wearing a classic maroon Morehouse sweatshirt and matching shorts, blending in perfectly with our J.Crew super ad.

Funny enough, the only person who didn't have on anything college related was Brandon, quite possibly the sole Stanford grad I knew who didn't constantly brag about his alma mater. So, while the rest of us were marching in coordination with each other, in more ways than one, Brandon stood out in a two-piece, Army green tracksuit, conveniently unzipped so that it subtly but seductively exposed his pecs through the white tank top he wore underneath.

It wasn't exactly surprising that he'd opted not to match our aesthetic, but it was noticed, and that was something I knew he took a certain amount of pleasure in.

In truth, Brandon wasn't exactly someone who liked fitting himself into neat little square boxes. In college, for example, he'd majored in biology, which I could only assume his family thought would lead him to being an illustrious and very rich doctor. But as they would come to learn, he had different ideas. After graduating from one of the most prestigious universities in the country, Brandon jumped headfirst into the job he'd had his heart set on since he was a little boy: personal trainer.

Eventually, he worked his way up to start his own business, one where he had the flexibility and autonomy to train multi-million-dollar athletes one day and a group of kids the next. But he'd also confided in me one night, after maybe a few too many drinks, that his parents had lovingly given him the side-eye for several years before they finally saw the value of his dreams. That had hurt him a little at first, but more than anything, it made him determined to show them he knew what was best for him. It also came to define more than just his career outlook. He lived his life that way as well.

In a society where men were often forced to choose one side of their bisexuality over the other, for example, Brandon never did. He was honest and transparent with everyone he dated, but he was also clear on one simple truth: he was the kind of guy who followed his heart and did what felt right to Brandon, no matter what. So, that meant he was never going to hide who he was in an effort to build a white picket fence with either a man or woman. If either were to love him, they'd have to love him wholly as he was or not at all.

Knowing these things about Brandon, how casually adamant he was about the things he believed in, was part of what drew me to him—it's probably what drew a lot of people to him, to be honest—but it's also how I knew, without a shadow of a doubt, that Keisha and Reagan were wrong about any romantic feelings he might have for me. The guy who fought for everything that he wanted, other people's opinions be damned, wouldn't hesitate to scoop me up if he had even the slightest interest in dating me. And that, regardless of what my girls seemed to believe, was one of the many reasons I couldn't let any silly attraction

I may have had for him change anything about my trajectory with Phillip.

Phillip was real, while Brandon was a fantasy. A fantasy better left in the friend zone.

With all the cars finally packed and ready to go, I slid into the passenger seat of Brandon's Mercedes GT 63 and made myself comfortable, pulling out my phone so that I could connect it to his speaker. Despite everything else, I truly did value our friendship, and I was excited to catch up with him for the next couple hours.

It was only about a minute or so later that he walked over to the driver's side of the car, opened the door and peeked in briefly.

"You're good, right?" he asked, eyes filled with the kind of sincerity that could melt a girl's heart if you let it.

"Of course."

I stared back at him, allowing my eyes to momentarily lock with his before raising my phone in the air to show what I was doing as I waited for him. For the past year, we'd been cultivating a shared playlist on Spotify, each of us adding a song to it whenever one randomly came up in discussion and got a visceral reaction from us both. The run time had accumulated to a little less than three hours so far, which to me, made it perfect for our road trip.

"Okay, cool. Just checking on you," he added before waving Jake over to his car. "I'll be ready to go in a moment, but I do like the way you think, Gig. Let's definitely get that going."

With a quick wink of reassurance, Brandon then raised his body out of the car door frame and turned to greet Jake.

"Bro, I just want you know that we got you," he said, gripping Jake's shoulders like the big brother he'd come to be ever since they'd met at an alumni chapter fraternity meeting when Jake first moved to New York. "You can relax, okay? I know you want things to be perfect for Rae, and I get it because the wedding's coming soon, and you don't want her to feel like her birthday is a nonfactor. But listen, you don't have to stress so much about pleasing your girl, man. Look at her. She's already having a great time."

Jake paused and looked toward Reagan, who was gleefully laughing along with Jenn as they unsuccessfully tried stuffing yet another duffel bag into his trunk. Knowing her, I was sure it was filled with a bunch of shoes she absolutely wasn't going to need but had to have with her just in case. I had to stifle my own chuckle as the two of them pushed and pushed, cracking the other up with every failed attempt, until finally the tiny bit of space they were trying to fit it into acquiesced to them. At last triumphant, they chest bumped and raised their arms in the air as if they'd just climbed the seventy-two stone steps in front of the Philadelphia Museum of Art.

My girls. They were a mess and a half, but I wouldn't trade them for anyone else in the world.

"Thanks, man," Jake replied, turning back to Brandon with the first genuine smile I'd seen him give all morning.

This also brought my attention back to them and the more interesting conversation at hand.

"I needed that reminder," he added. "And you're right; I know it's not all on me to make things go smoothly this week. I asked y'all to join us for a reason, because I know Rae, and as much as she loves me, she's in her happiest place when she's around her people."

"Exactly, bro. So, trust that we got you and her, and it's gonna be one helluva good time, all right? And, if that doesn't loosen you up enough, hell, I don't know, maybe get a kiss from your fiancée before you get behind the wheel.

That kind of thing usually boosts my spirits when I need it, and trust me, *you* need it."

Jake laughed and playfully shoved Brandon off him just as my phone started vibrating, tearing my focus away from their bro session. I looked down at my phone and saw some familiar culprits on my screen.

Reagan: Say friend, don't do anything we wouldn't on the ride up, okay?

Keisha: Nah, scratch that. Do everything that we would do!

*Gah, can't they tell I'm trying to listen in on Jake and Brandon? I don't have time for their shenanigans right now.*

I quickly typed back my reply, admonishing them yet again and reminding them about the very handsome man I was currently dating who didn't make me guess whether he liked me. Remember him? I asked before focusing my ears back on the discussion happening right next to me.

"Damn, I must be down bad, getting advice from the guy who hasn't dated anyone for more than a month since I've known him," Jake said with a laugh that told me whatever Brandon had said or done had finally settled him down.

"Ayee now, first off, that's not true. I was with Stephen for three months. And it doesn't matter how long I've been with somebody—I can still speak to the effects of a perfectly placed kiss from your partner and how it can make everything else seem like butter melting off you."

"That's some beautiful words, B. Thank you, man. Really."

Jake tapped Brandon on his chest, briefly pretending as if he were being serious before bursting into laughter again. To Brandon's credit, he seemed to be enjoying the interaction just as much as his friend, even as the butt of Jake's joke, leaning toward him and cracking a grin that looked equal parts happy and relieved. I caught myself smiling, too, as I watched them, marveling at the dynamics of their friendship. It was different from what I had with Keisha and Rae, but in many ways, it felt very familiar. Drenched in honesty and respect, but never so serious that we couldn't clown each other when the moment called for it.

Another text from Reagan jolted me out my thoughts, but not before I could have sworn that I heard Jake loudly whisper, "But save that kinda talk for Gigi, all right?"

*Not Jake, too*, I said to myself, looking back at my phone again. Foolishly, I'd considered him a neutral party, maybe even my ally, but I should have known better. There was no way Rae hadn't corrupted him with all her musings by now.

Reagan: We knooow, we know. And listen, we like Mr. Handsome.

Keisha: Yeah, he genuinely seems like a great guy.

Reagan: He's just not Brandon.

Before I could respond to the texts before me, I locked eyes with Jake as he nodded my way, clearly trying to discern if I'd heard him or not. I wanted to mouth back *every word, buddy—you're not really great at whispering*, but something in me thought better of it. I didn't really need him to know how much both of their voices had carried through Brandon's open car door, especially considering the personal nature of some of their discussion. Instead, I simply returned his smile and shifted my eyes, if not my attention, back to my phone.

"Aww man, c'mon, don't do this right now," Brandon whispered in response.

"All right, fine. I'll leave it, but you didn't do yourself any favors asking her to ride with you."

"We're friends, Jake. That's it," Brandon said firmly. "And besides, she agreed!"

"That's because you're both delusional," Jake answered, undeterred by Brandon's protests. "And by the way, about Stephen, yes, you were together for three months, but two of those were before we met. I only saw you with him for a month, so my assessment still stands."

"Man, whatever. Go kiss your girl, so we can get up outta here."

"Now, I'm the jerk if I say the same back to you, right?"

Out of the corner of my eye, I watched Jake as he walked away, pleased with his counter to Brandon and completely unaware that I'd heard them both.

As Brandon climbed back into the car, I quickly typed my final reply to the girls and then changed my settings so that their texts wouldn't show up on his car dashboard.

Me: Brandon isn't an option for me. Please let it be.

"You ready?" he asked, turning his head toward me and winking as he settled into the driver's seat.

"Never more."

With a quick, almost indiscernible breath in, I conjured up every good feeling I had about our friendship and flashed Brandon a reassuring smile that he returned in kind. All thirty-two teeth glistening in the sun, set off by the goatee that perfectly outlined his lips.

"Bet. And you got our playlist keyed up already, right?"

"Of course. Bruno Mars is just waiting for you to join him in song."

"See, you play, but you know I sound as good as he does on 'Just the Way You Are.'"

"Eh. In the shower, maybe, but that's it," I replied, laughing and shaking my head at the overconfidence he had in himself.

Brandon may have been a lot of things, but a singer was not one of them.

"I was thinking more like when I sing it with you, but…"

He paused and stared into my eyes for what felt like a moment too long before turning his full lips into a devious smirk.

"That *can* be in the shower if you want, though."

"Please. I think not, playboy. I'm staying as far away from you and showers as I can."

With a light shove to his right shoulder, I rolled my eyes to punctuate my sentence.

See? This was why the girls were convinced he had feelings for me, but the man was simply a flirt. Nothing more, nothing less. And every once in a while, I had to remind him that I wasn't like all the other people who hung on every word he uttered in hopes that his flirting would turn into something more.

"All right then, I guess our duet will have to remain in the car," he said with a shrug. "Good thing for me I've got all the time in the world to get you to come around and see me as the real musician that I am."

"The real musician, huh?"

"Yeah! We can't all be fancy as you and formally study music as a kid, but that doesn't mean I didn't do my own work. I'll have you know that my cousins had me practicing Jodeci songs every weekend when I was younger. And who do you think was K-Ci? That's right. Me."

Brandon pointed to himself and winked at me again, and I couldn't stop myself from doubling over with laughter.

"Lord, help me," I replied, catching my breath. "What am I going to do with you?"

"Enjoy the ride," he replied, raising his eyebrows to the car ceiling and then finally starting up the engine and pulling out onto the road. "That's what I tell all my girls and guys."

For more than an hour straight, Brandon and I loudly sang together every inflection, ad-lib and extended high note that showed up on our playlist, ranging from Dru Hill's "Beauty" to Groove Theory's "Tell Me." When there were two distinct parts, like in Monica and Brandy's "The Boy Is Mine," we each instinctively took one and matched the other's energy, bopping our heads to the beat and low-key dueling to see who was best. But when the song called for us to sing in unison, we shined like a well-oiled machine or as if we'd practiced our parts every weekend like he'd done with his cousins.

Brandon didn't actually convince me of his singing chops, but that was never the point, really. Most important was our continuous laughter that filled the interior of his car almost as much as the prevalence of the really awful notes he'd managed to hit time and again.

I'd nearly forgotten how rocky things had started off in Harlem when he asked me to pause our song fest so that he could ask me a really important question.

*Damn it*, I thought, bracing myself to have to explain Keisha's comment about giving us our own space from earlier.

"What's going on with the HUD proposal?" Brandon asked, briefly turning his head to me before refocusing on the road. "It's coming up soon, right?"

"Wait, that's your really important question?" I asked with an enormous sense of relief.

"Yeah," he said with a shrug. "I know how big of a deal this is for you, but I also figure we may not have a ton of time to ourselves once we get to the cabin. So, now's as good a time as any to tell me all about it. Right?"

"Yeah. You're right," I replied. "Well, the good news is we've almost finalized the proposal, and I'm happy to say my team has really worked together to put forth something that is solid, sensible, and lays out exactly what we can do and how we can do it. Our design team has also done some good work to showcase how the pilot program we want to start can be used to prove our case for expansion over the next several years."

"Hmm. Okay. Tell me more."

"All right. So, the idea is that we would use part of the money to build a new housing unit in Brooklyn that would house up to eight women and their children rent free for six months at a time. Then, we'd partner with an organization that does wraparound services, so that they'd have access to employment assistance and substance use treatment if needed. They'd be connected to a pro bono therapist who specializes in working with adults and kids, and we'd work with them to secure a lease by the time their six months were up."

Brandon listened closely as I detailed the remainder of the proposal, highlighting why we thought it made sense to own the land and the building to help avoid any NIM-BYism that might restrict what we're able to do if neighbors began championing for our removal strictly based on

some of the fears that come with a subsidized housing facility in your community. I also explained how we planned
to partner with the other service providers to sustain the
work over the course of the three-year pilot, and then use
the outcome data we collected to lobby and make the case
for city funding to be able to scale the program up. He even
laughed heartily as I finished my description with a seated
curtsy to try to tone down some of the seriousness.

But as I went on, I got the sense he could tell there was
more I wanted to say.

"Wow, Gig," he replied. "That's a very well thought out
and detailed proposal."

"Yeah," I said quietly. "I'm hopeful that when we present it next week, we'll have a real shot of becoming one of
the organizations they choose to partner with."

"I have no doubt that they will. You're brilliant, and your
proposal sounds like it would make a real difference to the
women who are able to join the program. It's just that…"

Brandon hesitated for a moment, not yet taking his eyes
off the road despite the fact that by now I'd fully turned my
body toward him in my passenger seat.

"What?" I asked, staring at him.

"Can I be honest?"

"Of course. I'd expect nothing less from you."

"It doesn't totally feel like you."

With a clear road ahead, Brandon finally turned his face
toward me and locked his eyes with mine. It was brief, but
in the stillness of the moment, I felt every goose bump pop
up on my skin.

"I'm not saying you didn't have a part in it, obviously. If
I know anything, I know the level of detail within it comes
from you challenging your team to think through every
scenario and be prepared for every question. But it feels

like something's missing. I don't know, it just doesn't have your heart in it, you know. You don't even sound excited when you talk about it."

"I am hopeful," I countered. "I think we have a real shot when we present it next week, and I believe in my team."

"None of that says you're excited, Gig. But listen, maybe I'm wrong. I don't want to put my feelings on you. So, tell me..." he said, looking at me once again with the kind of eyes it was really hard to lie to. "Are you?"

"No."

My response was almost as quiet as the car had become, but I knew he'd heard me all the same. And in *my* head, it sounded like a loud drum trying to awaken something I'd given up on in my pursuit not to fail.

"But excitement, thrill, big hopes and dreams, however you want to phrase it, that's not always feasible, Brandon," I countered. "This is a proposal I know my company can accomplish. What's the use of aiming for the moon if you fail?"

"Well, if you ask me, there's no point in doing anything less. You should be, at all times, only pursuing whatever makes your heart skip a beat. That's what brings real change in this world. That's what sets you apart from everybody else."

"Even if there's a greater chance of falling flat on your face?"

"Yes," he replied. "To me, that's not even a question."

I shifted my body so that I was once again facing forward and sank into the back of my seat as I thoughtfully considered Brandon's words and whether I agreed with him. His ideas couldn't have been more completely opposite from Phillip's, a man who prioritized goals and results over the potential of a dream.

I liked that about Phillip. I found comfort in the way he put action into whatever he said he would do and never oversold what he wasn't sure he could achieve. That had served him well in his career, and frankly with me, too, because I knew I could rely on him. In a world where so many people just said what they thought others wanted to hear, Phillip and his outlook on life were refreshing. Stabilizing, even.

And so, as a leader of a team with an immense amount of responsibility foisted on us, his advice had resonated with me, and I'd been inspired to follow his model to make sure we put our best foot forward by delivering an intentional and practical proposal that was failure proof. But Brandon was right, too. In the process, I'd removed any element that felt too big or too hard to accomplish.

The proposal was great, but it no longer represented me. It was Phillip's.

"I may have packed my laptop with me," I admitted, speaking up for the first time in minutes.

To Brandon's credit, he hadn't rushed to fill the silence in the car with the music from our playlist or jokes that might have taken away some of the discomfort I'd had to sit with. No, he'd let me have the time I needed to process, I think knowing eventually I'd say something again when I was ready.

"Why am I not all surprised by that?" he asked.

"Because you know me well."

"I do."

Brandon nodded his head and waited for me to continue.

"So, maybe, when everyone's gone to bed, and I have some quiet time alone, I can see where there's some room to sprinkle a little bit of me back into the proposal."

"Mmm—"

"That doesn't mean completely changing it," I interjected. "But what's the point in having a moon if you don't aim for it every once in a while, right?"

"Ha! I couldn't have said it better myself, Gig."

# *Chapter Nine*

True to Jake's plans, all three cars pulled up to the cabin, following one by one into its curved driveway, at about 12:30 p.m. It was a beautiful Saturday afternoon, sun high in the sky, with a slight breeze that made June far more palatable than the later months in the summer would be.

Without hesitation, we all stepped out of our respective cars and marveled at the house before us, statuesque with its wooden exterior, and even more magnificent than what was shown in the photos. Surrounded by multiple entry stairs—and a wheelchair-accessible ramp—the place looked like a giant could have lived there, standing tall among the most beautiful pink, violet and yellow flowers, with lush green pine trees flanking its backside and views of an even greater mountain in the distance. Next to it sat a bright red carport that we could fit all three cars in once we'd unloaded them. And just off the center of the middle of the house was a huge brick chimney, which got me super excited thinking of lighting up the fireplace when the air chilled in the middle of the night.

"Wow," I said, catching Brandon's eyes as we both looked on in wonder. "We're a far cry away from the city."

"Yeah," he replied. "But this is home for the next week."

"You're damn right it is!" Keisha shouted as she ran

up to me and twirled me around. "Gig, it's only been two hours, and I've missed you already. Please take me out of misery and come with me."

As if on cue, Reagan and Jenn joined her, swarming me and pulling me toward the house with them. I barely had time to look Brandon's way and mouth a quick *I'm sorry* before they dragged me up the steps, giggling about rooms and cocktail hours as we entered into the cabin. We walked right past the pile of groceries Jake had ordered to be delivered at twelve fifteen without any of us even deigning to bring them inside.

"Shouldn't we help get those?" I asked.

"We'll come back, don't worry," Reagan replied. "First, we need to hear about your car ride, and I think we've only got about ten minutes of privacy before the boys have unloaded all the cars. So, we don't have time to dawdle."

"Exactly," Keisha interjected. "It's gossip first, then groceries. The boys will understand."

"I'm not going to get away with just saying nothing, am I?"

I looked at all three ladies and watched in amusement as they tilted their heads toward me and squinted their eyes as if they were trying to see if something was wrong with me.

"Oh no, have you taken ill all of a sudden?" Jenn asked, raising her hand to my forehead to check my temperature.

"No," I replied, rolling my eyes.

I could already tell exactly where this was going.

"Well, is it amnesia?" Keisha asked, mockingly gasping to show her distress.

"It is not!" I laughed.

"Then *cher*, you must know who we are. But in case your brain is all mush from the time you just spent with the love of your life, I'm Reagan, and this is Keisha and Jennifer. We're all friends of yours."

Reagan pointed to each person as she mentioned their name, and then directed her attention back toward me. In a matter of seconds, the expression on her face turned from one of fake concern to a huge smirk that revealed how badly she wanted to burst into laughter.

"I hate you all, but yes, I know who are!"

"Okay then. So, you already know the answer is no."

Keisha grabbed my hand and pulled me toward the interior steps, racing us through the vast, open-air living room. Jake had already assigned our rooms and shown us the floor plan, so I knew the two first-floor bedrooms to our left side were reserved for the couples—Keisha and Julian, and Rae and Jake—but I didn't have a chance to see anything as I was swiftly hauled up another flight of steps to get to my room.

On the second floor of the cabin were four bedrooms, with the two in the middle sharing a bathroom. The two corner bedrooms were smaller, but each had its own bathroom, so they'd been assigned to Julian and Lucas. Jenn and I, on the other hand, had happily agreed to the ones in the middle, both of which had incredible views of the backyard and king-sized beds.

Keisha immediately took us into the middle left room and secured the door as the rest of us found spots where we could sit. Jenn took the desk chair, conveniently positioned next to the adjoining door that led to our shared bathroom. Reagan plopped down on the large window seat that overlooked the backyard and provided a cute little reading nook in the corner. I commandeered a space on the edge of my bed, not wanting to fully lie across it before I'd cleaned and inspected the room. And finally, Keisha, faced with nowhere else to sit, dropped down to the floor, butt first, crossing her legs as she waited in anticipation to hear all I had to say.

"Okay, now give us the deets before we run out of time," Reagan called out, her voice stern yet playful.

"And please don't bother pretending there are none," Keisha added. "We know better than that."

"Well, *I* don't actually know better than that," Jenn admitted with a shrug. "But Rae and Jake have done their best to catch me up, so I'm ready for the gossip, too."

Her confession was just the moment of levity we all needed and dually served to confirm my suspicions that Rae and Jake had indeed been talking about me and Brandon. More importantly, however, as I looked around the room, I was reminded that I was surrounded by women who only wanted the best for me, and that I could trust them with the truth. However inconvenient it might be.

I had a different relationship with each woman facing me. My friendship with Keisha was the closest, but my connection with Reagan had long ago grown from friend-of-a-friend to sister. And the more time I spent with Jenn, the more I absolutely adored her. I could see how she'd been the heart of Reagan's college crew—sweet and maybe a little unassuming, but with some spice that made me want to learn even more about her.

I took in a quick breath to gather myself, sensing there was no way out of my interrogation except through it, and then proceeded, for the next few minutes, to appease my friends in a bit of folly. I only hoped my plan would be enough to dispel any further Brandon notions and ensure a peaceful cabin trip for us all.

Knowing how much they would latch on to any little detail, I carefully mentioned some of the cuter moments between us that I assumed they would enjoy, like the ease that I felt with him as we sang some of the greatest love songs to and with each other or the time that Brandon's hand mistakenly brushed my thigh. At the last minute, I decided to also tell them about the way he'd challenged me on my team's HUD proposal, in a way that only Brandon could. If I was going to really make them believe I'd come over to their side, I knew it had to be based on more than a few casual winks in between songs.

"That conversation reminded me of one of the uniquely beautiful things about him," I said, holding my right hand to my chest as if I were truly a woman in love. "Brandon makes you want to see the world as pure and openhearted as he does."

"I knew it!" Keisha shouted out as soon as I paused to let them bask in all that I'd laid out before them.

With gleeful eyes, she raised her hand to meet Rae's for an impassioned high five that even I could not begrudge them for. In one sense, they had been right. The drive up to the Catskills with Brandon had certainly confirmed for me that he was someone I could always have fun with, someone I felt comfortable being completely myself around. But— even though I knew they weren't going to want to hear this part—it had also reinforced my belief that we should leave well enough alone.

I watched the three of them grow ever more excited, with Reagan and Keisha's light brown cheeks burning red with delight. Even Jennifer flitted her feet on the ground as if she was badly trying to stop herself from jumping up to dance. It was nice to see my girls so happy for me. What woman didn't want that, right? To be able to share in her joy with her closest friends and have their support and encouragement? If only those feelings had actually been real.

If I was completely honest, there was a very small part of me that wanted to explore the end result they were all pushing for. But the thing was, I knew things they didn't. And in order to make them truly understand how I felt and why I'd long since let go of any pretense of something beyond friendship for me and Brandon, I knew I was going to have to take them down the same rollercoaster ride I'd been on. I just hoped they would get it when I was done.

When it looked as if they couldn't beam any brighter, I slowed down my words and carefully began to bring them back down to reality, complete with a retelling of the end of his conversation with Jake. "Friends," I echoed for them, not as some kind of disastrous ending, but as confirmation of the beautiful thing we'd built that worked...*for us*.

Predictably, their faces fell. It was painful to see their reactions, but I was at peace with Brandon as my friend. In fact, for me, all he'd said to Jake earlier just solidified what I'd known all along.

Maybe it was a tall order to ask, but I didn't want any of my girls to be sad about that. I wasn't. If anything, I counted myself lucky. None of the people Brandon had ever dated were still present in his life, and very few of my exes were in mine. This way, I could be certain we'd have our whole lives to look forward to, together.

And... I could save a different, more sensual type of companionship, and all the risks that came with it, for someone who wasn't also one of the most important people in my life.

"Which is why you're dating Phillip," Keisha said quietly, her eyes piercing into mine with what seemed like understanding, *finally*.

"Yes and no," I replied. "Phillip is new and untethered to any other part of my life, so yeah, that helps a lot in that

I'm less worried about the fallout if things go wrong. But also, I'm starting to really like him. He's kind, and stable, and he treats me well. And for once, it feels good dating someone who doesn't make me question his interest in me."

I smiled, thinking about our last conversation before he left for DC the night before, and how, even now, I knew he was waiting to get a text from me saying that we'd made it safely to the cabin. Maybe that kind of clarity didn't come with all the bells and whistles that Brandon brought to the table, but it was nice all the same.

"Okay then. If he's really who you want, I can get on board with that. For real this time."

"Thank you."

I turned to Reagan to see if she was willing to do the same and instantly saw that she wasn't quite there yet. We both sighed as our eyes met.

"Can I just ask you one thing?" she requested.

"Sure. Why not?"

"Are you and Mr. Handsome exclusive?"

"No, not yet."

"So, I mean, we're all here for the next week, in this big, beautiful, secluded house. And Brandon's going to be down the hall from you the whole time. Would it hurt to just keep yourself open to whatever happens while you're here? You never know, maybe your friendship with him isn't a replacement for romance, but it's something amazing that you can build on?"

"Reagan." I shook my head at her continued resistance.

"I'm not pushing it; I promise," she said, raising up her hands in defense. "If nothing happens, then so be it. All I'm asking is will you stay open?"

"Okay," I replied softly, feeling as if I'd been sufficiently

Reagan-ed. "As long as you agree to consider that I might also be right."

"Deal."

She rose from the window seat, and walked toward me with her right hand out so that we could shake on it, as if we were two master negotiators settling on an arrangement. I gladly obliged and took her hand in mine, being sure to keep eye contact with her even as we effectively sealed our deal.

"Well, now that that's done, we should probably get back downstairs before the boys all lose their minds," she said, shifting her focus back to the other ladies in the room.

"Oh gosh, you're right," Keisha replied. "Because I can see Julian unpacking everything now and putting it all in the exact wrong place."

"And then you'll have to decide if you want to keep it there, knowing it's better off somewhere else, which will annoy the hell out of you, or listen to him whine about how you came behind him and moved everything—" Jenn added.

"Which will also annoy the hell out of me!"

"Exactly."

"Goodness. It's like we've all been cursed to love the same man," Keisha remarked as she, too, got up from her seat on the floor.

"No, we just all happen to love men," Reagan chimed in. "And even the best of them…"

"Are still just men."

Jennifer finished Rae's sentence, and we all chuckled in response.

"To the men…may we love and support them, but never take on their brains," said Keisha.

"Hear, hear," we all replied in unison, giggling once again as she unlocked my door and swung it open.

"Babe!"

Almost immediately, we heard Jake's voice calling for Reagan, which just made us laugh even harder.

"We could use you guys' help down here," he added.

"When I tell you I know my man," she said with a playful eye roll before poking her head out of the door and shouting back that we'd all be right down in a minute.

"And you're still gonna stick beside him," Jenn joked in return.

"You damn skippy I am," Reagan replied. "I can't imagine my life without that fool."

She paused and then looked straight at me.

"That's all I want for you, Gig. I hope you know that."

"I know."

"And I mean it. That could be with Brandon, Phillip or the freakin' Tin Man from the *Wiz*, for all I care."

I laughed and held back a small tear from falling out of my eyes.

"I'll be sure to tell the Tin Man he's got your blessing."

"Nah, *cher*, I'm still very much Team Brandon—that's who has my blessing. But… I'm staying open, too, as promised."

"Got you."

One by one, Keish, Rae and Jenn made their way through my door and down the steps, back into the living room and then into the kitchen. There, as far as I could tell from my room, the guys had started pulling the groceries out of the bags and were apparently quite flummoxed on where certain items should go, just like we'd assumed. Meanwhile, I lingered upstairs so that I could text Phillip before rejoining the mayhem awaiting me.

Me: Hey! We made it up here, and I have to say, the place is absolutely beautiful.

Phillip texted back almost immediately.

Good. I'm glad to hear that. Do you have a favorite spot on the grounds yet?

Me: Not yet. There's a reading nook in my room that's definitely in contention, but I hear there's also a babbling brook somewhere on the property. I can't wait to see that.

Phillip: Damn, a babbling brook is pretty hardcore. But can it top this?

Within seconds, an image of colorful flowers overlooking the Potomac River with a view of the Kennedy Center in the background popped up in my phone.

Me: Oh, I don't know. That might be tough to beat.

Phillip: No, it won't. All you'd have to do is send me a picture of you, and you'd beat it by a mile.

I laughed at his corniness but also the sweet way he'd basically asked for a picture without asking for one. I wasn't about to go looking for the brook just yet, but the reading nook was right in front of me. I walked over to it, carefully positioned myself so that the sun shone through my window to illuminate my skin and snapped a quick selfie. Then, before I could overthink my decision, I pressed Send on the unedited photo, and waited for his response.

Perfection, Phillip replied.

If anyone had seen me in that moment, I couldn't be sure which they might say was shining brighter, the sun or my face. How Reagan and Keisha thought Brandon, who flirted with everyone practically anytime he opened his mouth, could ever top that, I didn't know. Not when Phillip was very specifically interested in me.

Me: Thank you :). Really.

I should go before I get called out for being anti-social, though.

Phillip: Surely, we wouldn't want that.

Me: We would not lol

Phillip: Okay, have fun. We'll talk later.

Me: We will! Oh wait, how did the contract negotiation go?

Phillip: Signed and delivered.

Me: I knew it! Congratulations, Phillip! Sounds like we need to celebrate later as well.

Phillip: Thank you! And I'd very much like that.

I blacked out my screen and dropped my phone on the bed, skipping toward my door like a girl with a high school crush when…bam! I almost crashed right into my suitcase, which had apparently been carefully placed directly at my entrance. If I hadn't been so distracted, I would have easily seen it in time to avoid almost falling square on my face; but then again, I hadn't even noticed that someone had come right up to my door.

"Wow," I thought, dragging the oversize luggage into

my room. I owed a huge debt to whoever had been so kind to save me from having to lug it up those stairs by myself, but I also wondered what they'd seen that had stopped them from making their presence known.

After I took a couple minutes to hoist my suitcase onto the luggage rack that I found in the closet, I briefly looked about to see if anyone else was still moving around upstairs, hoping I could thank them for their efforts. It seemed to be just me, however, so I returned to my mission to rejoin the crew. Down the steps I trotted, past the three large blue sofas in the living room, and into the sprawling kitchen with a big grin on my face.

"Ayee! You're just in time, Gig," Jake called out, greeting me warmly almost as soon as I entered into the common area.

If there was one thing about Reagan's fiancé that always held true, it was that the man knew how to make anyone feel as if they'd walked into the Cheers bar when he was at his best. That was a gift not many people had. Reagan and Brandon had a similar charm about them, in that they knew how to disarm you and make you feel at home, but Jake was undeniably Sam behind the bar. He made everyone feel like they were his best friend, even if he wasn't theirs.

"I'm about to hand out assignments for today," he continued, twisting around to make sure we were all together and visibly counting to see if he got to the number eight.

"Just as soon as B gets back, I suppose."

"Whoa, I'm here," Brandon replied, strolling into the kitchen almost as soon as Jake finished his statement.

He quickly slid next to me on the outside of the giant marble island that took up almost a fourth of the kitchen area.

"Put me in wherever you need me, coach."

"Oh good," Jake replied, relief washing over his face again.

"Was it you who brought my suitcase to my bedroom?" I whispered, turning to Brandon as Jake began informing everyone of what he needed them to do for the next couple hours.

"Yeah," he answered sheepishly. "I just didn't want you to have to carry it upstairs."

"But you didn't say anything when you saw me in there?"

"I don't know. You seemed…occupied. I didn't want to interrupt."

"Oh okay."

I looked at Brandon to see if I could detect any emotion to match the slight hesitation in his words, but his expression seemed the same as any other time we were around each other—a combination of jovial and stoic all at once.

So maybe his reason really was as simple as what he'd said.

"Well, thank you," I continued. "I really appreciate it."

"It's no problem, Gig, really. Nothing that anyone else wouldn't have done."

That, of course, was where Brandon was wrong. Plenty of men, ones I could name without even thinking too hard about it, wouldn't have thought to do a simple act of kindness, unprompted and for no reward. And on the off chance they did, they would have at least painted a large banner beside my suitcase to ensure they got the credit for it.

But Brandon just always did whatever he felt was right.

*How lucky the person will be who finally captures his whole heart. I imagine he'll try to give them the world if he can.*

*And they'd better be deserving of it*, I responded to myself. *Or they'd have me to answer to.*

By the time we finished our brief talk, Jake had already given out the majority of the assignments, all dished out according to our strengths. He'd asked Julian to join him on the grill, while Keish and Jenn were assigned to food prep. Lucas, ever the interior designer, had been tasked with setup for the dinner table outside. And Reagan's job, despite her best efforts to help put everything together, was simply to sit and look pretty, with the occasional taste-testing request sure to come her way.

Finally, he turned to me and Brandon and explained that we had one of the most important assignments of them all: making drinks for not just the sunset dinner he had planned but also for the next few hours while we primped and prepped throughout the day.

"We're on it," I replied, resisting the urge to repeat Brandon's earlier "aye, aye, captain" comment.

It would have been funny, but I didn't need to give Jake, or Reagan, for that matter, any more reasons to see us as more than friends. I already thought it mighty suspicious that we'd been paired together as the bartenders for the day.

"You ready to get these drinks going?" Brandon asked, spinning toward me with a bottle of St-Germain in his hand as Jake casually slipped away and headed back over to Julian.

"Oooh, are you thinking what I'm thinking?"

I eyed him, biting my bottom lip, until we both started grinning, knowing instantly that we were on the same page.

"French 77," we said unison, our eyes lighting up with excitement.

"Well, look at that," Reagan chimed in as she slid herself next to me, practically joining her hip with mine. "Sounds like you two are making a great team already."

# Chapter Ten

"You guys, I just have to say, everything today has been so damn good," Reagan announced suddenly, interrupting a riveting a game of Truth or Dare as she raised her glass into the night air.

It was a little past 8:00 p.m., and the sun was just beginning to set, painting the sky with beautiful lavender-and-coral hues as it started descending behind the mountains. The eight of us, seated at the wooden dining table a few feet away from the main house, on a deck that eventually led to the hot tub and firepit we'd been eyeing since we did a group tour of the property, were pleasantly full from all the food we'd been eating and a little tipsy from the great-tasting cocktails Brandon and I had made.

Reagan, who liked to boast of her New Orleans drinking card, sat next to Jake with slightly glossy eyes that told a different story. But it was really the smile on her face, running from ear to ear, that seemed to be the reason for her dramatic interruption. Since she was the birthday girl, no one dared try to stop her.

"Jake has thanked everyone here a lot already," she began, swiveling her body to ensure she made eye contact with each of us at least once. "But now it's my turn. And

I know, I know…you all want to get back to the game, and we can in just a moment, but I want to say one thing first."

Her voice was modestly slurred as she spoke, but of course in a way that only Reagan could make endearing and kind of cute. In any case, who could blame her for being a little tipsy? Brandon and I had let her be our taste tester as we played around with different cocktail recipes for hours since Jake had refused to give her anything else to do. So, even after eating a plate full of grilled salmon, tuna, steak and chicken plus a watermelon-and-feta salad, several deviled eggs and shaved elote, a little garbled speech was bound to happen.

Besides, I think we were all kind of fascinated to hear what she felt she just *had* to say before we could continue.

"When he told me you'd all planned this trip for my birthday, at first, I have to admit, I was floored. Because, like, how are y'all that good at keeping this big of a secret from me so long? I was like, what else haven't they told me?"

She squinted her eyes jokingly and briefly pretended to be a detective searching for clues.

"But then… I was happy," she added, her voice going up an octave as she shrugged her shoulders, "because I realized, with you all here, I'd have no other choice but to be. And welp, let me just say, you have simply outdone yourselves, and it's only day one. I mean, between this amazing food and the table decor—Lucas, you're a literal genius—and then the driiiiinks…"

"Oh, we know you like the drinks, babe," Jake chimed in, wrapping his arm around her shoulder and pulling her in for a quick peck on her cheek.

"Hmm. I think that's supposed to be a joke about me, but I like *everything*, so thank you."

Closing her eyes momentarily, Reagan gently poked him in his chest and then turned her attention back to the rest of the table.

"All I'm saying is…as much as I have been so excited for the wedding later this year—and I am babe, honestly—there are a lot of days when I can't help but think about the fact that Chrissy won't be here for it. Just like she's also not here to see me be loved on by the most amazing man and the best friends a girl could ask for. And I could dwell on that, right? It would be easy to let my brain focus on who's not here. But you all make it incredibly hard to do that when I look around and I see right in front of me who is. I mean, Jenny, you came all the way from DC to be with us this week. Hello?!"

Reagan's eyes grew moist again, this time from the tears I knew she was desperately trying to hold back. Still, she kept going.

"So, anyway, I want to thank Jake for knowing that I needed y'all this week, and I want to thank all of you for your presence and your love. It really means more to me than you know."

She took a moment to swipe away a lone tear that had fallen down her cheek, but the look on her face wasn't one of shame or embarrassment. If anything, it was joy—the kind that people have when they've been through some tough times but have come through it to find a sense of peace that they didn't know was possible.

Some years before, Reagan probably would have never been as open and vulnerable to a table full of people, but experience, and likely Chrissy's death, too, had taught her it was okay to be honest when she needed help. Especially among her friends. I loved this for her, truly. The only problem was that her speech, as beautiful as it was, had managed to make everyone else around the table suddenly feel as if we had dust in our eyes. And on the very first night? I couldn't let that be the way we ended the festivities. So, I knew I had to stop her before we all started boo-hooing at the dinner table.

"Ahem, there's no crying in baseball," I said, inflecting my voice so that I sounded almost uncannily similar to Tom Hanks in *A League of Their Own*.

I winked her way and then tossed my rose-colored cloth napkin directly at Reagan, hoping that she would understand my silent message that she had my support but also that we needed to keep the party going. With the help of the summer breeze, the napkin floated just across the table, past the gold chargers and bundles of white silk flowers Lucas had twisted around a set of candlesticks he found, and landed right in front of her, as I'd intended. In response, she tilted her head toward me, smiled, scooped up the napkin and raised it above her head triumphantly.

"Oh, is it second-line time now?" she asked jokingly, waving the napkin in the air as if she was following a brass band on a crowded New Orleans street.

"It is not," I replied, laughing at her silliness but also relieved that we seemed to have turned the tide on the conversation. "But can we officially get back to the game, now? Or do you want us all bawling our eyes out for the rest of the night?"

"Well, tuh. I *was* just going to say that I love y'all, but now, I think I'll save it."

"Mmm-hmm. We love you, too. The whole table loves love. We're the epitome of love. Love knows nothing if not for us," I deadpanned.

"Okay, BYE, Giselle!" she shouted in response and tossed the napkin back my way.

When it barely made it halfway across the table, her nonplussed reaction finally incited the laughter from our group I'd been looking for. Something to stop us all from releasing puddles of tears in response to hers. *Thank God.*

"Lucas, I think it was your turn," Jake chimed in as we all settled down from our chuckles.

"Oh, yes," he replied. "Okay, so this one's actually for you, Jake. Truth or dare?"

"I'm feeling kinda lazy right now, so let's go with truth."

"All right then. Why did it take you so long to realize Reagan was the one?"

Oh brother, talk about not reading the room, I thought to myself. *After all the work I'd just done to get us back in a jovial mood, this was what Lucas repaid me with?*

I put my head in my right hand and braced myself for Jake's response.

"Damn, okay... What the hell was the dare going to be?" he asked, pretending to wipe his forehead as if he were starting to sweat.

While most everyone else was keyed in on Jake's body language, waiting to see how he'd respond, I looked past him to see Reagan's. Maybe predictably, she sat calmly next to him with a smirk on her face that read *Go ahead, babe, tell the people how you feel* but also gave off a true sense of confidence. It was as if she wasn't a lick bit worried about what he'd say in response. That kind of clarity was yet another reminder of what I wanted in a relationship.

"I mean, the truth is I knew when we were in college that there was no one else who challenged me, supported me and loved me like Reagan did. I would stay up and talk to her all night and still want her voice to be the first thing I heard in the morning. She was my guiding light on pretty much everything, but I was also young and an idiot, and

I didn't really know what love required of you back then. So, I let a lot of things stop me from fighting for her and for us...for years. Dumbest decision ever."

"That's real, man," Julian chimed in. "And it doesn't even have to be when you're young. Just last year, me and Keish were 'this close' to missing out on each other over reasons that don't even feel important anymore."

"He's right," Keisha added. "I mean, I literally walked away from him the first time we met because I had so many assumptions about who he was and how he would, of course, just hurt me like my ex had. And then, for months, I simply couldn't see past every wall I'd put up to protect myself. I had to knock them all down before I was able to let him in."

"Exactly," Jake said. "And that's the thing people don't really talk about a lot. Almost every day, you'll have moments when you can decide to let your fears, doubts or even external factors stop you from choosing the person who you want to be with. Ultimately, it's on you to pick the path that brings y'all toward each other, and not apart. Ain't that right, babe?"

Jake pulled Reagan closer to him, and she easily snuggled her head into his chest, as if there were no other place it belonged.

"Damn right," she said softly.

I wasn't sure if anyone else saw it, but she very distinctly looked my way as she responded, locking her eyes with mine, as if she wanted to make sure I, of all people, was listening to Jake's words.

"Thankfully, this beautiful Creole woman right here decided to give me a second chance," Jake continued. "Because, man, my life would be pretty boring right now without her."

"Eh, it was more like a tenth chance," she countered

softly with a small giggle, head still lying on his chest, in what was clearly her nook. "But who's counting, right?"

Jake laughed and squeezed her tightly before shifting his focus back to Lucas.

"I hope that's a good enough response, bro, because there's not much more that I can say beyond that."

"Yeah, I think that'll do," Lucas replied, nodding his head as he grabbed one of the pitchers from the center of the table and refilled his glass.

Filled with cachaça, lime and sugar—a classic caipirinha—it was the perfect summer drink, and one of three that we'd made for the evening. On his way back to his seat, I could have sworn I saw Lucas give Brandon a look similar to the one that Reagan had given me, but I decided it better to stay out of grown men's business and leave well enough alone. Plus, I had my own stare downs to contend with; I didn't need to be spending my time clocking anyone else's.

"Great," Jake answered with a noticeable sigh. "Then, that means it's my turn. Jenny from the Block, how about you? You haven't been put on the hot seat in a while. Truth or dare?"

Jennifer was the sweetheart of their friendship group, dating all the way back to when she, Robin, Reagan and Chrissy were in college. So, while I'd only known her for a couple years, I knew enough about how they all felt about her to know that Jake wasn't about to come at her crazy. But I was definitely curious about where he was going to take things after the last question had led to such vulnerable responses.

She must have been equally interested, as she eyed him suspiciously before taking a sip from her drink and responding with one clear word.

"Dare."

"Oooh, now that's what I like, Jenn. Okay!"

The two of them were seated directly across from one another, so Jake seamlessly raised his hand to give her a high five, which she met with enthusiasm.

"I dare you...to pick one embarrassing scene from *Coming to America* and act it out for us."

"You're kidding me," she replied.

"Nope. You get to choose, but you gotta pick one."

Jake and Jenn stared at each other defiantly as the rest of us around the table waited with bated breath to see which scene she'd choose. I had one that instantly came to mind and thought would be funny as hell, but I also assumed she'd never do it. Not the woman who was the dean of students at her elementary school and walked with such an elegant stride, I sometimes wondered if she was too grown to be friends with me.

"All right then," she said, rising up from her seat. "I'll be right back."

The seven of us watched intently as Jenn raced back to the house and then reappeared within a couple minutes with Reagan's birthday tiara on her head and one leg lifted off the ground.

"Oh my God, she's really doing it," I said with wide eyes and glee as Jenn proceeded to hop toward us on one foot, making a noise like an orangutan.

"I knew she would," Reagan chimed. "Jenn's got more spunk in her than a lot of people give her credit for."

"And when she's with this one," Jake added, nudging Reagan in her side, "you gotta watch out, because there's no telling what she'll do."

A little over an hour later, our laughs around the table had turned into extended and contagious yawns, but it seemed as if no one wanted to be the first person to say they needed sleep. That, or we were all secretly hoping that Reagan would notice our heavy eyes and dismiss us appropriately. Considering she'd nuzzled herself deeper into Jake's side as the night went on but was still somehow jumping into random conversations anytime anyone thought she was asleep, I wasn't exactly convinced she'd be our savior.

Thankfully, eventually, Jake came to our rescue.

"I think, maybe, it's time we call it a night," he said, glancing down at her face, completely at rest. "We've got that hike early in the morning, and there's no way we'll make it if stay out here much longer."

We all emphatically agreed, jumping up to begin clearing the table. As sleepy as we were, we still carefully stacked the dishes and decor in neat little piles and then dragged our tired bodies back to the kitchen, loading the dishwasher and putting everything else away. As each person finished their part, they said their good-nights, and after promising to be up on time in the morning, made their way to their respective rooms.

I was the last of the upstairs group to climb the fifteen steps that led to my room. But as soon as I walked in, I practically threw myself onto my recently cleaned and inspected bed, took in a long and drawn-out breath and finally released any stress or worry from the day. It had been fun, of course; but in the twelve hours since we'd met at Jake's, I had also been through enough emotional roller coasters to last me for the next week. Between Keisha and Reagan's prodding, then the amazing time I had with Brandon on the way up, which was capped by Phillip and Brandon unwittingly competing for sweetest gesture of the day, and later, Reagan trying to make us all burst into a sea of tears, I was all too ready to just run through my very mundane nighttime routine and go to bed.

In fact, all I really wanted to do was curl up into the crisp white sheets and the champagne-colored duvet that lay between me and the memory foam mattress that felt so plush under my body. But I needed to wash my face and take a shower first, and that wasn't going to happen if I lingered much longer. With another deep sigh, I heaved myself up from the bed, peeled off my Trojans sweatshirt and jean shorts and grabbed my travel bag that contained all of my nighttime essentials. Then, I pulled out my button-down, oversize satin nightshirt and laid it across the bed, imagining just how amazing that material was going to feel when it was combined with the softness of the sheets and my freshly showered skin.

The final items I needed for the night were my multicolored, satin, floral hair bonnet and my fuzzy house slippers, the latter of which I'd packed at the last minute after realizing that the wooden floors in the cabin might feel drafty once the sun went down. With my eyes barely able to stay open, I grabbed those last two objects from my suitcase and gratefully stepped out of my Birkenstocks and into the slippers, using the lack of friction on the soles to propel my tired limbs over to my and Jenn's adjoining bathroom.

I heard the shower water running as soon as I opened the door, but the steam was so heavy, I couldn't see much beyond my own two hands. Thankfully, I'd perfected my nighttime regimen to the point that, if needed, I could complete it with my eyes closed. Otherwise, I would have had to turn back around and wait until she was done. And as exhausted as I was, I just knew I wouldn't make it. I'd be asleep in less than five minutes.

"Hey Jenny, it's just me," I called out, stepping into the bathroom and heading straight for my side of the marble "his and hers" vanity.

It was topped by a supersized mirror that stretched all the way to the ceiling but was currently almost completely opaque from the steam.

"I'm just going to unload my toiletries and wash my face and stuff while you finish up. Hope that's okay."

A deep chuckle came from behind the shower curtain and pierced my spine right as I dropped my bag onto the counter.

"Now, I've been called a lot of names before, but Jenny has never been one of them."

If it had been any other voice, I might not have known exactly who it was. But this one? With its low and gravelly tone combined with hints of his time spent in Northern California and New Jersey, the place he'd called home for the past twelve years? I knew *that* voice like the back of my own hand.

"Brandon?" I asked.

The question was very obviously rhetorical, but in a strange way, I think I still needed confirmation.

"In the flesh," he replied calmly. "And you're cool to do whatever you need to do, Gig. It's your bathroom just as much as it mine."

*Mine.* Huh. The word batted around in my head as I silently questioned why Brandon seemed to be under the impression that he and I were sharing a bathroom. For weeks now, Jenn and I had been laughing about our different takes on bathroom etiquette. But apparently, something had changed in the time since we'd arrived at the cabin. I had a suspicion it wasn't a coincidence that I hadn't been looped in.

Unsure of what to do next, and slightly in a daze, I began pulling my toiletries out of my bag, feeling the need to ground myself with something real. Something I could control, steadily, one item at a time, unlike this moment I'd been thrust into unwittingly.

"Wait, so what are you doing in here?" I finally asked, my voice surely giving away every bit of trepidation I had about our current circumstances.

"Uhh, well, I take it from your reaction that Jenn didn't tell you she asked me to switch rooms while you were on the phone earlier."

"No." I sighed. "She did not."

*Well, that at least answered one of my questions.*

I stared down at the counter as he spoke and saw that I'd finished taking everything out of my bag. It was an unnerving realization, and I instantly felt my body freeze in response, with my legs and arms literally refusing to do the one thing they were designed to do. In fact, no matter how much I screamed internally, my predicament remained the same—stuck, motionless in front of the mirror. It was almost like someone had turned me into a medieval statue, posed to perfection with my hands plastered to the counter even as I heard Brandon shutting the water off and drawing the shower curtains back.

"Right. Well, sorry about that, Gig. I thought you knew. I thought it was kinda funny given our conversation on the way up here. But if it's a problem, I mean, we can always switch again. It's no sweat off my back."

The casual way in which he continued to speak, even as I intrinsically knew he stood naked behind me, was both comforting and infuriating. Of course, he didn't think it was a big deal. I hadn't, either, when I'd thought it was Jenn in the shower and not him.

So, why was I so bothered now that I literally couldn't move?

"No, no, it's all right," I said with a small gulp. "I just…

I wouldn't have barged in if I knew it was you in here, that's all."

"It's all good. What's a little nudity between friends, right?"

"Ha! Right," I replied, attempting to mimic his nonchalant tone but all the while dying inside.

What I wanted to say was *Of course, it's a big deal for you to be naked in front of me! Are you joking?* but I stopped myself before the words had a chance of coming out of my mouth. To admit that to him would have meant I'd also have to say why. And how could I do that without confessing that there were many nights when I'd dreamt of him standing before me, just like he was now, my eyes slowly tracing every inch of his body before he inevitably wrapped me in his arms and dove deep inside of me?

Another, maybe even more pressing reason for my lie was that I suddenly realized Brandon wasn't the only person without all their clothes on in the bathroom. I'd been so perplexed about potentially seeing *him* that in all the time I'd been standing there, in the same spot for several minutes, I'd completely forgotten I had on nothing but my lime-green bra, matching hipster panties and nude-brown, fuzzy slippers. And while he was behind me, concealed from me by the steamed up mirror and my inability to move, I was *in front* of him, completely exposed. Panic set in as I tried, unsuccessfully, to convince my body to get me out of there once again.

*C'mon!* I screamed internally. *All we have to do is make it back to the other side of the door, and this will all be over. We can go to bed and pretend like it never even happened.*

Despite my best efforts, my attempts fell short.

Now that the water was turned off, I was faced with yet another problem. Permeating silence. The stillness in the bathroom made it so that every movement Brandon made behind me flooded into my ears in surround sound. And my brain, in all her wonderous, imaginative glory, used those sounds to begin creating her own ideas of what I couldn't see, blending memories of times when we'd been in each other's presence with the fantasies I dared not speak of.

Each time I heard him doing something, whether it was stepping out of the tub or grabbing a towel from the rack closest to it, images flashed through my head, intent on showing me what I couldn't bring myself to turn around and view in real life. Like the way the water was probably cascading down his perfectly sculpted body, dripping from his chest to legs to his feet. Or what it might look like to see him running a large towel across his deep caramel brown skin as he attempted to dry himself off despite the steam in the room.

I closed my eyes in a feeble attempt to reset and think of anything other than Brandon's naked form behind me, but that simply made it harder for me to ignore the soft sounds of him wrapping the towel around his waist and walking toward me.

Brandon's stride was slow and steady, reinforcing how natural this all must have seemed to him. He was, after all, a man so confident in his own skin that he couldn't even fathom the idea of being completely thrown off by the potential of someone else seeing it. But for me, the anticipation of his approach only amplified all the sensations running through my body. I would not turn around. I *could not* turn around. And yet the tiny hairs prickling on the back of my neck didn't care if I actually saw him or not as he drew closer. They'd already been working together with my brain to send consistent pulses to my vagina that threatened to make me soak through my panties if I didn't pull myself together.

Finally, eventually, Brandon stopped, positioning himself directly behind me. I barely had time to process how close he was to me when he casually leaned over my shoulder and wiped a large portion of the mirror clean with his hand, just enough so that we could suddenly see from the tops of both our heads to the outline of his collarbone. As he did so, Brandon's chest very lightly grazed the upper corner of my back, instantly jolting me from fantasy into reality.

It would be no exaggeration to admit that my body literally quivered under his touch. But more importantly, with that one move, I was forced to finally look at him. To see how his almond-shaped eyes curved upward to meet the high cheekbones that carved their way down his striking jawline and the way a few of his locs, tied in a messy top bun, still dangled down toward his amazingly chiseled shoulders. In an instant, the mirror that had once been my saving grace, cloaking everything around me, became a magnifying glass, drawing my eyes to him in a way that I seemed to have no control over.

"Hey there," he said with a smile, momentarily locking eyes with me. "You know, when you look as good as we do, there's no point in hiding it, anyway, right?"

"Now, is that what you say to everyone who finds themselves standing in front of you with barely any clothes on?"

As if I was having an out-of-body experience, I could hear myself trying to keep up our normal banter even as my brain toiled over one thought and one thought only—how much I craved his touch, in spite of myself.

"Nah," he whispered in response. "Just you."

Brandon quickly dropped his eyes down to the counter, turning his attention to the toiletries I'd laid out before my limbs stopped moving. But I remained stuck in the mirror, watching the condensation drip away and widen my view of us, allowing my eyes to travel the length of his face down his neck and across his expansive torso through our reflection. With no willpower left in me, I found myself studying him, keying in on the way his lips were parted ever so slightly and the movement of his chest as he breathed in and out. If I didn't know any better, I might have been tempted to think he was struggling just as much as I was, desperate not to begin panting from how close our bodies were to each other. But Brandon had already made it clear that he was unbothered, so I swiftly disabused myself of that thought and tried not to focus on the tickle of his breath that I felt on the nape of my neck.

My eyes, with a mind of their own, wandered their way to the well-defined dips in his clavicles, which seamlessly offset the broadness of his shoulders. In another life, I could have easily used those same dips as handlebars to grip Brandon tightly as he stood with my legs wrapped around his waist and rocked in and out of me slowly and deliberately until I begged him for mercy.

*Dear God, I'm practically drowning in my lust for him.* I had to figure out a way to stop, and ASAP.

"Oooh, score," Brandon called out abruptly, effectively interrupting my thoughts. "Now, this is the real reason I said yes to the switch."

He leaned over me once more and grabbed my Perricone MD face moisturizer from the counter. Like a pro, he opened it ever so gently and scooped a couple fingers' worth into the palm of his hand before placing it back where he found it.

"We'll have to find a mutually beneficial win for you, Gig, but I can already tell you this one is mine. Women always have the good face-care stuff. I should have known you'd have the expensive kind, too. My skin's going to be glowing by the time this trip is over!"

*As if it wasn't already*, I said to myself.

Brandon had probably the most flawless skin I'd seen on a man, which, combined with the droplets of water still trickling down his chest and arms, made it increasingly difficult to turn my gaze away. I watched him as he placed small dollops of the moisturizer on very specific parts of his face, and then, making circles with his fingers, moved up his jawline and across his cheeks, meticulously rubbing the lotion into his skin.

"Umm, how often do you make it a practice to steal our stuff? Because you seem like you know exactly what you're doing!"

"Ha! Can you keep a secret?"

"I mean, at this point, sure. Why not?"

"Anytime I spend the night."

"What?! Brandon!"

"Sorry," he said with a shrug. "Y'all shouldn't have such good shit, and I wouldn't be as tempted."

"You know you can also just get your own, right?"

"Nah, what's the fun in that?"

He raised his eyes to meet mine in the mirror again and winked at me for emphasis. Thankfully, I was still semi-paralyzed in front of him, because otherwise, I might not have been able to stop myself from turning around, pulling him into me and sucking on his lips until there was nothing else that he could do besides pick me up, carry me back to his bed and ravish me for hours.

*Get it together, Gigi!* I admonished myself, dropping my eyes to the three slim gold chains Brandon always wore around his neck, one with a small cross attached to it and another with an angel. I'd hoped that the familiarity of them could help center me and remind me that I was standing in front of my friend, not someone who might have had any sexual interest in me. Instead, the chains only served to draw my eyes toward the small patch of fine hair that started at the top of his chest and ran down the middle, ending just before the apex of his nipples. Which were now standing at full attention. My mouth fell open instantly and a small moan escaped from it.

*Oh God. Oh no.*

I quickly looked back up, hoping Brandon hadn't noticed me gawking over him, and accidentally caught his eyes in the mirror again. Unlike before, when they were playful and nonchalant, this time they had a tender curiosity behind them, and I could tell he knew I'd been surveying him. I don't think it was something either of us wanted to verbalize, however, so we stood in silence defiantly, locked in each other's gaze, until he eventually cleared his throat and broke our eye contact.

The sense of relief that flooded over me finally provided my limbs with the courage they needed to move, and I picked up the first things I saw to distract myself from the embarrassment I felt building up inside of me: my toothbrush and toothpaste. It didn't make sense to try to run at this point; he'd seen everything he could of me up close and personal and had even caught me admiring him, too. No, I had to take my L like a big girl, and so quietly, I simply began brushing my teeth as Brandon kept his eyes on me.

I was almost done when I felt his fingers slowly grazing my right shoulder, sending chills throughout my entire body, and freezing me solid yet again.

"Hmm. This is a cute bra," he said, his voice dropping lower as he playfully snapped the strap on my shoulder.

"I guess that's another benefit I get by sharing a bathroom with you. You let me know when you're ready to say yours, Gig."

Without another word, Brandon shuffled toward his bedroom door and gently closed it behind him. It took me several seconds before I had the wherewithal to move again, but once I did, I practically ran to his side of the bathroom and locked the door, taking in a deep breath to stop myself from screaming out loud and effectively waking up the entire house.

*What the hell was that?* I questioned, as images of me standing before him, my body flushed with excitement, ran through my head.

Brandon, my friend, had just seen all of me...the way my hips dipped at my thighs, the tattoo that started at the nape of my neck and ended at the small of my back, how that part of my body curved to allow for my size-12 booty... and yet, he seemed almost completely unfazed. That was until he realized I wasn't.

I melted to the ground, and softly began humming Pink Sweat$' "Honesty" as I tried to comfort myself.

At some point, I was going to need to get up and take a very long shower, but for the time being, I was content to lie there as long as I needed to come back to life.

# *Chapter Eleven*

The next day, I sprang out of bed just as the sun began piercing its rays through my window and rushed to the bathroom door, hoping to commandeer the shared space before Brandon could get to it. If last night had taught me anything, it was that we were going to need to set clear boundaries for the rest of the week. But I had no desire to field that conversation bright and early in the morning, so my hope was that I could avoid it, and honestly him, too, by perfectly executing the grand plan I'd cooked up just as I was falling asleep.

It was a fairly simple idea—get into the bathroom as early as possible, lock the door to his side until I was done and then slip downstairs before he could even say hello—but it was predicated on one very important element. I had to wake up before he did.

Dressed in my nightshirt and bonnet, I swung the door open and peered into the bathroom, ready to put my plan into action. Only to see Brandon doing the exact same thing. It was almost as if we were mirror reflections of one another, each standing in their own doorway, visibly hoping not to run into the person on the other side.

*Welp, so much for that idea.*

At least this time, we both had clothes on, so maybe miracles still happened after all.

I watched from my doorway as Brandon proceeded to enter the bathroom, wearing a simple black tank top and a pair of matching boxer briefs. It was a far cry from the lone white towel that had draped recklessly across his hips the night before, but truth be told, the material of the boxer briefs wasn't exactly hiding much more. That made it dangerously difficult not to become distracted by the way his briefs gathered at the top of his thighs or the meaty bulge protruding in the front.

I was intent on doing my best, though. Because damn it, if I couldn't avoid him, at least I wasn't going to let myself be a statue in front of him again.

"Good morning," I said cheerily, walking into the bathroom and heading straight to the left side of the vanity again.

"What's up, Gig."

Brandon didn't turn his head toward me when he spoke. Instead, he quickly nodded into the mirror, briefly catching my eyes before returning his attention to the items gathered on his side of the counter. Without another word, he grabbed his electric toothbrush, added a small amount of toothpaste to it and proceeded to start brushing his teeth like it was perfectly normal for us to be standing side by side in our nightclothes, after having seen almost all of each other's body parts the night before.

Frankly, I would have been impressed except for how deafeningly silent it was outside of the hum of his toothbrush's motor. On the one hand, it wasn't even 6:00 a.m. yet, so I could totally understand not being up for idle chitchat. Heck, I usually needed a coffee infusion before I could properly engage with people in the morning, too. On the other hand, I couldn't shake the feeling that *his* quiet was more about not knowing how to be around me anymore.

I had no clue of how I should even begin to address that, nor did I really want to. What I wanted was for us to go back to the comfort and ease we had with each other before he'd caught me staring at his chest, practically drooling over myself. Clearly, that moment had changed something for him, but I was too tired and too scared of what he might say to broach the conversation just yet.

So... I didn't.

I simply began my morning routine as well, silently brushing my teeth and washing and moisturizing my face as he did the same. It was a strange juxtaposition. Looking from the outside in, it might have seemed like we were two people so used to each other that we could comfortably go about our day without needing to fill the quiet with meaningless chatter. But inside, I'd never felt more like a stranger to him than I did in that moment.

For the last part of my regimen, I finally freed my jet-black twists from the hair bonnet that kept them fresh while I slept and then used my hands to lightly shake them out so that they fell exactly how I wanted—loose and springy, as a portion of them draped diagonally across my forehead and the rest tickled the open collar on my nightshirt. Afterward, I closely examined the strands in the mirror and then took a step back to marvel at the results. At least one thing seemed to be working in my favor this morning, I thought. I'd take that if nothing else.

When I was all done, I glanced over at Brandon's side of the vanity again and saw him reorganizing his toiletries, carefully stacking each item so that they were placed in the order of his daily routine. Funny enough, as long as I'd stood frozen in front of the same countertop the night before, it hadn't been until I finally peeled myself off the floor that I saw how his stuff had already been meticulously set up on the right side of the vanity by the time I'd burst into the bathroom. If I'd been paying any attention at all, even with the steamy atmosphere, I would have easily seen the Tom Ford beard oil and shea butter lotion and known they weren't Jenn's. I'd missed them, though, and the damaging result of that seemed to be an awkwardness between us that felt as if it would never go away.

Another minute or so passed before Brandon finally looked up from the counter and turned his full body toward me. It was the first time he'd done so all morning, and instantly my heart jumped up for joy, all too ready for us to return to our regular banter so I could clown him for using my moisturizer when he had his own system of expensive products lined up on his side.

I straightened out my hunter green nightshirt, making sure that the hem of it fell at least midthigh, and turned to face him as well. Even through the tension between us, Brandon's eyes looked over me with care and tenderness. It was a hallmark of his and one of the many reasons I knew he'd broken more than a few hearts throughout the years. For, how could anyone truly think of him as just a casual dalliance, even if that was the agreed-upon arrangement, when he had the power to see into your soul with one extended gaze?

"Gig," he said, tilting his head slightly. "Green seems to be a good color on you. You should wear it more often."

With just sixteen words, Brandon shocked my limbs into a paralyzed state again as he pivoted and headed back toward his bedroom. His walk couldn't have taken more than thirty seconds, but every bit of it felt like torture, with me desperately trying to convince my legs, mouth, arms...

something to move. Eventually, he reached his destination, closing the door behind him without giving me so much as another glance.

As soon as I heard the door shut, the feeling came back to my limbs, but so did the realization that he'd left me, alone, in the bathroom yet again to stew over what had just happened between us.

"Damn it," I said aloud, grabbing my bonnet off the counter and heading back to my room.

This could not be how I spent the rest of my week, I thought. But that meant one thing—we were going to have to talk…about everything…before it was too late.

Twenty minutes later, I walked into the kitchen dressed in my best hiking gear—a red, tan, and brown lightweight flannel shirt unbuttoned to reveal my charcoal gray graphic tee that read Take a Hike with Me, and paired with deep teal skinny jeggings and my classic eight-inch Bean boots from L.L.Bean. I'd expected to see Jake when I entered, but I was pleasantly surprised to also find Julian and the rest of the girls already downstairs and eating breakfast. They each had on their own spin of a stereotypical hiking outfit, some with a long-sleeved shirt wrapped around their waist and others with a flannel hair tie serving as the fun accessory. What I loved seeing the most, however, were the variations of hiking boots, ranging from high-top tan Sorels with bright orange shoestrings to deep hunter green Nike Air Zooms.

"Good morning," I said, grabbing a banana from the kitchen island.

"Morning," they all replied, some with groggier tones than others.

"I just knew I'd be the first one down here, but look at y'all! All spruced up and set to go."

"Well, we figured we'd hear your mouth if we weren't dressed in time," Keisha replied.

"Huh, funny that *that* would be thing you'd think I want to discuss this morning."

I scanned the room quickly to make sure that Brandon wasn't hiding behind a door or something and then turned my attention to Reagan, Keisha and Jenn, who were seated in high stools along the island, giggling among themselves. Eyeing each of them individually, I purposely waited to say anything more until their chuckles morphed into an uncomfortable silence. I knew one of them would eventually break down and ask me how my night went; the question was which one would it be.

It took about thirty seconds, but eventually Reagan became the first to succumb to the pressure.

"What's going on, Gig?" she asked faux innocently. "Looks like you have something on your mind."

Close enough, I thought, ready to pounce but committed to dragging this out so they could feel even a sliver of the awkwardness I'd endured…at their hands, no less.

"You know, I was just thinking about how difficult it can be to know who's really got your back sometimes," I said, slowly and solemnly, holding her gaze with mine.

"Oh? Is that something you've been questioning lately?"

"Not really, no."

I paused for three seconds before continuing.

"Not until last night."

Reagan swallowed hard and nudged Keisha in her side.

"Well, what happened last night?" she asked.

"Really, Rae? C'mon, you know what you did. *I* know what you all did. Just admit it."

Looking at the three of them clam up, I was convinced I was going to have to withstand another staring matching until Jenn finally spoke up.

"Don't blame them," she said. "It was my idea."

I sucked my teeth in disbelief.

"I'm telling the truth, I promise! I just... After you and Reagan made your deal, we were headed downstairs, and it hit me. Wouldn't it be a whole lot easier for you to stay open to the possibility of you two if you suddenly had to share a bathroom with each other?"

"To be fair to Jenn, we immediately thought it was a genius idea," Keisha added. "You know, we just figured it might give you some more one-on-one time. What's the harm in that, right?"

"Everything!" I shouted before I could stop myself.

Realizing how loud that had come out, I lowered my voice again before continuing.

"You all have no idea what you've done. I damn near walked in on him in the shower last night, and this morning, you could cut the tension between us with an electric saw."

"Oh no," Reagan replied.

"Exactly. Trust me, whatever y'all thought you were doing, you did not do a good thing here."

"Damn, we're so sorry, Gigi."

Keisha leaned over the counter to take my hand in hers.

"We shouldn't have meddled."

"No, you really shouldn't have," I replied quietly.

"We're idiots," Reagan chimed in.

"You are."

"Idiots who love you more than life itself, but still...we definitely concede to the idiot part," Keisha added.

I rolled my eyes as I felt myself soften toward them

again. It was a sad fact of nature that I could never stay mad at these ladies for very long.

"Good," I said, letting a small grin start to form on my face as I casually dropped my hand from Keisha's. "Because you *are* still idiots."

"We know!"

Reagan raised her hands up to her face and batted her doe eyes at me.

"But you still love us, right?"

"Ugh. Of course!"

"Yaay!" all three exclaimed, jumping from their stools and forming a circle hug around me.

They squeezed me tightly for a few seconds before finally letting me go.

"And…for what it's worth, I can't imagine that things with you and Brandon won't right themselves," Jenn added. "Just give it some time."

"Does that mean you're down to switch rooms with him again?" I asked.

"Oh no, no, no," she protested. "Trust me, that will only make things worse."

"There's no such thing," I replied, shaking my head.

"Well, umm…can I ask about Phillip, since that such was a disaster?"

Keisha looked toward me, and I could tell that she was anxious to see how I'd respond, but this was a pivot I was all too happy to make.

"Sooo, I was supposed to talk to him last night, actually, but after everything that happened with Brandon, I just didn't have it in me. I figured he was going to be pissed, honestly. Phillip's never said he was going to do something and then didn't, and I basically blew him off last night."

I paused my story while I unlocked my phone and

scrolled to my messages app, then opened the text chain with Mr. Handsome as the contact.

"But then I woke up this morning to this…" I said, a smile growing on my face as I turned my phone toward them.

On the screen was a very silly image of Phillip biting into a large half smoke from Ben's Chili Bowl, covered in chili, mustard, and onions—their signature dish—and a text that read: I never thought I'd like something as much as I enjoy coming to DC and indulging in a juicy-ass half smoke, but I'm starting to think hearing your voice might just top that. Hope you have a great time hiking today. Can't wait to hear all about it.

"Oh my God," Jenn exclaimed, her mouth dropping in awe. "How cute is he?!"

"I know, right."

"Okay, I'm not gonna lie, Mr. Handsome did his big one with that, *cher.*"

Reagan giggled as I blacked out my phone screen and tucked it away. Last thing I needed was for the guys to become interested in what we were talking about, and then suddenly it's the talk of the cabin.

"I mean, it's corny, but it's good."

I couldn't stop myself from blushing as I thought about it more and just knew my brown cheeks were starting to flush with a rosy hue underneath them.

"So, wait, what did you say in return?" Keisha asked in a hushed tone.

"That I missed his voice too, and I was down to be the chili to his half smoke if he wanted."

"What?" Keisha burst out laughing as Reagan and Jennifer tried to restrain themselves. "Sis, what does that even mean?"

"I don't know, I just thought it was cute."

"And did he reply?"

"With the tongue emoji."

I shrugged, and immediately, they all lost it, jumping off their stools again, and squealing with glee. So much for not drawing attention to us.

"Oh, he's *really* good!" Reagan said, grabbing my phone from me to see the evidence herself.

"Yeah, you can't outwit him, Gig," Keisha added. "That's a big plus."

"Can't outwit who?"

The four of us turned to the kitchen's entrance to see Lucas and Brandon finally strolling in, a little less than five minutes before we were supposed to head out. Lucas's eyes were bright with curiosity as he awaited our response, but Brandon still looked like a shell of himself, as if he wanted nothing more than a chance to crawl into a dark hole and disappear from view.

"Oh, it's nothing," I replied, suddenly very thankful I'd already slid my phone into my back pocket before anyone else could see what was on it.

Brandon eyed me as he walked over to the island and grabbed an apple from the fruit bowl.

"Keeping more secrets, Giselle?" he asked.

*Wow, okay.* I stood next to the island, stunned into silence as I watched Brandon head toward Jake. I couldn't remember the last time he'd called me by my first name, and not one of my nicknames, so that was clearly intentional. But beyond even that, it was hard not to notice the snarky way in which he'd just addressed me in front of our whole crew.

"What the hell was that?" Reagan whispered.

I shrugged my shoulders and mouthed, *I told you*, simultaneously trying to hold back my tears from just how hurt I was by the interaction.

"Nah, I think you ladies *are* over there plotting something," Lucas added, thankfully bringing everyone's attention back to him. "I hope y'all don't think you're going to convince us to go skinny-dipping in this waterfall today just so you can run off with our clothes."

"In your dreams, Lucas!" Jenn replied, clearly used to his antics since college.

"All right," he said matter-of-factly. "Just remember that I was born in the day, not yesterday!"

"Oh my God, Jake, get your friend, please." Reagan rolled her eyes and playfully pushed him toward her fiancé.

"Look, I'm just saying that you can't outwit me. I done watched too many of these movies with group hiking trips in them. I'm ready."

"This coming from the man who doesn't even know that you can't get in the water at Kaaterskill Falls," Keisha added.

"Oh."

Lucas's one-word concession caused the whole room to laugh as he sat down next to Jake. He may have been a goofball sometimes, but I was grateful for the way he'd lightened up the mood. I wouldn't have thought that was possible after Debbie Downer Brandon had tried to ruin it.

What was up with him? I wondered. And was he actually mad at me for last night? This whole time I'd been thinking we were going to have to work through whatever awkwardness I'd caused with my ill-advised moan, but it seemed like the problem was far bigger than that now. Like there was anger in his tone for some reason.

Either way, as much as we needed to have a conversation about that, we didn't have time for it if we were going to make it out of the cabin on schedule. I'd have to find the courage and the space to talk to him later and hope that it wouldn't be too late by then.

"Well, since you mentioned the waterfalls, that feels like a perfect segue to go over our plans today," I said, bringing everyone's attention back to me, but for the right reasons this time.

I stepped in front of the island so they could all see me as Keisha, Reagan and Jennifer scooched over to the rest of the group. Now that Lucas and Brandon had joined us in the kitchen, I was able to view the crew in full, and it warmed my heart to see how much they'd all taken my suggestions for their hiking gear. It was no secret that this was going to be the first hike ever for at least sixty percent of the group, so to see them in the correct boots—and not some fashionable ones that would have them slipping and sliding along the trail—with the right kind of clothes on and with their bags fully packed, I was too geeked. Even Brandon, not known for wanting to follow rules on his best day, was dressed in a pair of Army green, fitted cargo pants with a long-sleeved dark gray shirt that hugged his sculpted arms in all the right places. If he hadn't come into the kitchen with an attitude like Mr. Hyde, I probably would have told him how great he looked and thanked him personally for participating in our group look. But alas, he'd have to deal with a group compliment instead.

"First, let me say that I'm loving all these different interpretations of hiking gear! And I know it's really early, but trust me, it's going to be worth it when we get to the waterfall and don't have to contend with eighty million other tourists. Now, I was really excited when Jake sent me and Keish the details about this cabin because the really cool thing is that there are hiking trails literally on the property. That means, for my folks who are less inclined to go hiking with me for hours, you can join us for the first part and then come back if you want. No judgment whatsoever."

"Wait, did you say hours?" Jenn asked, raising her hand like she was one of the kids at her school.

"Yeah, something like that," I replied.

"Like how many hours?"

"I don't know, maybe like three or four."

"Three or four?!"

Jennifer stood up, flabbergasted at the thought, which sent the room into a fit of laughter again.

"Like I said, you don't have to do the whole thing," I reminded her, trying to hold in my own chuckles. "But...you will miss out on the waterfalls if you don't."

"Hmm, we'll see, sis. I'm not making any promises."

"I hear you, don't worry."

I winked at her before continuing on.

"I've already plotted which trail will lead us through the property and get us on the path to the Kaaterskill hike. That will likely take us about an hour and a half. Then, it's about an hour more of hiking to get to the bottom of the falls. But that's why you all have on your hiking boots, right?"

I scanned the kitchen to peep everyone's faces, which seemed to be showing a mixture of excitement and worry. Brandon's, thankfully, appeared to be in the happy category. Any other day, that wouldn't have been a surprise considering his love for adventure and athleticism, but today, it felt like a win I could build on.

"Any other questions?" I asked.

"Nope!" Reagan replied with enthusiasm. "Let's do it."

"Okay, I like this attitude, Rae!"

"Yeah, you know me. I am woman...hear me roar!"

She balled up her right fist, and raising her arm, flexed her biceps in the air.

"That's the spirit," I said, laughing uncontrollably as we all grabbed our prepacked hiking bags and made our way toward the front door.

# Chapter Twelve

""Dooo youuu know what today is?""

I sang the query to Reagan in the melody of Tony! Toni! Toné!'s song "Anniversary" as the eight of us walked along the hiking trail still on the cabin's property.

"It's almost my biiirthday!" she shouted out in reply.

"Almost your biiiirthday!" the rest of the group joined in.

"Ayeee! Tomorrow will come and youuuu just can't waaaaait, it's youuur biiiirthday."

"Made just for meee."

Despite what had started off as an inauspicious morning, the hike was turning out to be a boost for the group's morale as we laughed and sang together, without any cares distracting us from the present moment we were sharing as a framily. It was good to see the smiles on everyone's faces, even as parts of the trail forced us uphill and wound us around trees so tall, they looked as if they rose into the heavens.

As the day's default guide, I took great pleasure in intermittingly pointing out things I saw along our walk, like the birds and squirrels gathering among the lush green bushes, but was also quite enjoying myself, leading what had amounted to our fake choir through the forest. That was how I'd ended up singing a knock-off variation of "Anniversary" as we neared the end of the path.

Lucas was just beginning to mimic the violin solo in the middle of the song when I heard the sounds of something much sweeter. It was like soft running water, lightly tapping along a series of stones, and I instantly knew we were close to the babbling brook I'd been hoping to see since we arrived at the cabin.

"Oh snap, there it is!" I called out, interrupting our birthday rendition as I ran toward it, practically leaping over some of the large branches that had fallen to the forest floor.

The rest of the group trailed behind me, with some coming along faster than others, but I didn't bother rushing anyone. They'd see just why we needed to veer off the trail momentarily once they arrived. When I finally got to it, I stood in silent wonder, completely mesmerized by nature's ability to carve out beautiful surprises in the midst of what might seem ordinary at first glance.

It was a sight to behold, as the shallow water gently cascaded over several large stones interspersed among the trees.

"Isn't it beautiful?" I asked, hearing someone come up behind me.

"It really is," he said softly.

There was that unmistakable voice, once again sending a shiver down my spine.

I turned to face Brandon and briefly met his gaze before Keisha, Reagan and Julian interrupted us, loudly complaining and laughing as they crossed over the final branch that stood between them and the brook.

"Damn, Gig, I know you were a track star back in the day, but we're all in our thirties now, okay? We can't be running through the woods like we're chasing freakin' Sha'Carri Richardson out here!"

Keisha tried catching her breath as she, Julian and Reagan joined me and Brandon by the brook, but she was so amused by her own statement that it took her several huffs and puffs before her breath normalized.

"You okay?" Julian asked with what seemed like genuine, but mild concern.

"Yeah, yeah, I'm fine," she replied, waving him off as she stood up straight.

I chuckled to myself as I watched their dynamic. Of course, he had to ask if she was all right, being a good boyfriend and all, but Julian also appeared to understand the thing that would save him from a lot of drama in the future—our girl Keisha liked knowing she could do things on her own, and so sometimes, you just had to let her be Miss Independent.

"This view helps," she added, leaning her head onto his chest once she'd sufficiently "saved" herself.

"Right?" I chimed in. "It's just so—"

"Calming," Brandon interjected, his face turned toward the brook with the warmest disposition I'd seen from him all morning.

"Yeah. It is."

Keisha and Reagan eyed me silently and then looked at each other, then back at me, employing the infamous Black girl telepathic messaging to perfection. What they didn't need to say out loud, but I heard very clearly, was something akin to *Girl! Maybe there's something still there after all. Talk to him!* to which I responded with a look that said *I plan to, don't worry.*

We were all starting to settle into our places along the

brook when the last of the bunch—Jake, Lucas and Jenn—finally joined us as well.

"So, this is why I almost just died, huh?" Lucas asked as they walked up to us.

Jenn playfully slapped him on his chest as she mouthed *Sorry* to me.

"I think what Lucas meant to say is this is really nice, Gigi."

She waved her arms around, pointing at the scenery around us.

"Calming, even," Reagan added with a nudge in my side.

"Riiiight," Jenn replied, looking between me and Reagan to try to figure out what she'd missed.

I shook my head and silently urged her to let it drop.

"But you know, some of us aren't as outdoorsy as you are," she added. "My idea of being one with nature is sitting on a blanket at Malcolm X Park in DC and listening to the drum circle while I eat jerk wings and a whole bunch of fruit."

"You literally have arms like Michelle Obama," I noted.

"Why does everyone seem to think that means I like to work out outside? Give me a yoga mat and some air conditioning, and I'm with you all day. But this, baby girl, while beautiful and, umm, calming, I guess, is not for me."

"Okay, okay," I said, not wanting to push anyone past what they were comfortable with. "I'm assuming that means you're probably heading back to the cabin from here?"

"Uhh yeah, y'all can have the rest of the two-hour hike. I think me and Lucas are going to go make some frozen drinks and enjoy nature the way I like to."

"Laying out in the sun in those lounge chairs by the hot tub?" I asked.

"See? Now you get me."

Jenn laughed and opened her arms out wide, wrangling me into a big hug.

"If it helps, I enjoyed this more than I thought would," she added.

"Actually, yeah, that does help."

We disentangled ourselves, and she and Lucas turned around to begin their backward trek to the cabin.

"Uhh, I think I'm going to go back with them," Jake announced, kissing Reagan on her cheek and then moving toward Jenn and Lucas.

"Yeah, me too," Julian added.

"What? C'mon guys!"

I threw my hands up, hoping no one else was about to bail on our main activity for the day.

"It's not that this hasn't been great, Gig—it has," Jake replied. "But as long as Rae is having fun, I could use the time to set up some more things back at the house."

"And I could just use the sleep," Julian chimed in.

"All right, I guess that's fine." I shrugged. "You three are still coming, though, right?"

I looked toward Reagan, Keisha and Brandon with pleading eyes, cajoling them to say yes.

"Of course!" Reagan replied. "Nothing's stopping me from seeing this waterfall you keep talking about."

An hour later, Reagan was clearly regretting her words as she and Keisha lagged behind me and Brandon. They were trying to keep up but their stride was getting steadily slower as we went along. When we finally reached the wooden trail sign for the falls, alerting us to how far away we still were, they both plopped down on the ground in exhaustion.

"Leave us!" Reagan cried out dramatically.

"Yes! Save yourselves!" Keisha added.

"We're not leaving you, fools," I replied, meeting Brandon's eyes as we both shook our heads and laughed at their theatrics. "One band, one sound, remember?"

"But this tuba is flat, *cher*. She needs a break."

Reagan dropped her hands behind her and swung her head back, allowing the two large braids in her hair to swing behind her. She looked pitiful, but also like a little girl who wanted to throw a tantrum, even if her ego wouldn't allow her to take it that far. She was, after all, turning thirty-three the next day. Keisha wasn't any better, sitting across from Reagan and gulping down the water from her one-liter Yeti bottle as if she thought she'd never drink again.

"We're so close though, guys. We've got maybe... I don't know...twenty minutes left?"

"I will die in twenty minutes," Reagan replied. "Like, literally, disintegrate before your eyes. You get that, right?"

Brandon chuckled off to the side, his chest rising and falling in spasms, completely giving away just how tickled he was by their antics. I thought they were amusing, too, but not so much that I was willing to have had us walk this far only to turn around empty handed.

"Okay, but you've come this far," I implored them. "You can't just go back now."

"Oh, I'm still going to see some damn water fall down a bunch of big rocks today, okay?" Reagan corrected me with Keisha mmm-hmming through her water bottle. "But mama needs a break. So, why don't you and Brandon go on without us, and we'll meet you down there?"

I looked at her skeptically. If this was another one of their attempts to try to force me and Brandon into time alone together, I was going to put my foot down. This really wasn't the time or space for that.

"I promise!" she protested. "Right, Keish?"

"Oh yes." She nodded her head in agreement. "Pinkie promise! We'll be there just as soon as our bodies allow us to move again."

"Well then, we can just stay and wait for y'all. It's no use in splitting up if we're going to the same destination."

"Gigi."

"Yes."

I looked at Reagan and waited for whatever matter-of-fact statement was coming next. Anytime either one of them used my name as a complete sentence, nickname or not, that was usually the end result.

"I need you to hear me when I tell you this and not take offense. I am asking you to leave so that I can recover in peace and not feel like Mom and Dad are frustrated and waiting for me to get ready for church."

"What?! I—"

"No, I know that wouldn't be your intention. But that's how I would feel. And it's been such a great day so far—thank you again, by the way—I want to keep it that way. You know?"

"Okay," I said, conceding. "If that's really what you want, then sure."

"Thank you, Gig."

Reagan curled her fingers into a heart shape and pulsed her hands toward me as she batted her eyes. The symbol had become the go-to way for millennials and Gen Zers to say "I love you" without using their words. But I knew Reagan was doing it to be silly and to make me laugh.

"Mmm-hmm," I replied, playfully rolling my eyes. "I love you too."

I turned to Brandon to see how he felt about everything, particularly finishing up the rest of the trail with just me after all we'd been through since last night. Thankfully, his anger had seemed to subside during the hike, especially once we took the break at the babbling brook. But he still hadn't fully returned to the Brandon I was used to, as he'd been sort of quietly blending in with the group for the past couple hours.

It wouldn't be as easy to do that once it was just me and him.

"What about you?" I asked. "Do you need a break, too?"

"Nah, I'm good to go, if you are."

He stared at me and shrugged nonchalantly, almost as if he was trying to see if I would be the one to chicken out. But I was perfectly fine with us being alone together, just as long as all parties were clothed!

"I'm good!" I replied defiantly.

"Wonderful, so can y'all both leave now?" Keisha asked from her seated position on the ground.

"Geesh! Okay, we're going!"

I laughed and wrapped my arm around Brandon's so that we could make a dramatic exit away from them and begin the final parts of the trail.

"We'll see you soon, right?" I asked, turning around once more to get another verbal confirmation from them as we walked away.

"Yesss, Mom!" they replied in unison, which just made me roll my eyes again.

As Brandon and I rounded the corner, I slipped my arm from his and softly apologized for roping him into my antics with those two.

"It's fine," he said, chuckling. "I know how y'all are when you get together. Nothing but shenanigans."

"Oh, is that what you call it?"

"You don't?"

He paused his stride just as we were about to turn onto the final trail that would lead us to the lower falls and eyed me with a distinct smirk on his face.

"I mean…"

I shifted my hands side to side in response. It wasn't as if I had a great rebuttal because we did, indeed, often get ourselves into foolishness when together, whether it was cutting up at a day party or meddling in each other's dating lives. Clearly, it had even been their well-meaning, bird-brained idea to put me and Brandon together in the adjoining rooms without telling me.

As upset as I'd been about that initially, if I was being truly honest, I had to admit that Reagan and I had basically badgered Keisha into giving Julian a chance, too—lovingly and jokingly, of course, though she may not have held the same sentiment about it at the time.

"Yeah, exactly." Brandon laughed. "That response is almost as bad as someone saying 'whatever' in a debate. You've already lost at that point, my guy!"

"Wha—"

I stopped myself as I heard the word coming out of my mouth, but not fast enough that Brandon didn't catch it, either.

"Mmm-hmm, like I said."

He continued laughing as we restarted our walk, heading down a trail that featured as many large rocks and wooden planks as it did concrete steps winding down toward the Falls. It was good to see Brandon genuinely smiling and enjoying himself again, even as we navigated through probably the most difficult part of the trail. I knew, of course, that I didn't like seeing him down, just as I wouldn't any of my close friends. But it wasn't until just then, when the Brandon I adored showed up again, that I grasped how much his mood earlier had also affected mine.

The truth was that I was happier now that he was, too. And that was an interesting realization to hold.

"Well, anyway, now it's just the two of us," I replied, winking at Brandon right before I started singing Bill Withers's iconic chorus for emphasis.

"How is it that you have a song for everything, Gig?" he asked in awe. "You're like a walking radio station, sometimes."

"Honestly? I don't even know. They just sort of come to me, I guess."

"It's pretty amazing."

Brandon dropped his dark brown eyes down to meet mine, and for a brief second, my stomach fluttered. It felt like he was seeing into my soul. But just as quickly, his lips turned up and a growing smirk formed on his face.

"Although... I just gotta say," he continued. "I thought you would have at least busted out the Will Smith version, and not the old-school one. What are we, sixty?"

"Woooow! Okay, first of all, don't do the legend Bill Withers like that. People under sixty listen to his music."

"Who?"

"Me!"

"Obviously, you don't count. You're a music nerd from Philadelphia! You listen to all the old-school stuff."

"I like good music," I replied, shrugging my shoulders.

"Uh-huh."

"You're telling me if 'Ain't No Sunshine' or 'Lean on Me' randomly started playing, you wouldn't sing along?"

I placed my hands on my hips and pursed my lips, waiting for him to try to lie to me.

"No, of course I would. Those are classic songs! But I wouldn't be walking on a hiking trail and have those be the first ones that came to my mind out of all the songs in the world right now," Brandon said, laughing, tears starting to fall down his cheeks. "It's just you, Gig. I don't know what to say—you're a special one."

It was hard to miss how his eyes seemed to have a twinkle in them again as Brandon belly laughed his way down the series of steps leading to the falls.

"Well, fine, I'll take that."

I clutched my hands together and batted my eyes, grinning at Brandon. It might have been a backhanded compliment but I refused to receive it as such.

"But also, don't fake on my hip hop knowledge, either. Especially when it comes to the Fresh Prince from Philly."

"Oh, so you know that version, too, huh?"

"Are you kidding me?"

I paused on one of the steps so that I could turn my body to the side, put my right hand on my hip and give him the proper look of amusement for daring to doubt me. Brandon tried to respond with his own defiant look, but I quickly shot that down as I flowed right into Will Smith's second verse, spitting his rhymes bar for bar in perfect cadence.

Brandon shook his head, chuckling in defeat. But he didn't stand off to the side for too long. About halfway through the verse, he jumped in, and suddenly, we were both rapping Will Smith's lyrics detailing his love for his son on the side of a waterfall. By the time we got to the end of the song, I was belting out the chorus like I was on a concert stage while Brandon was effortlessly rapping Will's last ad-libs where he tells his son that he's going to love him for the rest of his life.

When we were done, we fell into each other's arms,

cracking up at our silliness and just how fun that had been. Our amusement was buoyed even further when we heard a small round of applause coming from at least one of the other groups of tourists simply trying to make their way to the Falls.

"You see what I mean?" Brandon said as we started walking again. "Special."

"That applause was for both of us," I replied, politely correcting him. "My chorus doesn't sound as good without you doing Will's signature 'ha-ha's' in the middle of it."

"True true. You know what? I'll take that because I actually thought I did a pretty good job with those."

"You did!" I nodded my head. "Now, you weren't as good as me with the Fresh Prince flow, but the ad-libs, that was all you baby boy."

"See now?"

Brandon looked at me sideways as it dawned on him that I was still messing with him.

"I gave you a genuine compliment, and you dangled mine in front of me, and then took it back. That's not right."

"You also doubted my rap game," I replied, my cheeks starting to hurt from how much we'd been laughing, "and I tried to tell you not to."

"All right, all right. I will not make the mistake of doubting you again."

Brandon wrapped his left arm around my neck and pulled me in for a friendly peck on the cheek, rustling my twists with his right hand at the same time. It was the kind of move he would have casually done without a second thought before yesterday, but it felt that much more meaningful to me now. Like, something had been righted within our relationship, and all it had taken was us just being *us* again, having fun and playing off each other's strengths.

If Reagan and Keisha had schemed to give us this time to ourselves, at that point, I couldn't even be mad at them. I had my friend back, and that's what mattered.

"Okay, can I just say this is how I want us to always be?"

I looked up at Brandon as he loosened his grip on me, and we continued walking side by side. We'd already passed the midway point for the falls, where a lot of people chose to stop and observe, so I knew if I was going to bring up the elephant in the proverbial room, I was running out of time. I wanted this settled before we were fully down on the platform. That moment I wanted to be sacred and peaceful...and calming.

"I know things got a little weird last night, and I am sincerely sorry for my part in that."

"Gig." Brandon looked at me as he started to respond, but I cut him off before he could continue.

"No, I'm serious, B. Because you were so angry with me this morning, and I can't have that. Like, forget whatever weird version of us that was in the bathroom last night or even this morning. I only want *this* version of us."

Brandon tilted his head and chuckled softly.

"I wasn't mad at you, Gig. I—"

"Lies."

"What?" He looked at me quizzically.

"That's a bold face lie you just told right now, Brandon Clark!"

I clapped my hands on beat as I said the words "bold" and "face" and "lie" to make sure he knew that, despite the smile on my face, I was being serious.

"It wasn't a lie," he said, shaking his head.

"Then what was it?" I asked, turning my face toward him so that he could see I'd dropped the grin from it.

"It was...uhh... I mean..."

Brandon hesitated as he started and stopped at least three times, trying to deny what I already knew to be true. But if he really didn't want to admit it, it was actually okay with me. We could absolutely move on from it as long as everything was back to kosher with us.

"Mmm-hmm. Exactly. Like I said."

I smiled at him again with an "I already know!" look on my face as I resolved not to push him further on it.

"Honestly, though, it doesn't matter anyway because I just want us to be friends again. Deal?" I asked.

Brandon chuckled again and bit his bottom lip as he stared at me.

"On a scale of one to ten, how hard was it for you to not start singing Musiq Soulchild's 'Halfcrazy' just now?"

"Oh my God!" I replied, bending forward with my hands balled in a fist as I burst into laughter. "It was so hard! Like a fifteen at least."

"I knew it had to have been. Because 'I just want my friend back!' was right there."

"It was so right there!"

He pulled me toward him again as we walked down the last several steps and finally made it onto the lowest platform where you could take in the expansive view of the Kaaterskill Falls.

"All jokes aside," he said, his eyes penetrating deeply into mine. "If that's what you want, Gigi, for us to be friends—you got it."

"Desperately," I replied. "I can't do this life without you. I mean, look where we are right now, and look who's here with me."

I spun around with my arms out wide, waving at the amazing oasis we were now lucky to be able to witness. It was like nothing I'd ever seen before, with the waters rushing 260 feet down, crashing onto the most beautiful, gigantic stones and surrounded by greenery at every turn. The babbling brook had been beautiful and peaceful, but *this* was impressive and awe-inspiring.

"It's just you," I said. "It's just the two of us, so I can't lose that. Imagine if I'd tried to come here with just Rae and Keish. I'd still be stuck up there, watching them pretend to die."

"Yeah," he replied, grabbing me toward him again. "You're right, Gig."

Brandon wrapped his arm around my shoulder again, and I rested my head on his chest as we looked out onto the waterfall, both of us quietly taking in the tranquility of the moment.

*Dear God, thank you for giving me my friend back*, I prayed silently, relaxing in his embrace.

Just then, and to my absolute delight, Brandon began softly humming "Just the Two of Us" again. It was official, I thought, a smile growing on my face. We were back where we belonged. Finally.

# Part 3

"The first time I kissed you. One kiss, and I was totally hooked. Addicted to you. I could never love anyone the way I love you. I'd follow you across the universe."

—Ellen Hopkins, *Tricks*

# *Chapter Thirteen*

"Oh my God! Best. Birthday. Everrrrr!"

Reagan screamed with delight, shaking her wet and wavy ombre curls as we made our way into the cabin late Monday night, drenched from our day out on the Saugerties Marina. It had taken us forty minutes to drive back to the house, and yet, every single one of us was still soaking wet. Not a soul complained, however, because we were all far too excited about just how great the day had been. We'd spent the past several hours lounging around and partying on a full-service pontoon boat, just five minutes away from the Hudson River.

This was the second activity that Keisha and I had planned for the trip, and since we had a feeling that it would be filled with nothing but good vibes, drinks and food, we purposely timed it to happen on Reagan's actual birthday. In our minds, all we needed were some coolers of hard seltzers, a bunch of meat, cheese, and fruit—aka adult Lunchables—and our wacky cast of characters to ensure she had a great day. Truthfully, it ended up exceeding even our expectations.

"Ayeeee!" we all replied, sauntering into the living room with glee until we were immediately hit by the cold air blasting throughout the cabin.

"Oh shit!" Jake decried. "I guess we should have turned the air off before we left."

"Yeah, but it was just so warm at the time, it didn't cross any of our minds."

A shiver, and not the good kind, shot through my body as soon as I spoke, with the cold air a brutal reminder that I was standing in only my neon orange one-piece swimsuit and a pair of shorts. I wasn't the only one, however. A quick scan of the room revealed that we were all trembling from the cold as it met with our wet clothes and skin. Those of us with longer hair were even more at a disadvantage.

"Maybe we should finally light up the firepit tonight?" Lucas offered. "That way, we can keep the party going, but we'd be outside...and warm."

"I like the way you think, Lucas," Reagan replied, already starting to move toward the back entrance.

"Yess," the rest of us shouted in unison.

Honestly, he couldn't have come up with a better idea, I realized, because it would also give Jake a chance to slip away at some point, so that he could surprise Rae with her double-layered birthday cake, topped with buttercream and oh so many sprinkles. We'd been trying to figure out how to pull that off all day, and in one fell swoop, Lucas had made it ridiculously easy. Clearly, that was why we kept him around despite his silly shenanigans.

"All right," Jake said, running to his room as we all followed behind Reagan, "I'll get us some towels, too."

Less than a minute later, he was back, and handing out oversize towels, one by one, as we proceeded to the backyard. While some of us stopped to wrap ourselves tightly in the new material, desperate to get warm, others took off in a foot race to get to the chairs surrounding the pit. There were eight of them, the perfect amount for our group, but it was clear that people had their eyes on particular ones. I didn't much care as long as I could feel the warmth coming from the fire, and I could rest my back on a sturdy wooden frame.

By the time Jake and I arrived at the end of the deck where the firepit was located, there were two chairs remaining, one right next to Brandon and the other in between Julian and Reagan. It took everything in me not to roll my eyes, because it was so obvious which one had been left for him and therefore, also, which one was for me. I had half a mind to shake things up and grab the chair next to Rae; it's not like Brandon and Jake weren't best friends after all. But the truth was, I'd been meaning to tell Brandon some pretty big news all day and hadn't had a chance to yet.

Once the other pontoon patrons learned it was Reagan's birthday, our plans had gone from chill to explosive, as we were bombarded with free frozen cocktails, food that put our charcuterie trays to shame and even several rounds of mixed shots. The sudden camaraderie was also what led to us all getting so wet. Turns out it's pretty hard to resist invitations for group dance-offs and tubing races, all in the actual marina waters, when you've been drinking frozen cocktails with newfound friends.

I squinted my eyes at Reagan and Keisha as I walked past them and plopped down next to Brandon.

"Hey," he said, warmly staring into my eyes.

"Hi there."

"I feel like we've been around each other all day, but I really haven't talked to you that much."

"I know, same. Today was a wild ride, but not exactly one where you can catch up with anyone."

"Yeah, for sure."

I settled into my seat next to him, using half of my towel

to keep me warm and the other half to serve as a cushion between my back and the planks in the chair. The flames from the pit were already starting to rise, so I didn't feel the need to stay completely wrapped up, but coming out of the towel now meant I was face-to-face with Brandon in my swimsuit that not only had a plunge scoop neckline but also several cutouts between my stomach and sides. It hadn't felt that out of place among Reagan's black, bandeau-style bodice swimsuit that also had a ton of cutouts or Keisha's brick red one-piece with a V-neck top and a high waist that showed off her ample booty, or even Jenn's two-piece bikini with its crisscross top and Tuscan tan-and-white color blocking. But sitting here now, inches away from Brandon, when it seemed like everyone around us had sort of melted away from my vision, suddenly it seemed explicit in a way I couldn't quite explain.

It didn't help that I briefly caught Brandon drop his eyes and lick his lips as I turned my body toward him. That had, momentarily, sent the other kind of shiver down my spine, but thankfully, he brought me back to reality with the sound of his voice.

"Have you thought any more about the HUD proposal?" he asked, clearing his throat as he shifted in his seat.

He didn't know it, but that was just the question I needed to hear to stop me from allowing my eyes to trace his body again, now only clothed in his swim trunks and the towel that he'd draped across his lap.

"Okay, we must have ESP or something, because I've been wanting to update you on that all day," I said.

"Really? Okay, now I'm extra intrigued. Go on."

"Well, I had a chance to work on it last night once everyone went to bed, and I think I figured out a way to add a little bit of Gigi into the proposal without completely blowing up the idea that the team came up with."

"Oh shit, Gigi, that's great!"

Brandon's eyes looked like they were literally glowing, bolstered by the firepit flames and his enthusiasm, as he sat up straighter to give me his undivided attention.

"No, honestly, I can't thank you enough for calling me out on that. I think I was just so concerned about presenting them with a pipe dream that would never get approved that I lost sight of the whole reason my director wanted me to lead the initiative in the first place. I mean, sure, he knows I'm detailed, and I can rally the team, but he could have picked any one of us for that. I work with some incredibly bright people. He picked me because of my vision and my passion for the work, and I'd somehow forgotten that."

"Damn. Well, I'm proud of you for remembering it, and I'm rooting you on like crazy."

Brandon leaned in a little closer to me until I could almost smell the remnants of either his cologne or beard oil. I wasn't sure how that was still possible after we'd been at the marina for over eight hours, but there it was, all the same, threatening to distract me once again and make me forget the words I'd said to him at the waterfalls.

"You don't have to thank me, though," he continued. "This is all you. I'm just glad I was able to provide the spark to ignite that flame in you again."

"Yeah, me, too," I said quietly.

"And hey, if you want to run anything by me, I'd be happy to listen to it. As you know, I'm only a bathroom away."

He winked at me with a boyish grin that I couldn't help but smile back at.

"Ha! That's true," I replied. "And I just might take you up on that offer...as long you promise to keep your clothes on."

"I'll do my best."

Brandon slid back into his chair, slouching comfortably just as Jake came strolling toward the group, cake in hand with over twenty candles lit on top of it.

*Just in time*, I thought, turning my attention to the birthday girl as Jake slid the cake into her hands. The last thing I'd needed right then was a chance to be undone by the look in Brandon's eyes as he returned my smile. Filled with a combination of pride and awe, I could have lost myself in them if not for the welcome distraction, and that wouldn't have been good for either of us.

Reagan squealed once again as we began singing "Happy Birthday" to her, seamlessly moving from the original to Stevie Wonder's version without anyone having to give the direction.

"Thank you all," she exclaimed before pausing a moment to make a wish and blow out her candles. "Like I said earlier... Best. Birthday. Ever."

She scanned the circle of chairs, eyeing each person and giving them their own personal message. When she got to me, the sixth person in her line, she very distinctly winked at me and mouthed, *That wish was for you.*

Later that night, I found myself seated on my bed and poring over my last edits to the proposal when I heard my side of the bathroom door unlock from the inside. That was the signal to indicate that Brandon had finished taking his shower and was fully dressed—a new system we'd come up with since our truce at the waterfalls.

While I'd taken my shower first, Brandon's version of a congratulations reward, it still would come in handy if I needed to get up in the middle of the night and use the bathroom. I could rest assured, knowing he wasn't in there wet and naked again, if the door was unlocked.

"Hey," I called out, hoping I'd get his attention before he moved too far away from the door.

He opened it, slowly at first, and peeked through the crack in the entrance to my room.

"Was that for me or are you on the phone?" Brandon whispered.

"You."

"Oh, okay, good. I didn't want to assume."

The way he said those words, like maybe he had before, it brought me right back to the first day of the trip, when I'd found out Brandon was the one who'd brought my suitcase upstairs while I was caking on the phone with Phillip. I still had no idea if that moment had been awkward for him in any way, but I knew how I might have felt if the shoe were on the other foot. Even if, technically, I would have had no reason or recourse to be jealous. And truthfully, neither did he.

"All good," I said with a smile. "I was hoping I could take you up on that offer before you went to bed. I could use a second opinion on what I've done so far."

"Of course, I'm honored—and all ears."

Brandon swung the door fully open and paused at the foot of my bed as he tried to process the whole scene before him. There I was, sitting in front of my laptop crisscross style in the middle of the bed and surrounded by at least ten sketches and the last bits of all the pencils I'd used to draw them. Colored with immaculate details, I'd created every single sketch in only the past twenty-four hours, each one showcasing a different housing unit style we could develop throughout the five boroughs in the city. It was a feat that I hadn't accomplished since the burst of creativity that hit me following my brunch with the girls when I'd told them I was finally ready to get serious about pursuing a real relationship.

That time had been inspired by the kind of love I wanted to come into my life, while this was focused on the love and passion I already had. It wasn't lost on me, however, that both instances involved Brandon in some way or another.

"Wow, Gigi."

With a stride that was both calm and intentional, Brandon practically glided toward me, his face giving off that same look of awe he'd had by the firepit as he picked up one sketch after another.

"These are…amazing," he said marveling at each one as he shuffled them in his hands.

"Thank you."

My voice came out low and bashful, mostly because I was sure that, despite my best efforts, I was absolutely blushing from his initial reaction. But also because it had been a really long time since anyone had seen an illustration of mine, and everything in me wanted to burst with excitement.

"No, seriously. Like, these could be on a canvas somewhere and people would totally buy them. That's how good they are. You know that, right?"

"Well, I don't know if I would go that far," I replied, nervously chuckling at the thought.

"I would."

He picked up a few more that were closest to me, with their pale peach, brick red, and sea green colors jumping off the pages, and gently sat down in their place. His deep caramel brown skin, dressed in aquamarine shorts and a simple white tee, replaced the vibrancy of the sketches with something new, something different, something more… natural and grounded.

The energy on the bed almost immediately shifted as Brandon's five-foot-eleven frame stretched out next to me. But despite our newfound proximity, his focus was still tethered to the drawings in his own hands.

"You did these all while you've been here?" he asked.

"Yeah."

"But it's only been three days so far."

I giggled in response, tickled by the way he was processing everything out loud as his eyes darted from one building sketch to the next, each one showcasing its own intricacies in architectural style and flair.

"Ha! I know."

"And you weren't going to include these in the proposal at first? Gig, what a waste that would have been. I mean, I'd heard you were good, but this is the first time I'm actually seeing what you can do and… Wait, how is this the first time I'm seeing what you can do?"

Brandon finally looked up from the sketches and aimed his eyes directly toward mine, staring at me just long enough to steal my breath out of my chest as I attempted to inhale like normal. I swallowed quietly and returned his gaze, forcing myself to shrug off the intimacy of the moment, even as I noticed things like his left hand being mere inches away from my right thigh or how I could feel the heat generating from him.

"Don't take it personal," I replied, blinking to try to break the hold he was starting to have on me again. "A lot of people haven't. I faced so many disappointments when I first moved to New York, intent on being a full-time illustrator at someone's design studio or fashion company, that I guess I just stopped doing them for a while. Then, thankfully, I realized I also had this incredible passion for housing advocacy, and truthfully, it was probably easier to focus on making someone else's dream come true than to dwell on the fact that mine hadn't. And so, eventually, as with most creative things, if you don't use it, you lose it, right? That happened for me. Everyone talks about me being an illustrator, but for a long time, I'd lost my desire to draw anything. That was, until recently when I picked up my pencils again."

"Damn. I hate that a bunch of idiots weren't able to see your full potential, Gig. It's honestly their loss."

Brandon moved his hand and placed it softly on my thigh.

"Can I ask, what made you pick your pencils up again?"

"Umm…"

I hesitated as I thought about what I could say other than "you." But eventually, I found some words that felt like they could at least be serviceable.

"I don't know, really. Just one day, I came home, and I was so inspired, I could barely draw the imagery in my head fast enough. It was almost like an out-of-body experience for me, so much so, that by the time I looked up, it felt like I was seeing the sketch for the very first time. As if someone else had drawn it and not my own two hands. It's not too dissimilar from what happened here, as well."

"Well, shit, whatever the inspiration was, I'm glad it got you back into your craft, because if these sketches are any indication of what you've still got in you, the world needs to see that."

"Ha! It's funny you say that. I think that's exactly what I realized, too, after our conversation on the ride up," I responded, my voice rising barely above a whisper.

I cleared my throat so that I could speak louder, trying

to ignore how tender Brandon's touch felt as he slowly, maybe absentmindedly, rubbed along the lower part of my inner thigh.

"You know, I think I've spent so long being fearful of experiencing the kind of failure I did before that it never dawned on me that I could pursue both of my passions and figure out how to use them to support the other. I just didn't want to risk being disappointed again, and so I focused solely on logic and facts. Forget art and creativity, right? Forget thinking outside of the box, because that had let me down too many times. No, my goal was simple—outline something that couldn't be refuted, something that was tried and tested before, and therefore had to succeed. And don't get me wrong, there's nothing wrong with that approach. Obviously, we have to build a program with evidence-based practices, but—"

"What's the point in having a moon if you don't aim for it every once in a while?" he asked, a smile growing on his face as he purposefully interrupted me with my own question from before.

"Exactly. And someone I quite admire told me everything I pursue should make my heart skip a beat, so…here we are."

I stretched my arms out wide and waved them across the sketches, which had, in one day, become the physical manifestations of what my heart truly hoped my organization could accomplish. And, importantly, what I believed we had the ability to achieve, if we believed in ourselves. It was the first time I'd been willing to take that leap of faith with them.

"Aww girl, see? You're going to make me blush. Don't do that. I've got a reputation to uphold."

Brandon laughed as he inched a little closer to me, his

brown eyes beaming brightly, almost as if he held the entire solar system within his irises.

"That of the ultimate player who doesn't get flustered by anything or anyone?" I asked.

"What can I say?"

He sucked his teeth and then immediately dropped his eyesight toward my laptop.

"It's a blessing and a curse."

If I didn't know any better, I could have sworn that I saw a moment of sadness flash across Brandon's face. But before I had a chance to determine if I was seeing things, he'd turned his charm right back on, grabbing the Chromebook from my bed and swinging it so that he could view the screen.

"Okay, so, you've set me up beautifully," he said, eyeing the text before him. "I'm all in—I'm loving the sketches and the backstory. Now, give me the pitch."

"All right," I replied with a sigh, figuring that it was best to follow his lead and pivot our conversation back to the matter at hand. Besides, it was what I'd called him into my room for in the first place.

"Here's the gist of it. So, you remember, initially our proposal was going to focus on building *one* housing development in *one* borough and using that as a test case for what could be created across the city. That's not a *bad* idea, but it would take almost three years to impact nearly fifty adults plus their children. And then, even if enough people thought the outcomes were strong enough to invest in us, we'd still have to get additional funding to try to build more places like it. That's a drop in the bucket for the number of people experiencing homelessness in the city. Not even, really!"

I paused, feeling myself grow more excited as I got ready to finally reveal the new plan. Ultimately, I'd need to pitch it to my team to get their buy-in when I got back home. But if Brandon loved it as much as I did, my hope was that they would, too.

"But what if...we didn't spend all our money purchasing land and building something entirely new, and instead we focused on refurbishing what's already there, creating a multiborough living and treatment facility system? We'd have to do some targeted outreach in the designated communities so that they don't see us as interlopers, but we could do so much good if we get their buy-in. The facilities would still be designed around the concept of the Housing First approach, like the original proposal, and would operate off the evidence that people are more likely to get continued care and treatment and maintain employment if they first have stable, safe and affordable housing. But critically, we'd be able to serve more people for longer periods of time."

Brandon nodded his head furiously as he listened, like he was attempting to absorb every word I spoke before giving his final assessment. This only served to egg me on further.

"With the new proposal," I continued, "we'd cover the initial cost of rent for anyone living in these facilities. In the original version, that would last for six months regardless of whether they found employment during that time. But then they would have to leave once the six months was up so that the next group of people could move in. In this one, however, rent would be free for four months and then marginally increase based on a percentage of their income the longer they stayed. So, in month five, for example, they might begin paying fifty dollars a month for the next two months, then potentially seventy-five dollars a month two months after that, and maybe a hundred dollars a month for the remainder of their stay. Importantly, with that small increase in payment, they could live in the facility for up to a year while they received easy access to lifesaving treatment or services like children's therapy. We would also only require rent payments if our job recruiter successfully connected them to an employment opportunity. But for some people, this could be an opportunity to learn or relearn how to budget for rental costs in a secure situation. In a three-year program, this might allow us to impact over one hundred and twenty adults plus any children living with them."

"Wow, Gig, I'm kind of at a loss for words."

Brandon stared at me incredulously, as if he wanted to ask me why this hadn't been the plan all along, but by now, I figured he had to know the answer to that. It was my fear that had held me, and thus my team, back from producing anything close to this. The desire to push past that fear was now propelling me in a way I hadn't known was possible until a few days ago.

"Wait, there's more," I said, laughing at his reaction.

"Woman. How? Again, I'd like to remind you that we've only been here three days! Did you suddenly find a portal to extra hours that only you know of or something?"

"Sadly, no, I did not. What you're looking at is very much the result of hours spent working when all the rest of y'all were snoring up a storm."

"All right, well, now I'm even further impressed. Tell me more."

Brandon sat up straighter and waited in anticipation for me to continue.

"Okay, so, clearly, the sketches are of the different types of housing units I envisioned us being able to establish with the kinds of buildings that are already in each of the boroughs, right? For example, the two Brooklyn ones you're holding detail a large-scale brownstone that you might find in Stuyvesant Heights or Sunset Park or one of those brightly colored Victorian homes in a neighborhood like Ditmas Park. For Queens, there's the Tudor row house option or a single-family home like in Staten Island, too. But the way this all becomes a *system* of facilities is not just because there's one in each borough, right? My vision is that each one would be designated for a specific population, with the five working together to tackle some of the main priority groups who find themselves lacking shelter. Off the top of my head, that would, at the very least, be women with children, domestic violence survivors, people with mental health needs or co-occurring substance use disorders, and people who are returning home from incarceration. This way, the services they receive in the facility are tailored to the specific needs of each population, and we can more efficiently partner with clinicians and community advocates to support them in a truly meaningful way. Now, some of these groups might overlap in needs, but we could screen participants to determine which housing facility is best for them before they move in."

"Giselle Catherine Lewis, get up out of this bed right now and walk yourself straight out of that door."

Brandon grabbed one of the pillows off my bed and lightly tossed it at me before staring at me once again.

"I can't believe you were letting your fears stop you from *this*! This is life-changing stuff, woman. What the hell?!"

"I take it that means you like it?" I asked.

I knew I was bordering on sounding like the girlfriend who asks her partner multiple times if she looks pretty, but in this moment, I did really need to hear him say the words.

"Are you kidding me? Do I *like* it? I'm not sure there's one word I could actually sufficiently use to express my thoughts on all that you've done here, but 'like' surely wouldn't be the one."

I drew my hands to my face, not exactly attempting to cover up the excitement flooding through me, but desperately needing to do something with my hands other than grab Brandon and hold him tightly, whispering 'thank you' in his ear for as long as he'd let me. Not just for listening to me or complimenting my work, but for challenging me to run toward that whole heart-skipping thing that he'd talked about. It had been a really long time since I'd experienced that feeling, but damn, it felt indescribably good.

"So, I actually have one more idea that I want to flesh out before I go to sleep tonight," I replied, my body still pulsing with an energy that seemed to flow from Brandon to me, one that made me feel like I could take on the world as long as I tried. "I'm thinking of maybe having volunteers come in once a week to do some sort of creative activity with the children and any young adults, whether that's painting, reading, writing or otherwise, just something to give them a chance to be carefree even in a tough situation, you know?"

"There it is," he said, pointing toward me. "That's the heart of Gigi that was missing from the first one. Everything else you've pitched so far has been genius, but *that's* the piece that is uniquely you."

"I'm really happy to hear you say that, Brandon. I hope my team feels the same. The last thing I want is for them to think they wasted their time putting together the initial pitch, all for me to just come in at the end and change everything."

"Well, from what I heard, you didn't change everything. You expanded on what y'all had already established to make something bigger and bolder, and most importantly, that you can feel passionate about pitching. I don't believe they would see that as a bad thing, knowing you like they do. I'd be willing to bet, actually, that they'll be thrilled about some of these updates."

"Yeah, you're probably right. I had to convince more than a few of them that we shouldn't think too far outside the box. They were far more ready to do so than I was!"

Brandon's expression turned from joyful to inquisitive to stern in a matter of a few seconds, and I could tell he was examining me like a coach would his star athlete, trying to ascertain what exactly he found to be missing. In return, almost instinctively, I dropped my hands into my lap and began nervously flicking my nails, anxious about what he was going to say or do next.

"Hmm," he groaned, tilting his head and squinting his eyes. "Gig, can I be tough with you for a second?"

"Sure."

I couldn't immediately tell from Brandon's facial expression just how much I needed to brace myself, but my chest tightened all the same.

"I believe you can do damn near anything you put your heart and mind to," he said. "And this proposal right here tells me that you haven't even scratched the surface yet of what you can ultimately do to make a real change in this world. But one thing you can't do is stop yourself…ever again. I mean that. Not for anyone. Everything that makes you *you*…it's far too important for all of us, that you don't hold that back any longer."

*Wow, now that was definitely not where I thought he was going.*

As if his words were some kind of cue, I instantly felt my eyes growing wet as Brandon's words echoed in my head. Spoken by anyone else, I might have questioned their sincerity, wondered if it was just what that person thought I'd wanted to hear. But from him? I knew they were genuine. My heart seemed to know that as well, fluttering again for the second time that night, but for quite a different reason than before.

"Okay," I replied softly, nodding my head in agreement as I dabbed at the corners of my eyes.

"Promise me."

"I promise."

I raised my right hand and stuck out my pinkie finger so that we could "pinkie promise" shake on our deal. Brandon happily obliged, looping his large finger around mine and grasping our hands to his chest.

"Is this how you're so good at being a personal trainer?" I asked. "You give inspiring pep talks, and then you refuse to back down until your client agrees and completes some insane workout that they didn't know they had in them?"

"Maybe," he said with a shrug, dropping my hand. "But you don't need to be inspired by me, Gig. You are amazing all on your own. I just happen to see it. And I won't rest until you believe it, too."

Brandon's dark brown eyes wandered back over to mine, piercing through whatever armor I still had left around my heart and instantly making me aware of my body's reaction to it. Under the intensity of his gaze, every movement I made was magnified in my brain, like the way that my chest rose and descended, heavier with each breath I took, or the way my lips parted ever so slightly, on their own, begging to be licked.

"Gigi."

He said my name so softly, his tone so low and hushed, that it would almost have sounded like the beginnings of a lullaby except for the way it echoed in my head, plunging me into a sea of emotions and sensations that could only lead to one thing.

"Yes?" I asked, another moan escaping from my mouth. First the bathroom and now on the bed. *Crap.*

"That's the second time you've done that," he replied, his eyes dropping down to my lips.

"I know."

"What am I supposed to do about that? Am I supposed to ignore it? Because…"

If he'd been looking into my eyes still, Brandon might have seen the plea coming from them, imploring him to go ahead and finally release me from the misery of my own making. To kiss me and never stop kissing me as long as we had breaths in our lungs. But I realized he didn't need my eyes to tell him how much I wanted him. Every inch of my body screamed out *Please, take me now*, reverberating that energy off the walls in the room, and encircling us until there was nothing else to do but give in.

Brandon lingered his lips over mine as he dragged his fingers up the sides of my neck, teasing me with the whispers of his breath, like I might be snatched out of his grip at any moment. Then suddenly, gratefully, he drew my bottom lip to his with a low growl that sent my head into a tailspin, leaving me just cognizant enough to join in as he sucked me fully in, pulling and tugging on his lips with a fervor that matched his energy.

In an instant, everything around us melted away, and it was just us two once again. Brandon and Giselle. Carried away to another dimension, where the tiniest sliver of space that allowed us to breathe in and out as our mouths intertwined was the only thing we ever needed to survive.

# *Chapter Fourteen*

For the next minute, nothing else mattered as Brandon and I sucked and licked and pulled at one another, completely overtaken by the waves of pleasure crashing over us and sending indescribable chills throughout our bodies. We were like magnets who'd finally come together, and couldn't, even if they wanted to, release themselves again.

Eventually, however, even as our lips continued moving in sync, a horrible shout began ringing in my head.

*Stop*, the voice screamed out, joined by what seemed like the clanging sound of pots and pans to truly get my attention. *You're going to get hurt again.*

I tried to ignore it. Tried to focus on the smell of Brandon's beard oil or the way his tongue darted in and out of my mouth, expertly guiding me through a cycle where he teased me just long enough to make me crave him and then ultimately gave me what I wanted. That told me everything I needed to know about what he might do if given the chance to kiss and lick a different pair of my lips. But as enticing as all that was, it was no use.

The voice just screamed louder and louder, refusing to be ignored.

*Do you want to be curled up in your bed, crying over yet another failed relationship?* it asked. *Because that's the only way this ends. You know that. That's always how it ends when you've actually cared about the guy. So, what do you think is going to happen when it's Brandon Clark, of all people?*

That was the final straw. Unable to take it anymore, I cried out "Stop" myself, and then painstakingly tore my body away from Brandon and his beautiful lips, backing my way all the way to the edge of my headboard.

"Whoa. Gigi, what's wrong?" he asked, his eyes flush with confusion and concern as I drew my knees into my chest, trying to catch my breath and recover from the voice that had, of course, stopped ringing in my head now.

"I... I'm sorry," I whispered. "I shouldn't have... We shouldn't have..."

"No. No. Oh God. Please don't apologize..."

Brandon shut his eyes briefly in what seemed like his own attempt to regain some control of his faculties.

"Damn it!" he shouted. "This is all my fault. I shouldn't have put you in this predicament."

"No, Brandon, I..."

I stopped myself, unsure what I could possibly say to explain what the hell had just happened. Telling him about the voice screaming at me would probably only amplify how crazy I'm sure I seemed, but nothing else felt honest enough to be worthy of him. Of us.

"No, seriously, Gig. I know you're seeing someone, and so I should have left well enough alone no matter how badly I've been wanting to kiss you."

"Wait, you have?"

"Yeah," he replied softly, bowing his head in shame. "But that doesn't matter. You told me you wanted to be friends, and I'm supposed to honor that, not shit on it with my own selfish desires."

"Hey," I said, drawing Brandon's attention back to me.

The look on his face was so pained that there was no way I could just sit there and let him believe Phillip was why I'd pulled away from him. I still wasn't sure I had the right words yet, but I knew I had to say something.

"Let me be very clear. I didn't pull away because of Phillip," I continued. "I like him, yeah, but that's very new and we're not exclusive. I also don't think you're selfish or anything like that. I mean, clearly, I wanted this as much as you did. It's just that…this, us, our friendship, it's so important to me. Too important for me to risk it on something that, more than likely, would end in like three months, tops."

"What do you mean?" he asked.

"You and I don't have great track records when it comes to dating. Let's not forget that I've had a front row seat for every relationship that went nowhere and every heart you've broken over the past two years. And when it comes to me, I mean, I have *never* gotten it right, with anyone, no matter how much I've tried. Why do you think I just gave up for a while and resigned myself to using these dudes like they used me?"

"Huh," Brandon leaned his body back as he visibly thought through what I'd said. "We'll get back to me in a second, but it's interesting that you say you gave up. I don't see that with your interactions with Phillip."

"But Phillip's not you."

I said it so quickly that I had to catch my breath when I realized what I'd said out loud, but I also instantly knew there was nothing I could do to take it back. *Where was that damn neuralyzer when I needed it?*

"Is that a good thing or a bad thing?" Brandon asked.

"Well, you tell me. Because one misplaced moan almost ruined us two days ago," I replied. "That next morning, we were a shell of ourselves. It was awful. Now multiply that tenfold if we were to date and break up. That means not only do I lose my boyfriend, but I lose you? The man who I talk to almost every day? Who can make me laugh and then turn around and challenge me like only my best friends can? How could I withstand that and be expected to be okay in any way?"

"Do you hear yourself? You just jumped from one kiss to us breaking up. Weren't we talking about not letting your fears stop you all of five, ten minutes ago?"

"That's different, B, and you know it."

"I don't think it's as different as you think," he said softly, shifting his weight in the bed and then rising up from it in one fell swoop. "And by the way, you seem to have this skewed sense of my dating history, maybe because of the way me and the guys talk, but you should know that I've had my fair share of heartbreak as well. That said, I know you still have more work to do tonight, and I don't want to be the cause of you not finishing up your new proposal idea. So, maybe let's table the rest of this conversation for later."

"Okay."

I stared at him quietly as Brandon stood up straight and pulled the hair tie loose from around his locs, letting his hair fall down his shoulders and back while he inched toward me once again.

"Just one thing I'd ask you to consider," he said, leaning over me with his arm resting on the headboard. "What if you're wrong, and everything we've ever wanted is right in front of our faces? Would it be so weird to think that could last?"

"We?" I whispered, arching my head back so that I could try to see into his eyes again. As if they might tell me something I didn't catch before.

But this time, Brandon didn't oblige. Instead, he avoided my eye contact, leaned over further and planted his mouth softly and delicately on my forehead. It may have only lasted about two seconds, but it was long enough to remind me of the outline of his lips and how they'd seemed like the perfect match to mine even as his goatee tickled the corners of my mouth. It also effectively left me stunned into silence as I watched him turn around and walk back to the adjoining bathroom door, his stride just as long and confident as before. When he got to the door, still ajar from earlier, Brandon tugged on the knob, and then pivoted his body and turned toward me.

"Good luck finishing up tonight, Gig," he said. "I'll see you in the morning."

I didn't even have time to recover and reply before he disappeared behind the door and pulled it closed.

"Good night," I whispered, cursing that damn forehead kiss as I grabbed my laptop and attempted to refocus my thoughts on the HUD proposal and not how badly I wanted him to walk back into my room.

"All right," I said, speaking to myself out loud. "Where were we?"

I scanned the last paragraphs of the proposal to reorient myself, and the part he'd accurately assessed really struck at the heart of the artist still lingering within me.

"Ahh, yes."

As I read through it, my memory came flooding back, and suddenly, I was in the zone again. The idea about offering a creative outlet for any of the young people living in the facilities came directly from how important that had been for me as a kid. It was something I would always be grateful that my mom had recognized and supported for me. Yes, she wanted me to get good grades in school and excel in track and with my music studies, but she also saw the gift I had for art early on and encouraged me to pursue it until the day she died. Adding this piece to the proposal was just as much about honoring her as it was about connecting the parts of me that, for too long, I'd kept separate.

It did involve an additional step before I could present it to my team, however. We could, of course, partner with any group of volunteers to make this happen, but I knew Keisha's business plan that she was developing for school had a specific focus on helping young people find their voices through creative play, and so I wanted us to work with her.

For the next several minutes, I furiously typed out a plan to get her on board with the idea. It might also help to provide her new business with some initial capital in time for her to be a viable option for our program. It just seemed like a perfect alignment of our goals—as long as everyone agreed with me, of course.

By the time I was done, my eyes were as heavy as they were the first night of our trip, and I knew, without even looking at the clock on my phone, it was beyond time to go to sleep. I saved the presentation once more, to be abundantly safe, and then shut my laptop, placing it on the nightstand by the bed. I also gathered up the sketches Brandon had left next to me and added them to what was becoming my proposal pile, grabbed my phone and turned off the table lamp, all before sliding under the soft covers and laying my head down with a sigh.

As I melted into the comfort of the bed, the plush pillows sort of engulfing me in a sea of tranquility, I unlocked my phone screen and saw I'd missed Phillip's call about twenty minutes before. It was close to 2:00 a.m., I realized, but I knew we had another packed day planned for tomorrow, so if I wanted to talk to him, now was the best time. We'd been on the phone late at night before, so I figured, at the very least, it didn't hurt to try.

I pressed his name and closed my eyes as I waited for the phone to begin ringing, curious if he was even still up. A few seconds later, I got my answer.

"Hey, party animal," he said, picking up the call with a voice that sounded surprisingly wide awake. "Are you just getting in from a long day out with your friends?"

"Hi," I replied, softly.

I could feel the weight of sleepiness starting to wash over me, but I wanted to be present for our conversation, even if it meant just for a few minutes. It was the same courtesy he'd given me while on his work trips, so he definitely deserved the same.

"Not exactly," I said, clearing my throat in an attempt to stir up some energy. "Most of the group went to bed a few hours ago, but I've been up working on some revisions to the proposal. I had my phone on silent so I wouldn't be distracted. That's how I missed your call."

"Oh okay, that makes sense."

Phillip paused and I could sense the stiffness between us, like there was something he wanted to say but wasn't sure that he could.

"What are you still doing up?" I asked.

"Oh. I had plans downtown tonight, so I didn't get back home until about the time I called you."

"So, *you're* really the one who's the party animal," I joked, clocking how vague his response seemed compared to the guy who was sending me pictures of his whereabouts when he was in DC.

Now that he was back home, and I wasn't, something felt different. I couldn't put my finger on it, but it was there. Then again, I could have also been projecting following my kiss with Brandon earlier. And even if something was going on, Phillip and I were unequivocally not exclusive yet, so it wasn't a far-fetched idea that he may have been on a date with someone else he didn't necessarily want to talk to me about.

I breathed in deeply and settled my head further into my pillow, ultimately deciding to leave it be.

"Nah, I wouldn't go that far, but I had a good night," he replied. "I didn't realize you were still working on the proposal, though. I thought you'd tied all that up before you went out of town."

"Well, we had, I guess, but something about it was still nagging at me, so I brought my laptop with me just in case I got inspired out here. You know, between the fresh air and the solitude you can't really get in the city, I thought it might spark some new ideas for me."

*The people, too*, I thought, but obviously stopped myself from saying out loud.

"Gotcha. Well, it sounds like you did if you've been working on it for the past few hours, so that's good."

"Yeah, I'm really excited about what I have now, actually. And I can't wait to get back to the city to talk to my team about it, see if it's something they'd want to pivot to."

"Do you think they're going to feel like you completely took over the proposal, and now you just want to get their stamp of approval?"

*Ouch.* I opened my eyes and clutched my imaginary pearls. That was the kind of question I would have expected my inner voice to batter me with. I hadn't expected it from the guy I was dating. He hadn't even raised his deep tenor voice as he'd sprung that on me, but it stung all the same.

"Umm, I mean, I'm hoping that they don't," I admitted. "But, of course, that's always a possibility."

"Yeah. Well, especially since you guys have been working on something else entirely for the last month, right?"

The second question was what let me know I needed to be fully alert to continue this conversation. This had started off as me thinking I could talk to Phillip before falling asleep, strategically placing his voice in between Brandon's forehead kiss in hopes my subconscious would choose the latter for my dreams. But now, it had turned into what felt like me needing to defend myself in an interrogation gone wrong. I sat up in the bed and leaned my back on the headboard, trying to figure out how we'd gotten here so quickly.

What was most off-putting was how he'd seemingly immediately thought about my team's possible reaction without ever even asking me what changes I'd made or why I was so excited about them in the first place.

"We have been, yes," I protested. "But from the start, I had team members who wanted to do more, and I was the one who sort of stifled that energy. So, of course, it's not a guarantee that they'll love the direction I've come up with, but what's the harm in me at least trying? If it means we even just take one or two of the new ideas and incorporate them into the proposal, I'd think that would be worth it."

"Stifled, huh?"

*Crap.* Almost as soon as the word came out of my mouth, I regretted saying it and hoped he didn't think I meant that as a dig toward him or his advice.

"I didn't mean it like that. I'm sorry."

"It's cool. Here, I thought you were being a good leader and directing your team with a winning mentality, but I suppose 'stifling them' might be another way to look at it."

His tone sounded colder than I'd ever heard it before, and I instantly questioned why I'd even called him this late in the first place. Clearly, I was too tired and messed up in my head from the kiss with Brandon to speak with any sort of care and intention.

"Phillip," I said, trying to connect with him as best as I could without being in person or even on video. Either of those would have made it a lot easier to reset the mood and back us out of what I didn't want to become an ugly argument. Especially over something that really didn't impact us as a couple at all. The only reason he even knew about it was because of what I'd shared, hoping for advice and support. Ultimately, I still wanted his support, even if we didn't fully agree on the approach anymore.

"It's cool, Giselle. Honestly."

*God, why was it that people always resorted to calling me Giselle when they were mad at me?*

"Does the budget work with your new ideas added to it?" he asked.

"That's also what I want to talk to the team about," I replied. "I think so, but I'd like the accounting squad to double-check my numbers before we go too far down the rabbit hole."

"All right. Well, I'm glad you thought of that. I hope it works out for you."

"Do you?"

*Because that's surely not what it sounds like*, I thought.

"Of course, I do. I may not agree with you, but I still want you to succeed."

"Okay," I said with a sigh. "Thank you."

At least there was that, I supposed. How awful would it have been to realize that my picker was so flawed, I'd been dating someone for more than a month who couldn't wish the best for me unless I did exactly what he wanted.

"Not a problem," he replied. "In any case, I know it's

late and you sound very tired, so I'll let you go to bed. It was good to hear your voice again."

"Yours, too."

"You've got another three days before you're back, right?"

"Yeah, we get back on Thursday."

"Okay, cool. Well, hit me up when you get back. I'd love to see you again soon."

"I will. Hope you have a good night."

"You, too."

With those last two words, Phillip hung up the phone, and I slid back down onto the bed, wrapping myself into the covers as I closed my eyes once again, trying to get back to the serenity I'd felt prior to that call. To that moment right when my brain and body seemed to be in perfect harmony, and it felt like I could take on the world, just as soon as I woke up the next day.

I took in a few deep breaths, settling my nervous system, and allowing myself to feel the waves of peace as they washed over me.

*Sigh, there it was*, I thought, reveling in the sweet joy of it as my body melted into the mattress once again.

It was refreshing.

It was spirit filling.

And it made me feel wholly connected to God and the universe and whatever plans they had in store for me.

The longer I lay there, the more I felt myself drifting off to sleep, my breaths getting heavier, as my chest rose and fell in a soothing rhythm that lulled me into the land of my subconscious. There, Usher's "Good Kisser" played faintly in the background as the memory of Brandon's soft lips pressing on mine washed over me before everything went black.

## *Chapter Fifteen*

The next day started off slightly later than the previous mornings, a fact that I was particularly thrilled about considering all my late-night activities. I mean, between kisses and proposals and arguments—oh my!—I probably could have slept until the sun rose the following day and still have needed more z's. But that was definitely not an option. Not on this trip, at least.

At 11:00 a.m. on the dot, our white stretch limo pulled up to the front of the cabin, the driver just as cheery as could be and ready to take us to the first vineyard on our winery tour. Thankfully, the majority of us had just finished eating breakfast, a must when it came to coating our stomachs for the long day of wine sipping we had planned, and all but Lucas were fully dressed and prepared for the sunny, highs-in-the-80s kind of day. He bolted up the stairs almost as soon as he saw the white car rounding the corner toward the house, while the rest of us took our time gathering up the dishes and making sure we had all the accessories we needed for the day. Of note, there was a litany of sunglasses, portable fans, sunscreen bottles and even a couple wide-brimmed, beach straw hats in the midst.

The girls were, of course, radiant in their outfits, with Reagan and Jenn both rocking a cute white shirt that they paired with retro bottoms and Keisha glowing in a multi-colored, loose-fitting jumpsuit that alternated squares of white, blue, pink, orange, brown and green throughout. Her oversize, floppy, straw hat offset the jumpsuit perfectly. Reagan had opted to wear her hair loose and wavy instead of straightening it after our boat excursion, with only a simple cloth headband keeping the tresses away from her face but allowing them to billow down onto her button-down, white, cap-sleeved crop top. Jenn had added a bright red turban, tied up like a large rose in the front, on top of her short brown hair, giving her ensemble an immediate wow factor despite the classic simplicity of the rest of her clothing—a ribbed V-neck, white tank top that she tucked into her acid-washed, cotton, drawstring trousers.

For my part, I'd chosen to wear my two-piece, pale green, linen trouser set with a sleeveless crop tank top and matching high-waisted pants that fell about midcalf. I paired that with my pastel yellow, lightweight kimono duster, which featured bright orange-and-pink flowers surrounded by their green leaves and my own, much less oversize, beach hat as well.

The guys kept it simple, with a mix of linen and graphic T-shirts and tailored joggers, making it abundantly easy for Lucas to finish getting dressed and beeline his way back downstairs just in time for our scheduled departure.

One by one, we eagerly climbed into the limousine and settled in for the sixteen-to-twenty-minute ride that would take us to the Vineyard at Windham, a beautiful and sprawling, four-acre oasis nestled in the Catskill Mountains. With over twenty bottles of wine to choose from, some of which had been rated best in the state, it was the perfect way to kick-start a tour that included four wineries in total, within a span of seven hours. Hence the need for the driver.

By late afternoon, the eight of us were onto the third spot, the Middleburgh Winery, already feeling a little tipsy and hyped-up from the musical interludes during our rides in the limo. Jake had named himself DJ for the day and was certainly doing his part to keep us entertained as we traversed the Hudson Valley, bopping to everyone from Glorilla to Lil Wayne. But really, it was the initial view of the farmland, as we all hopped out of the limo and feasted our eyes on the vast acres of land before us, that kept getting me excited as we pulled up to each one.

Just like I'd done at the Windham and then again at the Blue Sky Farm and Winery, I climbed out of the limo at Middleburgh and took a moment to simply marvel at the wonders man could do with nature.

"It's beautiful, right?" Brandon whispered, coming up behind me as I looked upon the grassy hills, eyes glossy from all the tastings.

"It really is," I replied softly and then turned my head to face his. "Are you enjoying your day today?"

"Yeah, it's been a good day so far. I can't stop thinking about last night, though."

"Brandon," I said, staring into his deeply penetrating eyes.

"No, I know. We probably shouldn't go there again, but it is what I'm thinking about. Especially seeing you in green again today."

I chuckled quietly, remembering his bathroom suggestion to me from a few nights before.

"You know that I had my outfits planned already before I got here, right?"

"Yeah, I know. Doesn't stop me from being pleased about the happy coincidence, though."

"Fair. And, by the way, I haven't stopped thinking about

last night, either," I admitted. "Although, I'm not convinced that's a good thing."

"Hmm," Brandon moaned, his eyes visibly scanning my body from head to toe. "Well, from where I stand, it's definitely not a bad thing."

I cheesed in front of him, unable to stop my cheeks from lifting to the sky, and then playfully pushed him aside so we could stop coreminiscing and join up with the rest of the crew who'd made their way over to the entrance. They were in the middle of their own conversation, about weddings and their thoughts on marriage, as they waited for our guide arrive, all sparked by Lucas asking if Reagan and Jake had contemplated getting married in a venue like this instead of New Orleans.

"It was never a question for me," Jake replied. "I know how important it is to Rae for us to have our wedding in New Orleans, surrounded by her family in the city that makes her *her*, you know. I wouldn't want anything else."

"But wouldn't it be easier to get married two hours away instead of what's basically a destination wedding, just in the United States still?" Lucas probed.

"Man, you asking me if I want an easy wedding versus a happy wife? I'm picking the latter all day."

Jake and Lucas laughed as Reagan stood beside her fiancé with a look on her face that said, *I know that's right!*

"Obviously, there will be other things we'll need to compromise on, but actually, that *was* a pretty easy decision for me. It really just came down to, is it important to the woman I love? Bet. We'll make it happen then."

"And just to be clear," Reagan interjected, "I go through the same calculus with him. There's a reason I live in New York, now, right? I could have stayed in DC and forced us to continue making the long-distance thing work, but once

I realized it was important for him to be in New York, I figured out a way to get my job to move me where he needed me to be."

"It took a few years for us to get that joyful-sacrifice part of our relationship right," Jake said, laughing.

"If a few means ten, then yes," Jenn chimed in, silently counting the numbers on her fingers as she chuckled off to the side.

"Okay, Jennifer!" Reagan and Jake shouted in unison.

"No one asked you to turn into the Count on *Sesame Street*," Reagan added, fully unable to contain her giggles at this point.

"Okay, okay," Jenn replied, throwing up her hands in mock defeat. "No shade meant by it. We've all had our share of unlearning we've had to do in service of the health of our relationships. So, I'm actually really proud of you guys for working through all your stuff to get where you are now. Lifelong partnerships are not for the weak of heart—it takes a lot of honest communication, and I know for me and Nick, a big change for us was not expecting the other person to read your mind."

"Oh my God! Yes, that one's a killer," Reagan said, shaking her head. "It'll ruin even the best thing you've got going on."

I glanced at Brandon as our guide finally walked up and saw him deep in thought, looking as if he was intently taking in everything our friends were saying.

"Are you all ready for today's tour and tasting?" the guide asked, her accent signaling she was definitely from the local neighborhood.

"Oh yes," we all replied, eager to keep the party going.

"All right then, why don't you guys follow me."

Brandon turned his head toward me as the eight of us

closely trailed behind her. His eyes were warm and inviting as his lips turned up into a small smile that felt like
the sweetest silent hello that only the two of us could par-
ticipate in.

"Excuse us, guys, we'll be right back. We just have to
have a quick huddle off to the side."

Keisha grabbed my arm, practically lifting me up from
the wooden table where we were all seated, drinking the
last bits of our wine as we looked out onto the grapes growing along the rolling hills.

"Oh! Okay," I said, eyes wide open as the girls collectively dragged me fifty feet away, until they could be sure
our voices wouldn't carry over to the now-suspicious men
in our group.

"What's going on, guys?" I asked, looking to even one
of them to give me an explanation.

"Hmm, you tell us," Reagan replied, the first to chime
in, her head tilted as she attempted to study my reaction.

"I don't know what you mean."

"Ohh, you don't, huh?" Keisha asked. "Well, maybe this
will help you, baby. I caught you and Brandon giving each
other googly eyes earlier, right before we started the previous tour."

"Mmm-hmm, and I noticed a few interactions where
things seemed, let's just say...a little more than friendly,"
Jenn added. "At least once, when he was standing behind
you and whispering on your ear, I almost had to fan myself!"

*Damn*, I thought. They'd been clocking us the whole day,
and I'd been totally unaware, caught up in my own secret
world with him where we thought no one was noticing our
subtle winks and nods toward each other. I wondered if

Brandon was being subjected to a similar interrogation at the table. If Reagan had told Jake her suspicions, then the answer was probably yes.

She pursed her lips as she waited for me to react to all the accusations being lobbed at me.

"Well, *cher*?" she said, lifting her eyebrows and tapping her right foot impatiently as I stood quietly, unsure of how to begin my response.

"Umm, didn't you say you wanted me to keep an open mind this week?" I asked.

"Yes, of course."

Reagan rolled her eyes.

"But not without telling us!"

"Oh."

"Babee, if you don't start spilling the beans right now..." Keisha chimed in, her New Orleans accent coming out even thicker than normal as she tried to stop herself from laughing, "I'm going to have to fight you. And then I'm gonna actually be mad because my nails are done, and my jumpsuit is too cute to be rumbling and tumbling with my best friend at a damn winery!"

I smiled at the thought of Keisha Marianne Edwards, my bougie best friend from the bayou, doing anything that would even come close to messing up her ensemble or her nails. I would actually want to see that if it didn't involve me. I also realized I'd been caught red-handed by all three ladies and needed to just confess so they could stop trying to be super detectives, and we could all enjoy the rest of the day.

"All right, so...something *did* happen last night," I said, still hesitating a bit as I gathered up my courage.

"Duh," Rae deadpanned.

"Right," Keisha chimed in. "We obviously know that. But what?"

I stood frozen in front of them another few seconds until Jenn finally shouted out, "Well, don't leave us hanging!" which sent just the right bolt of energy my way so that my lips would move again.

"Umm...so...uhh... Brandon kissed me."

The words tumbled out my mouth slowly at first and then just as fast as I could get them out, but almost as soon as I'd said it, Reagan, Keisha and Jennifer jumped for joy, screaming and high-fiving each other like their favorite team had just won a championship.

"What?!" Keisha shouted. "Was it just out of nowhere? In the middle of the night? And how come you didn't tell us immediately?"

"Well, not immediately," Jenn corrected her with a smirk. "I imagine there were more *important* things at hand."

"True, you're right, not immediately. But long before now. You had the kitchen this morning. You could have pulled us aside at any of the wineries. Hell, I'm pretty sure my phone still works, so you could have also just texted us. Anything!"

"Now, that is fair," Jenn pointed out, siding with Keisha again. "A group text would have been real easy to pull off."

"I knew it!" Reagan whispered, rubbing her hands together as Keisha peppered me with questions and Jenn tried to remain the steady voice in the midst of the chaos. "I knew my boy would finally make a move. Go, Brandon!"

I stood in silence again and let them each process the news in their own way, vacillating between incredulous outbursts and questions I wasn't actually sure any of them expected me to answer. It seemed like they just needed to get them out of their body for relief. It took about another thirty seconds of mayhem before eventually, collectively, they quieted down and refocused their attention on me. Jenn was the first to try to calmly address me again.

"Okay, now that that's out of the way," she said, holding her hands out in a steadying formation. "What happens now?"

"Oh. I mean, I don't know, actually. It's not like we—"

"Wait, no, you don't need to know that just yet," Reagan interrupted. "It was a kiss, so it's totally understandable if you two haven't figured out anything beyond that. Wait, it was *just* a kiss, right?"

"Ha! Yes, it was just a kiss."

"On the lips?" Keisha asked. "Because if he hit you with a forehead kiss, and you've gotten us all excited over nothing…"

"Well, funny enough, he did kiss me on the forehead before he went to his room, but no, the main attraction was indeed on the lips… The forehead kiss was pretty deadly, too, though."

"I bet it was!" Reagan shouted out with laughter. "Okay, most importantly, though, how was it? The one on the lips."

She dropped her voice down low, almost to a whisper, like she was the one spilling all her secrets in a public winery.

"It was…" I paused to remember the taste of his lips on mine, the way his fingers felt as they made their way up my neck, even the thrilling feeling of him dragging my bottom lip with his teeth, and felt myself get chills just from the flashback. "Magical."

"As in it was full of tricks and surprises?" she asked softly, her eyes wide with excitement.

"As in it blew my mind and opened me up to wonders

I never thought possible," I replied. "You remember that Nikki Giovanni poem where she talks about the thought of her love sending indescribably delicious multitudinous thrills throughout and through-in her body?"

"Yeah," Reagan whispered.

"Well, it was like that with his touch but even more so because it also felt like I was floating in the galaxy somewhere, surrounded by all the stars."

"Damnnnnn, girl," Jenn chimed in. "That sounds like some powerful shit."

"For real," Reagan agreed.

"And y'all were able to stop from going any further after that?" Keisha questioned. "Your willpower might be even stronger than that kiss, baby."

"Well...it was kind of easy not to go further, actually... Because...eventually, I pulled away from him."

"Wait, why? What do you mean?"

All three women stared at me in horror, their expressions quickly changing with my newest admission.

"Was it because of Mr. Handsome?" Reagan asked. "Do you really like him that much?"

I chuckled nervously at the question, remembering how that was Brandon's first thought as well.

"No, it wasn't because of Phillip. I like him, but..." I shrugged.

"But he's not Brandon."

I laughed upon realizing we'd all said it unison.

"Yeah, I guess y'all have been saying that all along," I added.

"We sure have," Keisha replied. "But you know, you've been hardheaded as long as I've known you. It's gotta be something in that Philly DNA."

"Is it the same thing in the New Orleans DNA?" I countered. "Because it sounds to me like the pot calling the kettle black."

"Yeah, well, I'm from the Seventh Ward in New Orleans. If you were from there, you'd know I'm supposed to be a hardhead."

"All right, enough of that," Reagan interjected. "So, if it didn't have anything to do with Phillip, then what was it?"

"The same thing I've been telling y'all since forever. I'm starting to feel like I'm going crazy because no one is listening to me as much as I scream it from the hilltops. Brandon is my best guy friend. I don't want to lose that."

"But I guess I thought you said that before you knew that he had feelings for you, too. And that now that you know he does, things would be different," she countered.

"Well, one, I don't know anything beyond the fact he wanted to kiss me. That tells me nothing about his feelings toward me, if he'd want us to date, if he's ready for anything serious or anything else, really. And I'm not in the business of assuming what a man wants anymore."

"That's true," Jenn chimed in, back on my side for at least the time being. "We were just talking about not trying to read people's minds in a relationship."

"Damn it, Jenn, pick a side!" Reagan cried out before turning back toward me.

"The other thing is, and I've explained this before, with my track record and his, we'd be over before your wedding even happens."

"So, you really believe that because it hasn't worked out for you yet, it never will? Like really?"

"I hope that's not one hundred percent true, Rae, but the odds are definitely against me. Tell me, really, how could I not worry about that? All the evidence points to it. And so, while I'm not giving up the idea that it might change one day for me, I also don't know if I'm willing to risk our friendship on a wing and a prayer."

"But all love takes risk," Jenn said softly, clearly considering both sides and resisting the need to choose one over the other. "Anyone who tells you differently hasn't really been in love. Of course it's scary. You're opening up your heart to someone other than yourself and trusting they won't abuse it. But the payoff comes when you realize you've found the person that makes everything suddenly make sense. That's a feeling like none other."

"And it's worth the risk," Keisha added.

"So, so worth it," Reagan agreed. "Is that how you feel about Brandon?"

"Like suddenly things makes sense when I'm with him?" I asked for clarification.

"Yeah."

"Yeah," I replied with a sigh. "But what am I supposed to do about that?"

"I think you know, *cher*," she said. "You just gotta trust yourself enough to do it."

"Maybe."

"And we need to head back over to the boys before they get antsy and come over here to break this party up. You good?"

Reagan eyed me with compassion and put her hands on my shoulders. I didn't really have an answer for her, but I was ready for the conversation to end.

"I'll tell you what Chrissy once said to me," she added. "'There's nothing worse than an *amor cauteloso*—a cautious love.' You deserve so much more than that, Gig. Don't let the opportunity pass you by because of fear."

I mouthed, *Thank you*, and the four of us walked back

to the wooden table, where the guys had ordered another round of wine flights.

"It looked like y'all might need to re-up before we head to the next spot," Jake remarked, pulling Reagan into his side for a warm embrace.

"This is why I keep you around, babe," she said with a smile. "Excellent thinking."

As me and the girls sat back down, my eyes wandered over to Brandon's. Those were the same kind eyes that saw me so clearly, knowing things about me that even I didn't at times. He knew how to push me without making me feel dumb. He knew that my heart hadn't been in that first proposal. He even knew what kind of songs I liked and the way I preferred my coffee.

Things *did* make more sense for me when I was in his presence. I don't think I'd realized that until Reagan asked me.

I slipped my phone out of my trouser pocket as the crew began our final toast, just as our driver pulled up, signaling it was time to get back on the road.

Quickly, I unlocked my screen and went straight to Phillip's name in my recent folder.

Hey, are you free to talk later? I asked.

Of course, he replied. You can call me any time.

Okay, thanks. Talk soon.

"Hey," Phillip answered, his voice slightly groggy by the time I called around 10:00 p.m.

It had taken awhile, but after hours of hanging with the crew, I'd finally found a moment that felt appropriate to slip away while everyone else was pre-occupied. Maybe I was being too precautious, but I hadn't wanted to risk being interrupted while we were talking. More importantly, I also had no desire for the group to hear what I thought might become a very personal conversation.

So, score one for Taboo, because it made for the perfect distraction.

"Hi," I replied. "Sorry to call so late."

He laughed.

"This is a marked improvement from the other night, so you're fine. It's just been a long day."

"Touché. Well, either way, you sound tired, so I don't want to keep you too long."

"I appreciate it, but you're good, Gigi."

I paused for a second, sighing as I tried to figure out exactly what I was going to say to him. It's not like things had gone so horribly wrong between us; it was just that I'd realized maybe we weren't as compatible as I'd hoped.

*Or as Brandon and I are.*

The latter thought rang through my head like an uninvited guest, and I quickly shushed it away. I wanted to focus on the right words to say to a good man who just probably wasn't *my* man, and I didn't have time for Brandon popping up in my brain while I did so. Regardless of the fact that he was likely reason number one for why I had to talk to Phillip now.

"So, listen, I—"

"If it's all right—"

Phillip and I burst out laughing, breaking the tension between us, as we simultaneously realized we were both interrupting the other. It was a nice reprieve and briefly reminded me of our first phone dates when we spent hours talking, and accidentally interrupting one another, as we got to know each other.

"You go first," I said, grateful for a little bit more time to gather my thoughts.

"Thanks. I was just going to apologize for last night, really. You didn't deserve for me to be so harsh with you."

"Thank you, Phillip. That means a lot."

*Wow*, I thought to myself. This was why I'd started liking him in the beginning, A man who easily took accountability and apologized? I'm sure there were plenty, but I hadn't encountered too many of them.

"I have been wondering, though," he continued, "if maybe our outlooks on life are just too different for us to continue dating."

Oh.

*Wait, is he breaking up with me? When I'm the one calling to break up with him?*

I sat up straighter, gripping one of the pillows on my window seat and braced myself for impact. Sure, I'd been planning to end things with him, but I wasn't exactly thrilled about him beating me to the punch.

Phillip must have taken my silence as a nod to keep going because after a few seconds, he did.

"I don't mean that in a bad way, you know. I always have such a good time with you, and you know I think you're probably the most beautiful woman I've ever met. But when I think about who I want to build a future with, it seems like we'd want to be more aligned than you and I are. Right?"

"No, you're totally right," I said, finally finding my voice to speak again. "I don't know that I'd considered us having opposing outlooks on life, but I do agree that we maybe seem to have a kind of paper-doll connection."

"What do you mean?" he asked quietly.

"You know, it's fun to play around with, and at times,

can feel kind of perfect," I replied. "But when you really think about it, it's a little…two-dimensional."

"Mmm. Yeah, I can see that. Maybe if you were Barbie and I was Ken, things could have worked out."

"Maybe," I said softly, even though I knew the real problem had nothing to do with him.

For the next twenty minutes, Phillip and I took turns speaking lovingly about the time we'd shared together. We laughed about how uncomfortable the waiter at Barn Joo was around us and talked about how ridiculous my reply had been to his Ben's Chili Bowl text. We even reminisced about the first time he'd invited me over so that I could personally try his grocery store specialty—frozen pizza and wings.

It was probably the most comforting ending I'd ever experienced. And then when we were done, we said our goodbyes and knew that they weren't "see you laters."

# *Chapter Sixteen*

Around 1:00 a.m., I found myself wide-awake, restless in bed, desperately trying to find some position that felt comfortable enough to fall asleep. I tossed and turned, kicking one leg out from under my covers, only to pull it back in when I got cold. I cocooned myself within the soft sheets, hoping that would help, almost like a baby being swaddled. But that, too, had its issues as I quickly grew hot and anxious from the tightness of the cloth around me.

Eventually, I resigned myself to the truth—there was nothing physically wrong with me or the mattress. I was just so in my head, questioning if I'd made a huge mistake in ending things with Phillip, that my body was the thing suffering as a result. I quietly stepped out of the bed, slipped my feet into my fuzzy slippers and breathed in deeply as I attempted to let all of the tension that I had pulsing through me flow out and into the air. It seemed like a lost cause, but I had to try.

Counting by eights, I inhaled, letting my chest expand as it filled with air and then exhaled, slowly pushing it out of my mouth. As I did so, memories from our conversation flashed through my brain. As far as breakups go, the call had actually gone relatively well—an indication that perhaps my picker hadn't been so terribly off when it came to him.

But in the middle of the night, that just made it harder to trust I'd done the right thing. With the exception of our conversation the night before, Phillip had been everything I'd been hoping to find for so long. Stable, intentional, treating me with honesty and respect, and not running from the prospect of us building something long-lasting. If anything, he'd reminded me that there were guys out there still willing to step up and show me exactly how they felt, no guessing games or wild-goose chases involved. We may not have been ultimately right for each other, with his singular focus on practicality and winning at the cost of spontaneity and creativity, but he'd made me believe what I wanted was possible again. I'd forever be grateful to him for that, if nothing else.

The question, now, was if the man in the room next to me, separated just by a bathroom, was one of the guys who could show up just as intentionally or if I'd just played myself by giving up on Phillip and me too soon.

"I really enjoyed the time we spent together," I said before we'd ended the call.

"Yeah, me, too," he replied. "And hey, listen, if you think about something new you want to try in the city and you don't have someone to do it with, I'm only a phone call away."

"Thanks, Phillip, I appreciate that."

It was a nice thought and a polite way to end our call, but I think deep down, we both knew we'd likely never speak to each other again. And still, almost as soon as I hung up the phone, I started questioning my decision.

*Who breaks up with someone for another person before they even know how that other person feels?* my inner voice asked. Clearly the answer was me. The fool who might have just taken all her eggs out of one basket before confirming there was a second basket to place them in! My poor eggs were just piled alongside each other, waiting to see what would happen to them next.

I circled my fingers around my temples and took in one final deep breath.

"Okay," I replied to myself with a sigh. "The breakup was a little more nuanced than that, and you know it. First, he was intending to break up with you too! But even if that wasn't the case, you wanted to end things with Phillip because it's abundantly obvious you have feelings for Brandon. Continuing on with another man as if that wasn't true would have been unfair to both of you."

This was right, but it didn't make our ending any easier to swallow. With one thirty-minute call, I was fully single again, with no guarantee that would change anytime soon. And despite my protests to the contrary, I really didn't want to get back on Hinge.

In hopes that some chamomile tea could finally help settle my thoughts, I gingerly made my way through my pitch-black room and out my door, careful not to bump into or trip over anything that would cause a loud crash and interrupt the stillness of the house. Everyone else had gone to bed hours ago. The last thing I wanted to do was alarm someone out of their slumber just because I couldn't sleep.

While tiptoeing down the stairs, I noticed a small light coming from the kitchen. Because of the cabin's open floor plan, it was hard to miss, considering the rest of the first floor was just as dark as my room. I figured that one of us forgot to turn the light off for the night, but as I drew closer, I heard the distinct sound of feet shuffling and instantly knew I wasn't the only one in the house needing some sort of late-night snack.

"Hello?" I asked, stepping into the kitchen carefully just in case the person inside was an intruder and not one of my friends.

"Hi."

My stomach dropped as soon as I heard the low and gravelly tone in the person's voice.

It was Brandon.

*We've got to stop running into each other like this.*

"What are you doing down here?" I asked.

Brandon appeared from behind the kitchen's island with a small item in his hand and his long locs draping down his shoulders. Even with the light, it was still too dark to visualize much beyond his silhouette, but I could distinctly see his perfectly sculpted arms and the outline of his broad torso. I blinked a few times to try to adjust my eyes and view him more clearly.

"You're not going to believe this," he replied, "but I was actually making some hot chocolate. I'd planned to come knock on your door in a few."

"What?"

I giggled at the idea until Brandon's face started coming into focus, and I realized he wasn't joking. He shrugged sheepishly in response and then pointed out the two mugs on the counter. Behind him on the stove seemed to also be a small pot of water he'd just turned off, and in his hand was a hot chocolate packet.

I was immediately floored.

"Oh," I said, dropping my smile once I'd assessed everything in front of me. "You're serious."

"Yeah."

A nervous chuckle escaped from his lips as he moved closer toward me.

"I know it's late, but I was hoping you might still be up because there's some things I wanted to talk to you about. I guess I could have waited until tomorrow, but I couldn't sleep, so I thought, might as well try tonight."

"Oh?"

How ironic that we'd both been lying in our beds, restless in the middle of the night.

As Brandon drew nearer, my heart began pounding loudly in my chest, distracting me from anything else happening around me. Suddenly he was directly in front of me, and everything just stopped. It was like someone had unplugged a DJ's equipment and abruptly interrupted all the noise in the room, leaving just us in our own bubble, with his eyes pouring into mine.

"Well, I'm down here now," I added, unable to move under his deeply intense gaze. "What was it that you wanted to say?"

Brandon cleared his throat and briefly dropped his eyes to my slightly parted lips before returning them to the center of my face.

"You know the thing you said about our track records? I've been thinking a lot about that."

"I wasn't trying to offend you or anything," I interjected.

"No, I know. And you weren't wrong in a sense. I've dated a decent amount of people in the time we've known each other, never really taking the time to invest in anyone seriously. Some of that is because it's easy to live up to my reputation, to just be the carefree guy who plays around until it's not fun for me anymore. If I never make a commitment, I don't have to worry about getting hurt. I don't need to think about anyone's expectations of me. I can just float from person to person and focus mostly only on what I need."

"Yeah," I replied softly. "I can understand that."

"But the other reason is something I should have shared with you a long time ago. I just didn't want it to affect our friendship."

"What's that?"

I raised my eyes to his, peering into them as I waited for him to continue, sensing that he was doing his best to try to open up to me in a way he hadn't before, and wanting him to know that I would stand there as long as he needed me to. I wasn't rushing him.

Brandon's eyes softened in response and his face relaxed as he gently took my hand in his, running his fingertips into my palm.

"I've wanted to be with you since the day we met on the basketball court, Gig, when I saw you walk up with that pink-and-red shorts set and the most beautiful smile I'd seen on anyone ever. I know I was messing with you that day, but the truth is, I was stunned by your beauty. Then, when I started getting to know you, I realized you weren't just beautiful, but you were funny and brilliant, and I wanted to talk to you every day—wanted to be part of your life in any small way. But before I knew it, you were my friend, and I guess I didn't want to risk you telling me I was too much of a playboy to take seriously. So, I let it go."

"Oh, Brandon, I…"

"I know. It probably sounds crazy coming from the guy who's known for going after whatever he wants, full stop. And a lot of that is warranted. But you were different, Gig. You've always been different for me… I also knew how much you'd been played around with before, so I understood, you know, given who I was and what everyone knows me for, that we probably could never be. I put my feelings aside and decided to genuinely be your friend. I want to be clear about that. Our friendship hasn't been some sort of consolation prize for me."

"Same for me, Brandon. I can't imagine not having you as my friend."

"Yeah, I know," he said quietly. "There's just one problem now. Ever since the first night of the trip, when you stood in the bathroom with nothing but your bra and panties on and accidentally moaned in front of me, I haven't been able to stop thinking about you. And not as a friend, Gigi. So not as a friend."

He cupped my hand tighter, and I gulped in response. It was one thing for Brandon to randomly and maybe impulsively kiss me; it was another thing entirely for him to admit to his feelings for me. It sent chills through my body that I wasn't sure I could contain.

"I realized, in that moment, 'Damn, she might actually want me just as badly as I've wanted her,'" he continued. "Can you imagine how much that messed me up? Like, all this time I've suppressed my feelings for you, thinking I'm being this upstanding guy, and then I catch the way you were looking at me in the mirror... I told you I wasn't mad that next morning. I was stunned, trying to process what I'd seen, and thinking about how much time we might have missed out on because I didn't know how you felt. You weren't looking at me like a friend that night, Gig."

"You're right, I wasn't."

"How were you looking at me?"

I licked my plump lips and stared into Brandon's eyes, contemplating how honest I should be. I risked ruining everything between us no matter what I did. If I lied, he would see through it clearly at this point and might be so frustrated with me that he walked away. But if I told the truth, the whole truth...he still might eventually leave me, like everyone else always did.

"How were you looking at me, Gig?" he repeated. "Tell me."

"Like I wanted you to ravish me," I finally admitted with a sigh. "To stand behind me and unclasp my bra, dragging the straps down my arms until it fell to the floor. I wanted you to lick and kiss your way down my neck and my back until you reached my hips, where the only thing keeping you from being inside of me would be the flimsy green panties that cupped my cheeks. I was looking at you like I couldn't wait for you to slip those off of me and dive into me from behind while we stared at each other through the mirror."

"Is that still what you want?" Brandon growled.

"Yes."

"Then what's stopping you?"

Brandon dropped his hand from mine and leaned his back into the kitchen island, staring at me, daring me to finally go for what I want. My eyes followed the length of him, this time with him standing right in front of me. There was no mirror to provide a sense of cognitive distance between my desire for him and the five-eleven frame that seemed like it was whispering my name every time his chest rose with his breaths. And so, with a hunger I no longer wanted to quell, I leaned into him and pressed my lips onto his, sucking on his bottom lip until his mouth dropped open, leaving just enough room for me to slide my tongue inside.

In and out our tongues darted as Brandon pulled me closer into him until it felt like our skin might become fully attached. Then, with a low growl, he ran his hands up my spine and grabbed my twists from the bottom of my neck, slowly yanking my head backward so he could have full access to the length of my neck, licking and sucking on it until I became putty in his hands.

"This is what you want, right?"

"Yes," I replied, barely able to speak as waves of pleasure crashed over me.

"Say it again," he implored, whispering into my ear as he continued licking his way down the collar of my pink satin pajamas.

"Yes," I repeated, slightly louder. "A million times yes."

That was all Brandon needed to hear as he scooped me up and placed my bottom on the island. Standing in between my thighs, he greedily unbuttoned my shirt until my perky brown breasts were completely exposed to him.

"Damn," he whispered under his breath and then immediately clasped his mouth on my right nipple, sucking it tightly as his left hand grabbed the other one, pinching and rolling it simultaneously.

"Oh my God," I cried out, throwing my head back and opening my body up to him even more.

Brandon chuckled deviously in response, my nipple still in his mouth as he whispered, "Yeahhh, now that's what I want."

He slid his left hand beneath the waistband of my shorts, squeezing it under my panties until his fingers found the destination he'd been seeking. Already soaking wet and desperate for his touch. He paused briefly and looked up into my eyes before cupping one and then a second finger and plunging both inside of me.

Brandon expertly rocked his fingers in and out of me as my body writhed around on the kitchen island, a pulsing sensation building up within me, tightening every muscle and shooting spasms from my neck down to my toes, until finally, it exploded.

"Fu— Oh, oh, my God!"

The muscles in my body jumped uncontrollably as I tried to catch my breath and recover from the massive orgasm that had just run through me. I was sure I looked like a wild woman, perched on the island, half-undressed, and a fire burning inside of me that craved oh so much more. When I looked down at Brandon, however, all I saw was a satisfied smile stretched across his face.

"We should take this upstairs," I whispered.

"I couldn't agree more."

The next morning, I woke up to the sun rising through my bedroom window and the feeling of Brandon's arms wrapped tightly around my naked body. Facing him, I opened my eyes and silently studied everything I could see from where my head was placed, next to the top of his chest, nestled into a nook that was partly my pillow and partly the underside of his left arm. My eyes traced the curves of his eyebrows down to his nose, then wandered over to his cheekbones, which angled perfectly toward his goatee. And then, of course, that same goatee outlined the most magical lips I'd experienced in my thirty-two years of living.

"Wow," I said quietly. "So that wasn't a dream."

"Nah, it wasn't," he replied with a chuckle under his breath.

Brandon's eyes were still closed, but his quick response indicated he was only half-asleep.

"Good morning," I said. "I didn't realize you were up."

"Barely. But if waking up means I get to experience all of this again, then, yeah, I'm up."

He squeezed me in closer to him, cupping my butt with his large right hand.

"Brandon," I chuckled.

"Too much?"

"Maybe a little."

"Sorry. You have to forgive me. I can't believe we waited so long to do this. Now I just want to experience it over and over."

A sharp pang went through me as Brandon spoke, and I flashed to all the times I'd thought I was important to a guy in my life only to realize he just wanted to have sex with me. I really, really needed that not to be the case this time.

"When you say *this*..." I asked, "what is that exactly? Do you just mean us having sex again?"

Brandon opened his eyes and looked at me, his brown eyes catching mine in a move that only sped up the unraveling beginning to happen in my head.

"Gig—" he started, but I interrupted him. I didn't want to hear some beautiful words that would sound good at first but ultimately would really amount to one thing: I don't really want to be with you, not in any sort of real or meaningful way. I'd heard all the different variations before; I didn't need to hear it from him.

"I'm just asking because you said a lot of things last night but none of them were that you wanted to date me or be in a relationship with me. Don't get me wrong, the sex was spectacular. But I can't possibly just have a sexual relationship with you. Not you."

"Okay, wait a second," Brandon said, rising up so that his back leaned onto my headboard. "If I wasn't clear last night, let me be abundantly so this morning. I want to be with you, Gig, in a real relationship. No games. No more wasting time dating other people. Just me and you, riding this thing until the wheels fall off."

"Are you sure about that?" I asked, sitting up as well, but bringing the sheets with me to cover my chest. "Because I overheard you and Jake talking before we left for the trip, and you seemed pretty adamant that was not at all what you wanted with me."

"You overheard me and Jake… Wait, what do you think you heard?"

Brandon shook his head, looking confused, as if he was trying to remember the conversation I was referencing. It would have maybe been kind of funny, except I knew it word for word.

"He was teasing you about me being your girl, and you repeatedly shot him down, saying that I was a friend and nothing more."

"What? Giselle, I told you everything changed for me in that bathroom. So, yeah, I'm sure I did say those things to Jake, but that was before, when I thought that was what *you* wanted from me."

"How do I know that's not still how you feel? Maybe we're both just caught up in the moment right now, and—"

"Because I'm telling you it's not," he interrupted. "I am sure of what I want, Gig. I've never been more sure in my life. I want you, plain and simple. I've always wanted you. You see me like no one else does. You're not looking to change me, and I don't want to change you. I just want to be with you. The only question now is will you trust me at my word, and will you let me show you that I mean what I say?"

I stared into Brandon's eyes and remembered the conversation I'd had with the girls about love being worth any risk. Some of the risks I'd taken in the past had left me mentally and emotionally battered, afraid to try again because

I might end up right back in the same position. But with Brandon, I had a chance for a different outcome. As long as I allowed myself to actually go toward it, despite my fear.

"Yes," I replied softly, my lips turning up into a sly smile.

"Wait, what's that you said?"

Brandon leaned toward me, stopping his face mere inches away from mine.

"A million times yes," I said louder, giggling into his shoulder as he grabbed me toward him, pressing my body into his.

"Good," he whispered. "Because we've got a lot of time to make up for."

Instantly, Brandon pulled the sheets off me and buried his head into my chest, peppering me with light kisses until he found his sweet spot once again. I threw my head back in ecstasy as he tightened his lips around my nipple, content to ride the waves of pleasure building up in me once again.

Brandon and I made our way down the steps and toward the kitchen a couple hours later, ready to join the rest of the crew for a day of antique shopping in Woodstock. Keisha and I had intended for Day 5 to be more laid-back than some of the others, so we weren't exactly on a strict schedule, but still, we figured most of our friends would be eating breakfast by the time we arrived.

All eyes instantly focused on us as we walked in, my taupe, knitted, two-piece shorts set slightly dipping down my right shoulder, the result of the already-loose fabric being stretched out even further as Brandon kissed me just a few moments before.

"Oh, look who's up!" Reagan announced teasingly.

"And what a coincidence, joining us all at the same time," Keisha added in that singsongy tone of hers.

"Now, Keish, that *is* pretty interesting, don't you think?" Reagan continued. "That Brandon and Gig would be the last ones downstairs today, and somehow, show up together."

"Almost hand in hand, really," Jenn chimed in.

Brandon and I looked at each other amusingly as the girls continued. I wasn't sure about him, but I was at least curious to see exactly where this was going.

"I do think that's interesting," Keisha said. "But you know what else I find fascinating?"

"No, girl, but please, do tell me."

Reagan leaned back into her chair and waited for Keisha to continue as all the guys chuckled off to the side.

"We all found two mugs on the counter this morning when we came in, which is kinda strange considering we've been putting the dishes up every night."

"Ooooh," Reagan replied, egging her on. "Well, how do you think those mugs got there then?"

"Oh, you see, I don't know," Keisha said, and then swiftly turned her head to me and Brandon. "But I think they do."

Reagan giggled and turned to us as well.

"You think *they* do?" she asked. "Well, let's see. Hey, Gig and Brandon, do either of you know what happened with these mugs last night? I mean, what could have been so pressing that someone forgot to put them up when they left out of the kitchen?"

I looked at Brandon again and tried to discern if he was ready for us to go public with our friends so soon. But honestly, keeping it a secret wasn't really an option. It was pretty clear they knew something was up. So, with a big smile on my face, I threw caution to the wind, and pulled him toward me, grabbing his face with my hands as I pressed my lips on his. Thankfully, he took my cue, and kissed me back, cupping my butt underneath my shorts as we smooched for several seconds.

When we finally pulled back, everyone's mouths were agape across the kitchen.

"Just that," I replied with a wink.

"Yeahhh, our bad," Brandon added, his cheeks flushing. "We may have been a *little* distracted last night."

"Oh. My. God!"

Reagan was the first person to verbalize all their reactions, jumping up from her seat as she whispered to Jake, "I told you so."

Jake politely brushed her off and turned his attention back to us.

"So does this mean what we think it means?" he asked. "Are the two of you together...finally?"

"Looks like it," Brandon replied, grabbing my hip and pulling me toward him.

"Thank God!" Lucas shouted out, his voice carrying all the way from the back corner where he was sitting. "It's about time."

A collective "Amen" rang throughout the room as I stared into Brandon's starry eyes once again.

"I guess it is, huh?" I said to him quietly.

"Hey, I say we're better late than never," he replied with a wink.

"I know that's right," Keisha exclaimed, overhearing us and throwing her arms around Julian for emphasis. "But now, we have to celebrate. Who's down for a lil champagne with their breakfast?"

# *Epilogue*

Dressed in pleated citronelle pants and a matching ribbed top that tied at my waist and popped beautifully on my skin, I walked into Fort Tryon Park with Stevie Wonder's "Overjoyed" playing in my ears, adding an extra bounce in my step.

"God, I love this park," I whispered to myself, marveling at the rows of bright flowers that flanked the various walking pathways, leading to everything from the Cloisters Museum to the lush, green, grassy areas of land that made it possible to lay under the sun for hours.

No matter how many times I came to it, it never got old to me.

Humming along to Stevie, I made my way down one of the pathways, where a view of the Hudson River could be seen for miles as it separated Manhattan from the state of New Jersey. The path dipped and curved as it followed the outline of the river, raised far above it and separated by a highway, but still using its shape to contour the walkway until it connected with one of the four grassy areas available in the park.

Stevie's voice faded out as I veered into the grass, eagerly walking toward the man with the deep caramel brown skin seated on a blanket, with a wicker basket and champagne in front of him, and his locs beautifully flowing down his back.

"Hey," I said softly, pulling my earbuds out and placing them into their cartridge as I stepped into his periphery.

Brandon immediately jumped up and whisked me into his arms, swinging me around as he planted soft kisses all along on my cheeks and my chin.

"I'm so proud of you, Gig. You guys are going to make such a big difference with this new program. And clearly HUD knows it."

He spoke each sentence in between kisses, squeezing me tightly until finally, he stopped spinning us and gently placed me back on the ground.

"Thanks, Brandon," I said, giggling as I slipped out of my hot pink, pointed-toe mules and stepped onto the blanket. "I can't believe they really said yes. I mean, they *loved* it, babe. Like, I don't even have the words for how excited they seem to work with us."

"Of course, they loved it," he replied. "How could they not? You put so much of your heart into that proposal, Gig, and then working with your team, you had the numbers and the data and the stories to back it up."

We sat down onto the blanket, and Brandon handed me a champagne flute before popping open the bottle and pouring me a full glass.

"You deserve this. And you know what? I know your mom would be just as proud of you as I am."

"I hope so," I replied.

"I *know* so."

Brandon raised his now-full glass to meet mine and stared at me with eyes so tender and kind, I could have melted at the sight of them if not for the excitement pulsing through my veins.

"To the cutie from Philly who just might help change the world," he said. "I love you, and I'm honored to stand by your side as you do so."

"I love you, too, babe."

We clanked our glasses, and I looked out over the full scene in front of me—the azure blue sky above us sprinkled with only a few white clouds, the bright yellow sun shining over the Hudson River, the green grass that tickled at our blanket and the five-foot-eleven man casually draping my legs over his lap. It was almost a picture-perfect, real-life copy of the drawing I'd created several months ago. The one I'd discarded because I didn't think it could ever actually happen for me.

Now, it was real. It was everything I ever wanted. And it was all mine.

I shifted my body and laid my head on Brandon's chest, looking out over the Hudson River, as I breathed in all the good things that had come to me in the past few months.

Reagan and Keisha had been right after all, I thought, chuckling to myself. I did deserve every good and amazing thing that I desired. And I was finally getting them, not because I was oh so special, but because I'd stopped letting my fears prevent me from going after them. And that felt damn good.

\* \* \* \* \*